THE AGES OF LULU

THE AGES OF LULU

Almudena Grandes

Translated from the Spanish
by Sonia Soto

GROVE PRESS
New York

All characters in this publication are fictitious, and any resemblance to real persons, living or dead, is purely coincidental.

First published as *Las Edades de Lulu* in 1989
by Tusquets Editores, Barcelona, Spain.
English translation first published in Great Britain in 1993 by Abacus.
First Grove Press edition, June 1994

Published simultaneously in Canada
Printed in the United States of America

FIRST PAPERBACK EDITION

Library of Congress Cataloging-in-Publication Data

Grandes, Almudena, 1960–
[Edades de Lulu. English]
The ages of Lulu/Almudena Grandes; translated from the Spanish
by Sonia Soto—1st ed.
Originally published: Barcelona: Tusquets Editores, 1989.

I. Soto, Sonia.
PQ6657 .R32E3313 1994 843' .914—dc20 93-43641
ISBN 0-8021-3348-7 (pbk.)

Grove Press
841 Broadway
New York, NY 10003

10 9 8 7 6 5 4 3 2 1

I suppose it might seem strange but that image, that innocent image, turned out to be the most illuminating factor, to have the most violent impact.

They, their beautiful faces, framed the first actor, whom I could not at that moment identify, so confused had I been left, earlier, by that radiant intertwining of bodies. The perfect, glossy flesh seemed to sink, satisfied, into itself, without injury, both subject and object of a complete, rounded, autonomous desire, so different from those mean, tight little anuses, permanently contracted into a painful, inconsolable grimace.

Sad, I thought then.

They were looking at each other, smiling, and they were looking at the open buttocks offered to them. Round the edges, the skin was firm and pink, soft, glossy and clear. Somebody had carefully shaved the whole area beforehand.

I had never seen anything like this before. A man, big and muscular, a beautiful man, on all fours on top of a table, his bottom raised, his thighs set apart, waiting. Defenceless, cringing like an abandoned dog, a pleading, trembling little animal, eager to please at all costs. A battered dog, hiding its face, not a woman.

I had seen dozens of women in that same posture. Including myself, a few times.

It was then that I wished for the first time to be there,

on the other side of the screen, to touch him, examine him, force him to lift his head, and to look him in the eyes, to wipe his chin and smear him with his own saliva. I wished then I had a pair of those horrible patent platform shoes like the cheapest tarts wear, hideous, unwearable stilts, so I could teeter precariously on their stiletto heels – they're such vulgar weapons – and move slowly towards him, and use one of them to penetrate him, and wound him and make him scream, and enjoy it, to pull him off the table and go on pushing, tearing, sinking into his immaculate flesh, so disturbing and so new to me.

She got there before me. She parted her lips and stuck out her tongue. She closed her eyes and set to work. Always in profile, like an Egyptian handmaiden, she diligently ran the tip of her tongue over the narrow pink island surrounding the desired channel; she licked its contours and slipped towards the inside, finally entering it. Her companion watched her and smiled.

But soon he did the same. He too opened his mouth and shut his eyes, and with his tongue caressed the vibrant flesh, the edge of the abyss. At the same time, with his free hand, the only one within the camera's field of vision, he softly struck the stranger's rump, which started to move rhythmically, backwards and forwards, as if in response to some secret signal. The hole, soaked in the saliva of others, contracted several times.

From time to time, inevitably, their tongues met, and then paused a moment; they intertwined and licked each other, then separated again and returned to their original task.

She let her fingers, with their extremely long nails, painted dark red, the colour of dried blood, slide slowly up and down, leaving light whitish traces behind them, marking out her territory. He, meanwhile, was kneading the pale flesh with one hand, pinching and stretching it, pressing marks into the skin. Neither of them let their tongue pause even for a moment.

Suddenly, the camera left them, abandoning me to my miserable fate.

After the first jolt of wonder and delight, I'd experienced the indefinable sensation of changing skin. I was very excited, but I understood. He looked adorable like that, wretched, hunched, his face hidden. I wanted him. I wanted to possess him. It was an unprecedented feeling. I am not, I cannot be, a man. I don't even want to be. My thoughts were blurred and confused, but I still understood, I couldn't help understanding.

Then, barely a moment after my metamorphosis, the familiar feeling of behaving badly.

A damp cold feeling, an unpleasant shiver, my skin covered in goose-pimples. I've just got out of a horribly lukewarm bath, and the tiles are freezing, and there's no towel. I can't dry myself; I have to stand there hunched, rubbing my body with my hands, my fingertips chapped and wrinkled like the chick-peas in the family *cocido*, the inevitable Saturday stew.

I feel defenceless. I want to return to the womb, to soak in the comforting fluid, to curl up and sleep and sleep for years.

That's how it's always been, the same repugnant premonition of repentance. Ever since I can remember, always the same, although back then, all those years ago, I suffered more. Stuffing myself with chocolate; fighting with my brothers and sisters; lying; failing at maths; turning out the light, avidly parting the hidden lips with my left hand and rubbing that which I cannot yet name with the tip of my right index finger, describing endless light circles, which finally bring me to the point of fission. I break in two, I am pierced by an indescribable sword and my thighs spread apart forever. I can feel the crack running up my back. I come. I open up, I split into two separate beings. Like an amoeba. Elemental, happy and slimy.

When I am one again, a single more evolved being, the

tiles feel icy and I have nothing to dry the drops of horribly tepid water, which make me want to cry.

But the stranger has returned; my body has once more become a warm and comfortable place.

There he was in front of me, in all his splendour. His acolytes were still by his side, but they were no longer preoccupied with him. They were smiling at each other, as they had at the beginning.

Almost immediately they started to kiss with a wild intensity which was unusual in a pornographic film. I had seen them talk earlier, and exchange signs and grunts from time to time, as if they really knew each other well. Maybe they did, I don't know. Anyway, the kiss, their surprisingly sincere kiss, soon ceased, as abruptly as it had begun. They resumed their original formation, and once again, it was she who took the initiative.

Suddenly, without warning, her eyes fixed on those of her companion, she inserted one of her pointed fingers into the stranger, who, this time, didn't seem to notice the change in the situation. Her nails were so long and sharp that there was something animal-like, almost repulsive about them. I assumed she was causing him pain – she must have been causing him pain – when, even though he had obediently engulfed the whole finger, right up to its base, she continued to push, twisting her hand around the opening, while she lightheartedly scolded the other man, who was watching her with an amused expression.

She chattered and gesticulated in an exaggerated fashion, like a little girl excited by a surprise. She puckered her lips into a pleading little pout, and slightly tilted her delicate blonde head, showing the pointed tip of her little tongue.

She inserted another finger, the second, into the stranger.

Then she started to move her hand faster and more energetically, and her arm began to tremble, her whole body moved with her hand. Her gestures became more explicit, even more feminine, her lips contracted into a ridiculous, brutal grimace. And she penetrated the stranger with a third finger.

It was intoxicating.

I couldn't feel anything like compassion, although I clung to the idea that it must all have been very painful for him. He's being punished, I thought, as arbitrarily as he was rewarded earlier. It was just. A little pain, and so ambiguous, in exchange for so much beauty.

The sight of the stranger, finally penetrated, clouded my brain.

Only afterwards, once I had regained my composure, did I reject the pleasurable hypothesis of punishment and suffering. I remembered all my petty, voluntary torments, in which possibly all children indulge, but which I haven't yet been able to give up. Winding a rubber band around one of my fingers, more and more tightly, until the skin turns purple and my flesh begins to burn. Or digging all my nails into the palm of my hand, pushing as hard as I can and then seeing the uneven marks, like small purple half moons. But the best, inserting a fingernail into the narrow slit between two teeth and pushing upwards, against the gum. The pain is instant. The pleasure immediate.

The stranger started to move again. He was probably writhing with pleasure.

Then the other one, the man with blond hair and a blue eagle tattooed on his forearm, gave up his role of passive onlooker and stood up. With his left hand, he lightly touched the stranger, whose face, hidden by his huge shoulders, I couldn't yet see. His right hand clasped a magnificent shaft.

The woman very slowly removed her three fingers. She looked one last time at the blond man, now completely upright, and disappeared off to the right, walking on her knees like a repentant sinner.

The two men were now alone.

It was then I realized that the stranger was most probably going to be sodomized.

I felt oddly elated. Sodomy, sodomize, two of my favourite words, frustrated euphemisms, much more disturbing, more revealing, than the insipid obscenities they replace to such advantage: to sodomize, a solid, corrosive verb which sends a violent shiver down the spine. I had never seen two men fuck – men like seeing two women fuck, but I don't like women – I'd never thought I might see two men fuck, but at that moment I felt strangely elated, and remembered how I liked pronouncing the word, 'sodomy', and writing it down, 'sodomy', because the sound of it evoked in me a notion of pure virility, primal, brute virility.

The two sodomites, the stranger and his present lover, had both obviously pumped iron in a gym. Perfect bodies, supple muscles now tense, glossy skin, immaculate tans; beautiful, young Greek gods off a Californian beach.

Perfect flesh.

There was nothing feminine about them.

The blond man came and stood immediately behind the stranger. The movement of his right hand accentuated the enormous proportions of his penis. It was huge, red, lustrous, and erect. The thick purple veins, distorted by the tight skin, looked about to burst, a magnificent portent, but he continued very calmly to caress himself, his feet firmly rooted to the ground, his eyes serenely watching his hand as it moved, a serious, even severe look on his face, while his companion on screen continued to wait, on all fours on top of the table.

I too was waiting.

For a moment I had a horrible suspicion that in the end it would all be reduced to this ridiculous pantomime. A couple more jerks back and forth and the blond man would come on top of the stranger, outside him, splashing his skin with spurts of utterly pointless semen, spurning the delicious, obsessive flesh, the subject of my miserable initiation, if that was what such an absurd performance could be called, threatening as it did to end before it had even begun.

The blond man masturbated slowly, diligently. At the

same time, with his free hand he monotonously stroked the stranger's rump. Suddenly, without altering his expression, he lifted his hand and then let it fall again.

The slap rang out like the crack of a whip.

That was another sign, the awaited secret signal. It was repeated very, very fast. The blond man parted his lips. He was smiling again.

The stranger shuddered beneath the blows, which became more and more violent, bursting in my ears with the Biblical power of the trumpets of Jericho. His skin was becoming red; his legs were giving way; his smooth, hard body pounded by all those infernal exercise machines, now shook powerlessly. His bottom was trembling like the thighs of an ageing virgin on her wedding night.

The volume of the soundtrack, a ghastly mixture of old piano favourites, gradually diminished, until it had faded altogether. It was replaced by the sound of the slaps. The stranger was breathing heavily. The blond man hadn't lost his composure. One of them shouted and they moved apart.

This time the interval was very brief, and startling. The stranger's face suddenly filled the whole screen. He was beautiful, far more so than his tormentor – he had dark hair, brown eyes, and perfectly drawn, almost feminine, lips and eyebrows, but a broad, strong jaw. The secret had been revealed; he was no longer a stranger; he had just been born, so he needed a name.

I called him Lester.

It suited him, the name of an English schoolboy, of a beautiful adolescent tortured by the perverted cane of his dry old stick of a schoolmaster in a shabby frock coat, with a pitifully small penis, who savoured in advance any of the little rascal's pranks, so he could make him stay behind after lessons, bend over a desk, take down his trousers and unleash on his firm white bottom a torrent of mean little blows of his cane, while his pathetic, limp prick, jumped around inside his trousers. Lester, the picture of the perfect sodomite, who felt pangs of nostalgia as an adult for the rites of childhood and sought a new master, a blond man, stronger than him, who'd really show him how things were done.

There he was, Lester. His cheeks were flushed, almost purple. He was sweating. The streams of sweat had left strange streaks down his face, like those traced by tears. He gazed into space. He continued to wait.

When the camera returned to the blond man, he was again stretching out his hand, but gently this time, and he placed it on the reddened skin. He caressed it for a moment and then pressed into the perfect, deliciously swollen flesh, parting the way with his thumb.

The hole seemed enormous.

He leaned forward. Lester sank down even further, his head to one side, his cheek resting against the table. I lost my head.

The remote control handset was on the table. I picked it up and wound the tape back. I went back to the beginning, when the woman was still with them.

I tried to reconstruct the sequence step by step, making sure I kept a cool head and understood it all properly, serious and attentive as I always am when I set myself a task which is beyond me. I wanted to know them, but I was able to stop in time. After all, they were just actors, they fucked for money; any attempt to get a glimpse of what they were really like was bound to fail. There wasn't any point in delaying the moment further.

There they were, both of them, still two separate, distinct figures. Then, with amazing ease, totally oblivious to me, to my convulsions, the blond man entered, literally entered, the child-man, he rested one hand on his waist, grabbed him by the hair with the other – I loved that, Lester, you dog – and started to move inside him.

I watched them, and I couldn't understand my own feelings. Little by little, the blond man was no longer blond. In my head, his hair turned black, flecked with stiff white hairs; he suddenly gained a few years, and then he had a name but I didn't dare pronounce it – I didn't even dare think about him.

The camera focussed on Lester's face. He was sweating more now, his eyes half closed, lips drawn; he was having a great time.

I said it over and over to him, quietly.

You're a bad boy, Lester. You shouldn't have done that. You're so cruel. You've made Daddy cross and this time you're really going to get it. Poor Daddy! Still so young and energetic, spends his life tending that lawn, and you've wrecked the whole thing in an instant. Now you won't be going to Eton this year, and Daddy will punish you, he's doing it already. Look at him, look at yourself in the big dining-room mirror, Lester. I'm sure he never wanted it to come to this . . . but he's always so decent, so strict. You deserve a spanking – you asked for it when you dug holes in the lawn with the funnel from the kitchen to make your stupid golf course.

I've heard him say it before, this means the supreme punishment. *Daddy's going to penetrate you with the funnel, Lester; he's going to stick that big perforated aluminium funnel up your bottom and he'll pull it out covered in blood. You've no idea. But there's a good side to everything, you'll see. The funnel will open up a hole so big that when Daddy comes at you with his cock, to get some compensation for the irreparable damage you've done to his lawn, you won't feel a thing, and that's good, I'm telling you – and I know from experience, little brother, dear Lester . . .*

The events on the screen brought me back to reality. The blond man, blond once more, was coming. As soon as the first jet of semen had spurted out – conclusive proof that none of this was rigged – he once more penetrated the man who had, after all, never ceased being a stranger.

But my body was on fire.

A thick thread of transparent saliva hung from my bottom lip.

It had been a strange day, odd from the start, and not only because of the heat, a dry, African heat, very unusual for the middle of September.

My sister-in-law Milagros phoned me first thing. She wanted to know if I could spare her a few minutes, and to tell me in passing about Pablo and how things were going well with his new girl. That's what she called her, his girl, a pale little muse he'd dug up in some intellectual coterie in the provinces. She was extremely young.

The agency wasn't doing very well. I knew Susana had got me a job there because I was her friend, and not because they really needed anyone. According to her, Milagros needed my time more than I needed her money, but even so, I answered that I was very busy, that I couldn't take on another book, and I felt bad about it all day.

I detest behaving in a capricious manner, but I just can't help it.

Things got complicated during the morning. I couldn't find a typist who was available; the typesetters were late with the proofs for the ad for the Germans; and one of our most faithful clients cancelled a job of considerable size. I spent the whole morning on the phone for nothing.

Work was going badly.

At midday I got a call from Ines' school. The form mistress wanted to see me because she was concerned about my daughter's behaviour. Apparently she was extremely antisocial for a child of four.

Pablo had his answering machine on.

I'd thought of inviting him to dinner with the pretext that we needed to discuss the sudden social inadequacies of our common heir, to see just how far I'd lost my power over him, but I didn't dare leave a message.

Chelo called me first thing in the afternoon.

She felt even worse than I did. She was in one of her wet depressions which set her off secreting tears, snot, dribble; her tongue gets thick; she makes unintelligible sounds, sordid visceral sounds, which somehow jump down the telephone line. The victim enjoys, savours her final tears on the sacrificial altar; the blade caresses her delicate neck, ready to administer justice, the supreme injustice.

This time it was some story about her exams. You really could call them 'her' exams, she'd been trying to pass them for so long.

I hung up on her.

I can't take it, I just can't take her bouts of hysteria.

It seems I'm not a sensitive person. I've got used to having that reputation.

I can still remember it all perfectly.

When I got home from school, Marcelo was in bed and Pablo was sitting at his feet.

He was twenty-seven and had just published his first book of poems, after the huge success of the critical edition of the *Spiritual Canticle*, but I wasn't impressed by all that yet.

He was big and tall, and his hair was already going slightly grey.

I'd known him ever since I could remember, and I loved him in a vague, comfortable way, with no expectations.

A fashionable singer-songwriter had come to Madrid to give a long-awaited concert, quite an event for the oppressed democratic opposition. Pablo was saying he had to go. My brother was insisting that he didn't have the energy to move; he had a horrendous hangover.

So I suggested I go – this was a reflex by now. I adopted an eager expression, clenched my fists, tried to make my eyes shine, and repeated like a little parrot that I'd love to go, just love to, really love to.

This had never worked before.

But this time Pablo looked me up and down and asked my brother what he thought. Marcelo, who looked, to my surprise, more suspicious than anything else, thought a moment, reminded him of my age and then told him to do whatever he liked.

Pablo looked at me again. I was calm because I knew he was going to refuse.

But he didn't.

He stood up, took me by the arm and started to hurry me along. If we didn't leave immediately, we'd get there late, and there was no guarantee that the concert would last much more than ten minutes. If we missed the beginning, we'd probably only arrive in time to hear the police sirens.

I put up a bit of a struggle. I hadn't had time to change, so I was still wearing my school uniform, and only the jumper was new, and my size. I was already taller than all my sisters. The skirt I'd inherited from Isabel, and it was much too short, several inches above the knee. The blouse was Amelia's, another hand-me-down, the buttons threatening to burst at any moment. At the beginning of term, my mother had been less willing than ever to spend any money, I mean, it was my last year. My stockings were worn out, the elastic was loose and I couldn't take two steps without them gathering round my ankles. My shoes were hideous, with rubber soles an inch thick. And everything, all except the green duffle coat, which had once belonged to one of my brothers, was a hideous brown colour.

When you're the seventh of nine children, especially when the last two are twins, you don't get anything new, not even your school uniform.

It was no good. He didn't want to wait one minute, even though we had plenty of time.

'You look very pretty just like that.'

As we were going out of the door, Marcelo called me and told me it would be better if Pablo left first, while I went and told Amelia some story, that I was going over to Chelo's house to revise, or something.

I didn't really understand his warning, but Pablo seemed to. He stopped and stared at him, and then said something even more odd.

'Come on, Marcelo, what do you take me for?'

My brother laughed, and didn't say anything more.

He left first. When I came down, he was waiting for me at the entrance.

The duffle coat was slightly longer than my skirt, and its rough edges brushed against my thighs as I walked. Christmas wasn't far off. It was cold.

I fastened my top button and put on the hood. I glanced at myself in the small mirror built into the wooden shop-front of an old grocer's, and decided that the hood didn't do anything for me. I realized too that not even the tip of my uniform was visible. I might have been naked under that big green jacket.

Pablo had a secondhand SEAT 1500, fairly dilapidated, but still, it was a car. I was very excited. This was the first time I'd ever gone out with him, the first time I'd gone out in the evening, and the first time I'd ever gone out with a bloke who had a car.

The journey took us a long time. La Castellana was packed with cars crammed full of children and provisions, whole families en route for a weekend in the mountains. He talked without stopping. He was openly malicious, telling me gossip, and jokes, and highly exaggerated stories, the kind of conversation with which he used to disarm my mother in the past, when he came round and found Marcelo grounded.

So then I thought he was treating me like a little girl.

I caught him looking at my legs a couple of times but I couldn't draw any conclusions from that.

Once we'd parked, quite a way from the marquee, he turned to me and delivered a set of instructions. On no account was I to leave his side. If the police turned up, I mustn't get scared. If fists started to fly, I wasn't to scream or cry. If we had to run for it, I was to take his hand and we'd get the hell out of there, no arguing. He'd promised Marcelo he'd get me home in one piece.

He was deliberately dramatizing the whole thing, to excite me with the prospect of danger and flight.

He asked me if I'd be able to behave like a good, obedient little girl.

I said yes, very seriously. I'd swallowed the whole story.

He leaned over and kissed me twice, first lightly, in the middle of my left cheek, then on the edge of my jaw, almost on my ear.

He'd made the most of my situation as a young damsel in distress to place his hand on my thigh. He was already unusually adept at fondling women with style.

When we got to the entrance, we launched into the ritual round of greetings, kisses and congratulations. I felt ridiculous amongst that crowd, with my green duffle coat and my stockings falling down round my ankles. Pablo seemed absorbed in his own social success, so I let go of his arm and tried to hang back. But in spite of appearances, he was keeping a close eye on me. He grabbed me by the wrist and forced me to stay by his side. Then, still not looking at me, he took my hand, not like couples do, with their fingers intertwined, but literally took my hand and squeezed it between his forefinger and thumb, like you take hold of a small child to cross the road.

He would never hold my hand any other way.

A middle-aged man with a sarcastic expression, a well-known author whose visible lack of enthusiasm made him stand out from the crowd, as if the whole event was really of very little consequence to him, was the only one to take any notice of me. He looked at me at length, smiling. When we passed by his side, his smile grew wider and he turned towards us, talking in a very quiet voice.

'Well, well, well! Pablito!'

Pablo burst out laughing.

'He liked you. Do you know who he is?'

Yes, I knew.

People were starting to file in, and we went to stand in the queue. Soon after, the trouble started. The bouncers on the door, the security people, blocked the entrance and started shouting that no one was getting in without paying. Those causing the row, a group of fifteen or twenty young people, answered that they weren't going to budge. Things stayed like that for quite a while, until someone started to push from the back of the queue.

The first charge shoved me out of my place. I was now immediately behind Pablo, right up against him, the back of his head touching my nose. The people at the back started shouting again, as if rallying their strength, and set off another avalanche. The six buttons on my duffle coat, little pieces of brown plastic streaked with white, which I suppose were meant to look like the horns of some animal, dug into his back.

I asked him if I'd hurt him. He said yes, a little. I unbuttoned my duffle coat. It was hot in the crowd. The people at the back were still pushing. The air turned thick with the smell of bodies. Pablo took my wrists and made me put my arms round him. He must have felt my body against his, and my breath on his neck. I felt good. It was as if the situation gave me more freedom. I didn't dare kiss him, but I started to rub against him. I was only doing it for myself, so I'd have something to remember from the evening; I was sure he hadn't noticed. I moved very slowly, pushing against him and then moving away, pressing my breasts into his back and biting tiny sections of his dark red jumper until the rough wool squeaked against my teeth.

The commotion stopped as suddenly as it had begun. It

felt cold again. I let go of Pablo as quickly as I could. And he started to behave very oddly.

He looked at his watch, stood staring at it for a few moments, then moved out of the queue and headed off in the opposite direction in a very determined manner.

'Come on, let's go.'

I obeyed, not really understanding what had happened.

'Do you smoke joints?'

His voice sounded different; I didn't recognize it. I remained silent because I didn't know what to say.

'Answer me.'

Yes, I smoked joints, but I didn't tell him so. I no longer trusted him. I shook my head, very seriously.

Still walking, he took a lump of dope out of his pocket, warmed it up and passed me a cigarette.

I didn't dare ask him what he wanted me to do with it. I licked the paper, unstuck it and emptied the tobacco out into the palm of my hand.

He stopped a moment to take it from me and roll a joint. He lit it, took two drags and handed it to me.

I stopped and shook my head again.

'For God's sake Lulu, you're acting like an idiot!'

He, Chelo and my father were the only people who still called me that. Marcelo tended to call me 'duck' or 'duckling' because I was, and still am, very clumsy.

I took the joint, had a couple of drags and handed it back.

We walked on, smoking. After a while I plucked up the courage to ask him, 'Why didn't we go in?'

He smiled at me.

'Do you really like that guy?'

'No . . .' This was only partly true. In fact, at that time I didn't even know that he sang in Catalan.

'No, I don't like him either. So . . . what was the point of going in?'

We reached his car but he carried on walking.

'Where are we going?'

He didn't answer. We turned down a very narrow street. A few paces from the corner there was a red awning with gold lettering. Pablo opened the door. As we went in I noticed the two droopy bay trees standing on either side of the door, and the yellowish light given off by the oil lamp fixed to the wall. Inside it was dark.

'Careful, duckling! There are some steps here.' But I still nearly fell over. Pablo drew back a thick leather curtain and we went into the bar.

I felt paralyzed with embarrassment. Most of the men were wearing ties. The average age of the women couldn't have been much under thirty. They were all sitting, mostly in couples, at tiny round tables with reddish table-cloths. The lighting was subdued and the music very low.

My hair had come loose from its pony-tail and was falling over my face. I was agonizingly aware of my uniform. Everybody was looking at me.

This time it was true. They really were all staring at me.

We sat at the bar. The stool was high, round and very small. My skirt stretched tight across my thighs. This made it seem even shorter. I crossed my legs which made it even worse, but I didn't dare move again.

Pablo was talking to the barman, who was looking at me out of the corner of his eye.

'What do you want?' I thought a moment, but I really didn't know. 'You're not going to tell me you don't drink either . . .'

The barman laughed and I felt terrible. Trying to put on a deep voice, I asked for a gin and tonic.

Pablo addressed the barman, with a smile.

'Her name's Lulu . . .'

'Yeah, it suits her . . .'

'My name's really Maria Luisa.' I don't know why I felt the need to offer an explanation.

'Lulu, say hello to the gentleman.' Pablo could hardly speak, he was laughing loudly, I didn't understand a thing.

'I'm hungry.' I couldn't think of anything better to say. I was hungry.

I was given a little plate of chips which I started to wolf down.

'Well-brought-up young ladies don't eat so quickly.'

Once again he was friendly and smiling, but his voice still sounded different. He was treating me with a disconcerting mixture of firmness and courtesy, he who had never been firm with me, much less polite.

'I know, but I'm hungry.'

'And well-brought-up young ladies always leave something on their plate.'

'I know . . .'

He was drinking neat gin. He emptied his glass and ordered another one. I'd finished mine and was about to do the same.

'That's enough drink for you tonight.' Before I'd had time to open my mouth and protest, he repeated firmly, 'You're not having any more to drink.'

As we left the waiter said goodbye with great ceremony.

'You're a delightful girl, Lulu.'

That made Pablo laugh again. By that time I was fed up with his enigmatic laughter, fed up with being treated like a little white lamb with a pink bow round its neck, and fed up with not being in control of the situation. It wasn't that I couldn't imagine possible outcomes, but rather that I dismissed them out of hand because they seemed so unlikely. It seemed so unlikely that he should want to waste his time with me. I couldn't understand why he was, in fact, insisting on wasting time with me, what he was doing it for.

Outside it was very cold. He put his arm round my shoulders, a sign which, in my state of utter bewilderment, I chose not to interpret, and we walked on in silence until we reached the car.

As he was opening the door, I asked him another question. That night was loaded with questions.

'Are you going to take me home?'

'Do you want me to?'

I did, really, I wanted to get into bed and go to sleep.

'No.'

'Good.'

Inside, he looked at me for a moment. Then, in a perfectly synchronized movement, he put his left hand between my thighs and his tongue in my mouth, and I opened my legs and opened my mouth and tried to respond as best I could, as best I knew how, which wasn't very well.

'You're soaking . . .'

His voice, his tone both of pleasure and surprise, sounded very far away.

His tongue was hot, and tasted of gin. He licked my whole face, my chin, my throat, my neck, and then I decided not to think any more, for the first time, not to think – he'd do the thinking for me.

I tried to let myself go and throw my head back, but he didn't let me. He told me to open my eyes.

He turned towards me and placed his left leg between my legs, pushing upwards, forcing me to move against his cotton trousers.

I felt hot, I felt my sex swelling, swelling more and more, as if it were closing of its own accord, just from the swelling, and it was turning red, redder and redder, it was turning purple and the skin was shiny, sticky, thick; my sex was becoming enlarged with something other than pleasure, nothing like the easy pleasure, the old domestic pleasure, this was nothing like that, but rather a new, annoying, irritating, even unbearable sensation, but which I couldn't do without.

He unbuttoned my blouse but didn't take off my bra. He just pulled it down, fixing it under my breasts which he stroked with hands that seemed enormous.

He bit one of my nipples, just one, and only once, clenching his teeth until it hurt, and then his hands left me, although the pressure of his thigh was becoming more and more intense.

I heard the unmistakable sound of a zip being undone.

He took my right hand, put it round his cock and gave it two or three tugs back and forth.

That night, his cock also seemed enormous, magnificent, unique, superhuman.

I continued on my own. I suddenly felt sure of myself. A hand job, that was one of the few things I did know how to do. The previous summer, in the cinema, I'd practised quite a bit with my boyfriend, a nice boy about my age who'd left me completely cold.

I tried to concentrate and do it properly, but he put me right straight away.

'Why are you moving your hand so fast? If you carry on like that I'll come.'

I didn't understand his warning.

I thought you had to move your hand really fast. I thought he wanted to come and then we'd go home. I thought that was the normal thing to do, but by some strange sense of intuition, I didn't say so.

His hand grabbed my wrist and set a different rhythm, a slow, heavy beat, and then guided my hand down, I was touching his balls now, and then up again, so I had the tip of his foreskin between my fingers, really slow. We carried on like that for quite a while. I watched my hand, I was fascinated, he watched me and smiled.

My anxiety, and the initial violence, had all disappeared. Now everything seemed very smooth and slow. My sex was still swollen, opening and closing.

'I've always had great confidence in you.' His voice was tender.

That bit of slippery reddened flesh had turned into the star of the evening. He was no longer touching me, he wasn't doing anything to me. He'd been moving imperceptibly, so as not to get in my way, until he was back in his initial position. He was back in the driver's seat, his body arched forward, his arms hanging back.

He moved his mouth close to my ear.

'Have you . . .?' he didn't finish his sentence. He fell silent, thinking, as if choosing his words carefully. 'Have you ever sucked a guy's cock before?'

I stopped moving my hand, lifted my head and looked straight into his eyes.

'No.' This time I wasn't lying, and he knew it.

He didn't say anything, he just went on smiling. He put out his hand and turned the key in the ignition. The engine started. The windows were all misted up. Outside it must have been freezing; a curtain of vapour was rising up from under the bonnet.

He leaned back against the seat again, looking at me, and I realized that everything was collapsing, the whole world was collapsing around me.

'Makes me feel sick.'

'I can understand that.' He put his foot on the accelerator and pressed down a couple times.

I bit my tongue. I always bite my tongue in the fraction of a second before I make an important decision.

I lowered my head, shut my eyes, opened my mouth, and then decided that there was nothing wrong, after all, in making sure first.

'You won't piss on me, will you?'

He found that very funny; he found nearly everything I said or did that night very funny.

'Not if you don't want me to.'

I was dead serious.

'No, I don't.'

'I know that, you idiot, I was only joking.'

His smile didn't reassure me much, but there was no going back now, so I put my head down again, shut my eyes, opened my mouth once more and stuck out my tongue. Better to start with the tip of my tongue first; the idea of licking it was more bearable.

Pablo arched more, stretching out like a cat, and put his hand on my head.

I grabbed his cock with my left hand and, starting at the

base, pressed my tongue against the skin and held it still a moment. Then I started to move along it, very slowly. Most of my tongue was still inside my mouth, so as I moved, I was brushing the surface with my nose, passing over it with my tongue, and then my bottom lip followed the trail of saliva. When I reached the end, I moved back down, towards the base, then came upwards again very slowly.

Pablo was sighing. His hairs were tickling my chin.

The second time, I dared lick the tip.

It tasted sweet. All the cocks I've ever tried in my life have tasted sweet, which doesn't exactly mean they tasted good. It was hard and hot, definitely sticky, but all in all, to my surprise, it was less revolting than I'd imagined, and gradually I felt better, more sure of myself. The idea that he was at my mercy, that I'd only have to close my jaws and clench my teeth for an instant to finish him off, was rather comforting.

I ran the tip of my tongue over its slit, then down over what felt like an invisible seam, to the thick rim of flesh, then stopped just beneath it, and followed its circumference. I was doing it all very slowly – at times like these I've never had to be told anything twice – and I was beginning to think I was making rather a good job of it.

Objectively, doing this wasn't giving me any pleasure, except perhaps for the contact with a new flesh which my tongue could explore in much greater detail than my hands.

Objectively, it wasn't giving me any pleasure, but I was getting more and more excited. Somewhere inside my head, far back enough so it didn't bother me, but near enough to be noticeable, throbbed the fact that I was under-age, six years to go before I was twenty-one (at that time, coming of age was at twenty-one – I couldn't give a shit, nobody could vote anyway) – memories of the summers of my childhood, the dramatic episode at the lake, when I fainted in the water and Pablo saved my life; me spying on him and my brother touching up two girls on the swings in the garden; and my mother's voice, telling her friends, 'Pablo's one of the family, he's almost like another son . . .'

Marcelo, at home, must have been thinking we were still messing around with matches. I made sure I didn't forget that I was in a car, in the middle of the road, sucking the cock of an old friend of the family, and I felt waves of intense pleasure. I pictured myself, a fallen woman. It was wonderful. I remembered the habitual sermons – *boys only play around with girls like that, they don't marry them* – and I was also aware of the peculiar relationship between us. After the kisses and caresses necessary to win me over, he was now almost entirely passive. Sitting upright and fully dressed, he was letting me get on with it. I was flung over him, half naked, cramped and uncomfortable, but quite content with the situation.

My mother used to say that she would have let me go to the ends of the earth with him, and I was starting to imagine it already.

Just as I was starting to wonder if I felt sufficiently familiar with it to put it in my mouth, he again made the decision for me. His hand, which had been resting on my head, pushed down abruptly. He caught me unawares and I swallowed a good chunk. Instinctively I withdrew my lips but his hand stayed put, pushing down inexorably. We repeated the game five or six times.

It was fun, trying to resist.

My mouth was full. I could feel the small bulging veins, the slight unevenness of the wrinkled skin, which went up and down according to the movement of my hand. It tasted sweet and it tasted of sweat. The tip was knocking against my palate; I tried to swallow the whole thing, to put it all in my mouth, and had to contain the urge to retch.

Pablo took out my hairband, slipped his hand under my hair, and gripped it just above the nape, catching a handful of hair very close to the roots. He gripped it and pulled it towards him, again guiding me. His knuckles pressed into my head. It hurt, but I didn't try to stop him. I liked it.

Now he was moving too, moving gently in and out of my mouth.

'I always knew you were a dirty little girl, Lulu.' He spoke slowly, slurring his words, as if he were drunk. 'I've thought about you a lot lately, but I never thought it would be so easy . . .' This had an immediate impact on my sex. It would end up exploding if it carried on swelling at this rate.

I kept my eyes closed and concentrated fully on what I was doing. I was leaning so far forward that I was almost lying on my side on the seat, my legs curled up, the handle of the window against my thigh, trying to make sure that my hand moved in time with my mouth, openly defying my innate clumsiness. I was so engrossed that it was some time before I noticed the significant change in our situation.

We were on the move.

At first I assumed I was imagining it, so many things had happened that night, and were still happening, but suddenly the car filled with light. I opened my eyes and looked up, and there were all the street lights of La Castellana, staring back at me.

First of all, complete astonishment. How could he have moved the gear lever without me noticing? In fact the lever wasn't under me; it took me some time to remember that in this kind of car the gear lever was next to the steering wheel.

Then, terror. Panic.

I sprung up like a Jack-in-the box. When at last I was back in the right-hand seat, I realized that I was half naked. I covered myself up as best I could, with my jumper and my hands, no doubt managing to look ridiculous.

Pablo slammed abruptly on the brakes. We came to a halt in the middle lane, amidst the strident hoots of a bus which narrowly missed us on the right. As it passed I caught a glimpse of the driver, tapping his finger against his temple.

I agreed with him.

'What do you think you're doing?' I was really frightened. 'You could have killed us.'

'So could you.'

'You can't just stop like that, in the middle of the road . . .'

'You couldn't either, but you managed.'

Suddenly he no longer seemed like an adult. He'd lost all his self-assurance and had turned into a vexed, sulky teenager. His plan had failed and it was touching to see him now, with his fly undone and a serious manner, staring with an offended expression at a fixed point in the distance. For the first time in my life, for the first and last time in my life with him, I felt like a woman, a grown woman. It was a pleasant feeling, but I couldn't linger over it long. Pablo was furious.

I tried to calm down and make a proper assessment of the situation. I turned towards the window and checked that all I could see of the passing drivers was their torsos, their bodies cut off slightly below their armpits.

I wasn't sure what to do.

'I'm going to take you home. I'm sorry, I'm drunk.'

I suddenly felt a terrible urge to cry.

The sulky teenager had disappeared. His voice was grave and serene, the voice of an adult apologizing without meaning it – sorry, I'm drunk – a polite formula for a little girl who hadn't measured up, after all, to what was expected of her. He looked at me for a moment, smiling, and it was a formal, pleasant smile, without a hint of complicity, the smile of a condescending adult, a friend of the family, who'd known me since I was a baby, sincerely sorry for having overstepped the mark.

I suddenly shrank. I tried to make myself as small as possible and started to cry. I just couldn't hold back the tears. We were now going quite fast, my house wasn't very far, after all that, we were nearly at my house. My mind was a blank, I couldn't think but I had to try and do something fast – time was running out, it was slipping through my fingers and this was important, really important.

I turned and looked at him. He had at some point done up his flies without me noticing.

I flung myself at him, my whole body swung over to the left, and I started to undo his trousers, but I was very nervous, I was crying, and my fingers were constantly fumbling. I managed to unfasten his belt and in my haste I knocked myself on the cheek with the buckle. I was still crying, but from rage now because I wasn't managing to do things fast enough. I undid the button, unzipped his flies and took it out, and it was small, nothing like the magnificent weapon of only a few moments ago. I put it in my mouth and I could fit the whole thing in, and I started to do everything I knew, and more; I wanted to please it at all costs, but it wouldn't get bigger, the bloody thing wouldn't grow, and like that, small and soft, it made it all the more difficult.

It was in my mouth again and I sucked it, and suddenly I thought I like it now, but no, it wasn't that, I didn't really like it, it was just that it had to get bigger, it just had to. Every so often I took it out of my mouth and licked it as I'd done at the beginning. I ran my tongue over the whole thing, I covered it in saliva, from the tip to the base and back again to the tip, and then I put it back in my mouth, massaged it vigorously between my lips, swallowed it and moved my tongue inside my mouth, just my tongue, as if I were sucking the blood from an imaginary wound, and then, from outside, holding it firmly in one hand, I delved beyond the base, into the narrow space between the skin and the flesh, until my mouth was full of hairs, and then I went back to the beginning again . . .

The first thing I noticed was that we'd started to go much more slowly, and that we were constantly moving from side to side, changing lanes. Then I felt his hand on my head, once again. I only realized at the end that he had a hard-on again; I'd given him a hard-on again.

We stopped. Traffic lights. I didn't dare lift my head even for a second, but I opened my eyes and tried to guess where we were. An iron bridge crossed the street at a right angle above us. I'm a native of Madrid. I know La Castellana like the back of my hand.

The fantastic neon Father Christmas on the Corte Ingles must have been waving at us. I put it in my mouth and moved up and down it, mechanically, to give myself time to think. We still had quite a way to go anyhow. You had to take this route to get to my house, and to his.

From then on I tried to work out every inch of the way, blindly, and there was no longer a street, there were no people, and even if there were it didn't matter, it was just a distance, and that distance was all that mattered now.

The first clear sign was the sound of the fountain. I was starting to think I'd never hear it; we were moving so slowly that the huge grey mass had started to seem never-ending.

We drove on, leaving the sound of the fountain behind. Then the first pleasant surprise. He'd gone past the turning for the shortest route home on the right. We were carrying straight on.

A few minutes later I glanced up to make sure we'd reached Colon. I was certain no, we weren't going back to my house. Then, surprised, we weren't going to his place either.

Where was he taking me? Water. We left the Old Lady of the fountain behind and carried straight on. This was getting like the joke of the country bumpkin who only knew how to drive in a straight line.

There was one more fountain to pass – the sound of water again – but that was the last.

We turned left, took another few turns and then, wham, the front of the car gave a jolt. That time I really did very nearly swallow it.

The engine was switched off, but I didn't dare stop. Pablo took me by the chin and helped me up, then put his arms round me and kissed me.

When we moved apart, he leaned back a moment and looked at me. He didn't say anything. I worked out that he was trying to guess if I was scared.

'This isn't my house.' I tried to sound clever.

'No.' He laughed. 'But you have been here before.'

When we got out, I saw that he'd parked the car at an angle up on the kerb. He's always had a knack for doing that.

The house, a dark, grey building, about a hundred years old, didn't ring any bells. The entrance, an attractive modernist structure, led up to a pair of huge wooden doors with stained-glass panels. The brass door handle surmounted by a dolphin's head did look vaguely familiar though.

He went ahead of me. He stopped at a door with a gold plaque in the centre and then I remembered.

We were at his mother's workshop, the 'atelier' as she liked to call it. She was a a fairly well-known dress designer who brought out about four or five collections a year, and repeated like a little parrot the bit about creative tension, the social responsibilities of the creative artist, and the impact of 'prêt-à-porter' on contemporary urban lifestyles, silly cow. Years ago before it all went to her head, my mother had been a client of hers. I sometimes accompanied her to fittings, and I'd sit in a huge armchair and leaf happily through a pile of thick French magazines, full of beautiful models with enormous earrings and showy hats.

He walked ahead of me. As he passed one of the sofas in the hall, he picked up two big square cushions with the tips of his fingers, without stopping. At the end, a big double door opened onto the fitting room. He turned on the light, threw the cushions on the floor, gestured casually for me to come in and then disappeared.

The armchair was still there, in the same old place, I could have sworn it was the same one, just covered in different fabric.

'Lulu . . .'

I'd forgotten the mirrors, even though the walls were

covered in them, mirrors reflected in other mirrors which in turn reflected others, and in the middle of them all, there I was, with my horrible brown jumper and pleated skirt, from the front, from the back, from the side . . .

'Lulu!' He was shouting now, from I don't know where.

'What . . .'

'Do you want a drink?'

'No thanks.'

. . . There I was, a little white lamb with a pink bow tied round its neck, like on the label of the washing powder they showed – still show – on the TV ads.

Pablo came back holding a glass and sat in the armchair and looked at me.

I was blushing but it didn't show – it never does, my skin is too dark – and I was still standing in the middle of the room. I hadn't moved because I didn't know what to do or where to go.

'Honestly, I've never seen such hideous shoes in all my life.'

I didn't need to look down because I knew exactly what they looked like and they really were hideous.

'Don't they let you wear heels at school?'

No, of course they didn't, stupid question, you couldn't wear high-heeled shoes at a convent school, not even in the sixth form, even though we were allowed to go out and smoke during breaks.

'No, they don't let us,' I answered anyway.

'Take them off.' His words sounded like orders; I liked that, and I took them off. 'Come here.' He patted his thigh.

I went up to him and sat on his lap, fitting my legs between his body and the arms of the chair. Before, instinctively – I've never understood why, and it doesn't matter – I lifted my skirt at the back, so that it hung over his knees, and the back of my thighs came directly into contact with the fabric of his trousers.

He was really surprised by this gesture.

'Where did you learn to do that?' His face again showed a mixture of pleasure and surprise.

'Do what?' I didn't understand, I hadn't been aware of doing anything special.

'To lift your skirt up before sitting on a bloke's lap. It's not natural.'

Maybe he was right, maybe it wasn't natural, but I didn't know what he was talking about.

'I don't know, I don't understand.'

'It doesn't matter.' It didn't matter. He was pleased. He smiled and kissed me gently on the lips. 'Now take off your jumper and be a good girl; you mustn't say anything or laugh. I'm going to make a phone call.'

I took off the left sleeve first, then pulled it over my head. I was just finishing with the right sleeve when I froze with horror.

'Marcelo? Hi, it's me.' It must have been my brother at the other end of the line; there aren't too many Marcelos around. 'Yeah, it was fine . . .'

He pulled the jumper out of my hands, lodged the telephone under his chin and started to undo my blouse, just two loose buttons. I didn't move, I hardly breathed, I was paralyzed, completely stunned.

'No, it wasn't bad, really, the guy's a pain in the ass, you know that, but everybody had a good time, they shouted, they cried and they went home happy.' He adopted an epic tone, like a TV commentator during a national league match. 'In short, you missed another glorious episode in the history of Spanish Socialism, comrade, another glorious day, it was truly moving . . .' I could hear my brother cracking up with laughter at the other end of the line. Pablo was laughing too; even I couldn't have lied better.

He slipped his hands round the back and unfastened my bra, a huge Belcor, typical Seventies style, flesh colour, with a raised check pattern and three little fabric flowers in the middle, the sight of which had thrown him into mute spasms of exaggerated horror. He covered the receiver with his hand, slipped a finger under the shoulder strap and whispered in my ear, 'Is this part of your mother's cunning scheme to make sure you're all virgins on your wedding night, or what?'

He took off my blouse and bra, constantly moving the phone from one side to another.

'Aah, now Lulu . . ., taking her was my good deed for the day . . .' He looked at me and smiled; he looked beautiful, more handsome than ever, enjoying playing the inveterate, arrogant seducer of young girls. 'Another little Commie, mate; I've converted one more, with no induction course, no Gorky, nothing. She had a fucking brilliant time, I mean it.' He spoke slowly, watching me and emphasizing each word, speaking for both Marcelo and me at the same time, and he ran his glass over my nipples, leaving behind a wet trail, unnecessarily – my breasts had been erect since he started, although the ice-cold glass did feel confusingly pleasant. 'You can't imagine it, she raised her fist in the air, she shouted like a mad thing, then sang the Internationale all the way in the car, the whole works, you get the picture?' he looked at me, 'and I've never seen anyone move their lips so enthusiastically, she loved it . . .' He was smiling and I smiled back; I wasn't scared any more, I wanted to laugh now, although I wasn't allowed.

I tried to hurry things up and undid the top clasp on my skirt, but Pablo shook his head and made it clear that I should fasten it again.

'The thing is we met up with lots of people, we've been out drinking, and now she's so pissed she can't stand up,' he put his hand under my skirt and started to stroke the inside of my thighs with the tips of his fingers. 'Fuck off, Marcelo! How should I know . . .' He slipped his index finger under the elastic and started to move it up and down, very slowly, following the line of my groin with his knuckle. 'What are you on about? I didn't take her drinking, we just went for one drink, that's all, and she got pissed all on her own. She's old enough, isn't she? What are you, crazy or something? I wasn't going to spend the whole evening watching her every move, was I, even though she's your little sister. She disappeared a couple of times, she must have sipped some from my glass and other people's, I don't know . . . She was really excited, she downed quite a bit, and when she got here she was out of it, she couldn't even stand up. She's fast asleep now. We put her to bed and I thought she could stay here, if that's all right; I really don't feel like taking her home now.' He was running the tip of his finger up and down the slit of my sex, and with his other hand, without letting go of the phone, he pulled me towards him. I had to rest my hands on the back of the armchair to keep my balance. 'What? No, we're in Moreto . . . fuck off, Marcelo, what difference does it make? No one need know. Didn't she say that she was going to do her homework at a friend's? Well, she can stay the night at the friend's and that's that. I mean, out of sight out of mind, don't you think? Even your mother's antennae aren't that long . . . No, I don't know where her school is, she can tell me herself, I seem to remember she has a tongue . . . Look, Marcelo, I swear I haven't touched her, it hadn't occurred to me.'

He moved so that his face was at the level of my breasts.

I assumed he wanted to suck them or bite me, like he had before, in the car, but he didn't do any of that. He put his face in between them and rubbed it against my skin. I could feel his cheek, his closed mouth, and his nose, which felt huge, moving over me, pressing my flesh, nestling against it as if he were blind and armless, like a newborn baby who has nothing but his sense of touch and the deceptive sensations on his face, to guide him to his mother's breast, and when he spoke again, I could at last make out a hint of excitement in his voice.

'No, I couldn't go home, Merceditas is revising. She's got an exam tomorrow and I didn't want to disturb her. Anyway . . .' He gave me a conspiratorial look. 'I've got a chick here . . . Yeah, you know her, but she's shaking her head . . . She doesn't want you to know who she is . . .' His face took on a weary expression. 'Your sister? Look, can't you think about anything else? Your sister's sleeping off her hangover two rooms away. I can hear her snoring from here. She doesn't have a clue about what's going on.' Marcelo must have said something funny because Pablo laughed. 'Look, mate, don't get all high-minded on me. What the fuck does Lulu care if I'm cheating on my girlfriend? Why should she be offended? She might think she's in love with me, but she's still a child. It's only in novels that guys go to bed with little girls, and she'll realize, I suppose, I mean she isn't silly.' I blushed even more; my face was burning. 'How old is she anyway? All the better for her if she sees us; she's old enough to be wanking her eyes out.' For a moment I didn't react. 'What? You're joking . . .'

He opened his mouth and took firm hold of one of my nipples, pulling at the flesh from time to time with his teeth. Then, suddenly, he moved away from me, leaned back and stared at me, his eyes open wide and his mouth gaping, passing his tongue over the edge of his teeth. His finger changed position. He took it out from under the elastic and placed it in the centre of my sex. His movement was unequivocal. He was no longer rubbing me or caressing me. He was masturbating me over my knickers.

'What the fuck's a recorder?'

I wanted to die of shame. I would never have thought Marcelo capable of doing such a thing, but I was wrong. He told him. The whole thing. Pablo was staring at me in disbelief. I felt terrible. I stared at my lap.

'Fucking country, it's a disgrace!' That was like a mantra for them; Marcelo and he repeated it left, right and centre, over anything. 'A recorder . . . Good old Lulu, what a girl!'

I was torn between two very different feelings. On the one hand I was dying with embarrassment, I couldn't look Pablo in the eyes, and at the same time, I felt I was about to come, without having to use my hands, because he was doing it really well, in spite of the fabric, or maybe just because of it, his finger was exerting just the right pressure; it didn't hurt, or chafe my skin, unlike the clumsy, exasperating fondling of all the others.

'How did you find out about it? She told you! Whose recorder was it anyway? Guillermito's! Good for Lulu! Slowly but surely . . .'

Still touching me, he took me by the chin and made me lift my head.

'Look at me,' he whispered almost inaudibly.

I looked at him. He was smiling, smiling at me. I looked down again.

'I'm not surprised it gave you a hard on, mate; I'm getting hard as a rock just hearing about it on the phone . . . Yes, very amusing, something new after all these years. So what did you do? If I'd been in your shoes I'd have fucked her there and then . . . Yeah, I know, I've always been a worse brother than you, or maybe a better one, who knows. Anyway, poor Lulu,' giggles, 'don't worry, I'll take her to school tomorrow. I'll give you a ring, see you.'

'A recorder . . .' He'd hung up. He was talking to me. 'Look at me.' And his finger stopped moving.

I didn't dare look at him, or move, although I missed him between my legs.

He took me by the shoulders and shook me.

'Shit! Lulu, look at me or I swear I'll get you dressed and take you home right now.'

The same threat, the same result.

I raised my head again and looked at him. I was getting out of a bath full of lukewarm, tepid water, and I didn't have a towel to dry myself . . .

His eyes shone. There was an almost animal look in them. He was hurting my arms.

'Which way up did you put it in, by the mouthpiece or the other end?'

'The top.' The words came out involuntarily.

'Did it feel good?'

'Yes, but it was a bit narrow. I couldn't really feel it to tell you the truth, only the mouthpiece, that was all I could feel. Anyway, Amelia caught me at it almost straight away, I'd hardly had time to feel it, really, Pablo, I swear to you . . .'

He started to look blurred. Two huge tears welled up in the corners of my eyes. His tone changed, his grip loosened, and he spoke. He said almost the same as Marcelo had that night, when I went in, terrified, to tell him, because his room was the only place in the whole world I could go.

'I'm sorry, I didn't want to frighten you. There's really no reason to be scared. Come on, look it's OK, it's just that it's funny, Guillermito's recorder. I can still remember it – when the twins were born, you hated them, you weren't the baby any more and you hated them, so you got your own back, with his recorder, that's the only reason I laughed, honestly. Other girls aren't so inventive, they make do with a finger. You're a big girl now, perfectly healthy; you're exercising your rights and . . . and . . . I can't remember, feminists have an expression for it, I can't think of it now. It doesn't matter anyway, it's OK, it's natural . . . Everybody does it, although women don't admit to it.' He wiped my tears with his fingertips. 'Stop crying, now be a good girl and tell me all about it, and I'll buy you a real dildo somewhere, just for you.'

'I've never had anything of my own.'

'I know, I'll give you one so it reminds you of me when you use it. Not a very original idea, I know, but I like it.' He must have addressed this last remark to himself, because I didn't understand what he meant. Anyway, I nearly always thought about him when I masturbated, although obviously I couldn't tell him that. 'All right?'

I nodded, not knowing exactly what we were agreeing on. I'd never been so confused in all my life.

'Stand up.'

I got up.

We kissed for quite a while, rubbing against each other.

He rolled my skirt right up to my waist, baring my stomach. In the mirrors I could see a strange image of myself.

'Sit down and wait for me, I'll be back in a minute.'

He headed towards the door, and then, in spite of being dazed, I realized that I had something important to say. I called him, he turned, and leaned against the doorframe.

'I've never gone to bed with a guy before . . .'

'Who said anything about going to bed, stupid, at least not for now. We're going to fuck, that's all.'

'I mean I'm a virgin.'

He looked at me for a moment, smiling, and then disappeared.

I sat down and waited. I tried to analyze my feelings. I was hot, turned on in the true sense of the word. Turned on. I smiled. I'd been slapped hundreds of times without understanding why, for saying it. It was one of my favourite expressions. Turned on, it sounded so old fashioned . . . I repeated it very low, watching my lips move in the mirror.

'Pablo's turned me on.' It was funny.

I said it again and again, all the while realizing that I looked good, really pretty, in spite of the blackheads on my forehead.

Pablo had turned me on.

He was standing there, with a tray full of things, watching me move my lips, maybe he'd even heard me, but he didn't say anything. He walked across the room and sat down facing me, his legs crossed like an Indian. I thought he was going to eat my pussy – after all, he owed it to me – but he didn't.

He took off my knickers, pulled me abruptly towards him, making me lean my bottom on the edge of the armchair, and opened me up even wider, placing my legs over the arms of the chair.

'Come on, start, I'm waiting.'

'What do you want to know?'

'Everything, I want to know the whole story: whose idea

it was, how Amelia caught you, what you told your brother, everything, come on.'

He took a sponge from the tray, plunged it into a bowl of warm water and started to rub it against a bar of soap, until it was frothy.

I started to tell him, speaking like an automaton, but watching him and wondering what would happen now, what was going to happen now.

'Well . . . I don't know what to tell you. Chelo mentioned it to me but apparently the idea was really Susana's.'

'Which one's Susana? Tall girl, with very long brown hair?'

'No, that's Chelo.'

'So who's Susana?' He dipped the sponge in the bowl so that it filled with foam.

'She's short, very thin, she's got brown hair too, but it's more blondish, you must have seen her at my house.'

'Yeah, go on.'

I couldn't believe what he was doing. He'd put out his hand and was soaping me with the sponge. He was washing me as if I were a little girl. That threw me completely.

'What are you doing?'

'None of your business, go on.'

'It's my cunt, what you do to it is my business.' My words sounded ridiculous, and he didn't answer. I went on, 'Well, Susana does it a lot apparently, I mean put things up her, so she told Chelo that the best, the thing she liked best, was a flute, so we decided to try, although really I thought it sounded disgusting in a way, but I did it; Chelo didn't in the end, she always bottles out. Anyway, that's it; now you know, that's all there is to tell.'

He placed a towel on the floor, exactly beneath me.

I couldn't help looking in the mirror, at my pubic hair magically transformed, all white.

'How come Amelia caught you at it?'

'Well, we all share a room, her, me and Patricia . . .'

'Patricia, she and I . . .' he corrected.

'Patricia, she and I,' I repeated.

'Good, go on.'

'I thought I was the only one at home, on my own for once in my life. Well, Marcelo was there, and José and Vicente, too, but they were watching TV, and as there was a match on, I thought . . .' He took a razor-blade out of his shirt pocket. 'What are you going to do with that?'

He gave me his best 'don't worry' sort of look, although he kept a firm hold of my thighs, in case I tried anything.

'It's for you,' he answered. 'I'm going to shave your cunt.'

'No way!' I flung myself forward with all my might and tried to get up, but I couldn't. He was much stronger than me.

'Yes.' He seemed as calm as ever. 'I'm going to shave it and you're going to let me. All you've got to do is keep still. It won't hurt. I've done it loads of times. Go on with the story.'

'Why are you doing this?'

'Because you're very dark; you're too hairy for a fifteen-year-old. You don't have a little girl's cunt. And I like little girls with little girls' cunts, especially when I'm about to debauch them. Don't worry, just let me get on with it. I mean, this isn't much more undignified than shoving a flute up you, or a recorder, or whatever it's called . . .'

I looked for an excuse, any excuse.

'But they'll notice at home and if Amelia sees she'll blab to Mummy, and Mummy'll . . .'

'How's Amelia going to find out? I didn't know you got up to things together at night.'

'No.' I was so hysterical that I didn't even have time to get offended by what he had just said. 'But she and Patricia see me get dressed and undressed, and the hairs show through things.' That calmed me down; I thought I'd had a brain-wave.

'Oh, right, well, don't worry about that. I'll leave your pubis almost exactly the same; I'm only going to shave the lips.'

'What lips?'

'These.' He slid two of his fingers over them. I'd thought he was going to do the exact opposite, and his idea seemed even worse, but I'd already decided not to think, for the umpteenth time, not to think; at the rate we were going my brain would blow a fuse that night.

'Hold them open with your hand, will you please?' I obeyed. 'And go on telling me. What did you do when Amelia saw you?'

I felt the cold touch of the razor-blade, and his fingers stretching my skin, while I went on, spitting out the words like a machine gun.

'Well, I don't know . . . Before I knew it, there she was in front of me, screaming my name. She ran out of the room, with the umbrella, and slammed the door . . .' The razor-blade glided smoothly over what I'd just learnt were also called lips. I felt no pain – it was more like a strange caress – but I couldn't get the idea out of my head that his hand might slip. I could hardly see his face, only his black hair, his head leaning over me. 'So I ran after her. Luckily she didn't go into the sitting room. She went straight out the front door, with the umbrella; she must have come back just for that. Then I thought the only person I could trust was Marcelo, so I went and told him. I was still holding the recorder . . .' The razor-blade moved outwards; it was scraping my thigh. 'He was in his room, there was a whole load of papers on his desk, I don't know what he was doing with them. He laughed his head off, and told me not to worry, he'd shut Amelia up, she wouldn't squeal if she knew what was good for her, and then he said the same as you did just now . . .'

I thought he wasn't listening, that he was making me talk for the sake of it, like when they operated on my appendix, to keep my mind busy on other things, but he asked what exactly Marcelo had said to me.

'Well that, that it was normal, everybody wanked and it was no big deal.'

'Right . . .' His voice became deeper. 'He didn't touch you?'

I remembered what he'd said before on the telephone – if I'd been you I'd have fucked her there and then – and I shuddered.

'No.' He must have finished the right lip because I felt the icy shiver of the razor-blade on the left one.

'Has he ever touched you?'

'No. What are you getting at?' His insinuations sounded completely crazy.

'I don't know, you're so fond of each other . . .'

'And do you touch your sister?' He burst out laughing at this; I was scared his hand might shake.

'No, but then I don't find my sister attractive . . .'

'Do you find me attractive?' My friends said you must never ask a guy straight out like that, but I couldn't help it. He leaned back and looked straight into my eyes.

'Yes, I find you very attractive, and I'm sure Marcelo does too, and maybe even your father does, although he'd never admit it.' He smiled. 'You're very special, Lulu, a round, hungry little girl, but a little girl nevertheless. Almost perfect. And if you let me finish, you really will be perfect.'

It was then, in spite of the outlandishness of the situation, that my love for Pablo stopped being something vague and comfortable, and that I started to hope, and to suffer. His words – *You're special, an almost perfect little girl* – were to echo in my head for years. I lived for years, from that time on, clinging to his words as if they were a life-line.

He leaned over me again and insisted very quietly.

'Anyway, I think we ought to get it on one day, the three of us, you, me and your brother . . .' The blade moved outwards again, this time on the other side. 'There you are, Lulu, almost done. That wasn't so bad, was it?'

'No, but it really itches.'

'I know. It'll itch even more tomorrow, but you'll look much prettier.' He'd leaned back for a moment, to look at his handiwork I suppose, before disappearing once more between my legs. 'Beauty is a monster, a bloodthirsty deity which demands constant sacrifices, as my mother says . . .'

'Your mother's an idiot,' I blurted out.

'No doubt she is . . .' His voice didn't falter in the slightest. 'And now, keep still a moment please, whatever you do, don't move. I'm just finishing you off.'

I could imagine the look on his face perfectly, even without seeing it, because everything else, his voice, the way he spoke, his gestures, his boundless self-assurance, were all so familiar to me.

He was playing. He'd always liked playing with me. He'd taught me most of the games I knew and he'd trained me in the art of cheating. I'd learned fast; we were almost unbeatable at cards. He would cheat, and he would win.

He picked up a towel, dipped a corner into another bowl and squeezed it out over my pubis, which was almost unchanged, as he'd promised. The water dripped down. He did this again a couple of times before starting to wipe me to get rid of the hairs which were still stuck there. I thought I could do a better job myself, and much more quickly.

'Let me do it.'

'No way . . .' He was talking very slowly, almost whispering, he was completely absorbed, his eyes riveted to my sex.

He kissed me twice, on the inside of my left thigh. Then he put his hand out and took an amber-coloured glass jar from the tray, opened it and dipped in his fingers, the index and middle fingers of his right hand.

It was cream. A thick, white, fragrant cream.

His fingers slid over my newly shaved labia, leaving the cream on my skin. I shivered again; it was ice cold. Then I thought how there was still a lot of the winter to come and that the hairs would take a long time to grow back. It wasn't going to be very pleasant. Pablo was calmly gathering together all the items he'd used in the operation, putting them back on the tray, which he pushed to one side.

Then he too moved to my right, uncovering the mirror opposite me.

My sex looked like a little mound of red, swollen flesh. On either side of the central slit stretched two long white trails. The sight of it reminded me of Patricia as a baby, when Mummy put cream on her before changing her nappy.

Pablo was looking at me and smiling.

'What do you think? You look lovely . . .'

'Aren't you going to rub it in?'

'No, you do it.'

I stretched out my hand, wondering what it would feel like. My fingers touched the cream, which had become soft and warm, and started to spread it up and down, moving evenly over the slippery, smooth bare skin, which felt hot, like my legs in summer after they'd been waxed, until the two long white marks had completely disappeared.

Afterwards, I found it hard to stop. The temptation was too strong, and I let my fingers slip inside, once, twice, over the swollen sticky flesh. Pablo moved closer, inserted his finger very gently, then removed it and put it in my mouth. As I was sucking it, I heard him murmur, 'Good girl . . .'

He was kneeling on the floor, in front of me. He took me by the waist, pulled me towards him abruptly, and made me fall off the armchair.

The shock was brief. He handled me with great ease, in spite of the fact that I was – am – very big.

He made me turn round and kneel, my cheek resting on the seat, my hands barely touching the carpet. I couldn't see him, but I could hear him.

'Stroke yourself until you feel you're about to come, then tell me.'

I'd never imagined it would be like this, never, but there was nothing missing. I limited myself to following his instructions and unleashing a surge of familiar sensations, wondering when I should stop, until I felt my body beginning to split in two, and I decided to speak.

'I'm going . . .'

So then he penetrated me, slowly but firmly, without pause.

Ever since his announcement, his warning – We're going to fuck, that's all – I'd decided to endure whatever I had to endure, without uttering a sound, to bear it right to the very end. But he was tearing me. He was burning me. I was trembling and sweating, sweating a lot. I was cold.

My resistance was short-lived.

Before I knew what I was doing, I was asking him to take it out, to give me a moment at least, because I couldn't, I just couldn't bear it any more.

He didn't answer or take any notice. When he reached the end, he stopped and kept still inside me.

'Don't stop now, duckling, because I'm going to start moving and it's going to hurt.'

His words demolished any remaining hopes. It would be no use protesting, but I couldn't just stay still, in suffering. I'm not one to put up with pain, at least in big doses. I hate it. So I decided to follow his instructions, yet again. I tried to regain the rhythm I'd lost. He was setting a different tempo from behind. Holding fast to my hips, he moved in and out of me at regular intervals, drawing me towards him and away from him along the incandescent rod which now no longer remotely resembled the harmless toy on a spring which had filled my mouth a few hours before, and much less the famous recorder.

The pain wasn't fading, but, while remaining intense, it was acquiring different nuances. It was still unbearable at the entrance, there it felt as if I were being torn apart. I was surprised not to hear the tearing of skin, now tense to the point of transparency. Inside, it was different. The pain faded into more subtle tones, which intensified as I fell into rhythm with him, moving with him, against him, and my own handling was beginning to take effect.

The pain didn't disappear, it remained present the whole time, throbbing until the end, when my pleasure shook itself free from it, grew and finally overpowered it.

As I felt the final spasms, and my legs stopped trembling and disappeared completely, Pablo slumped on top of me, giving a muffled cry, both piercing and hoarse, and my body filled with warmth.

We stayed like that for some time, without moving. He'd hidden his face in my neck, covering my breasts with his hands, and was breathing deeply. I was happy.

He moved away from me and I heard him walking round the room. When I tried to move I realized that my whole body ached. I turned over with difficulty because something like the stiffness you get after a long run, but much worse, was paralyzing me from the waist down.

He helped me stand up. When I put my arms around his neck to kiss him, he picked me up by the waist, pulling my legs round his body and started to carry me, without saying a word.

We went out into the corridor, which was long and dark, typical of old flats, with doors only on one side. The door at the end was ajar. We went in, he somehow managed to turn on the light, and he put me down on the edge of a large bed. He took off my skirt and stockings, smiling. Then he lifted up the bedcover and pushed me underneath. He took off his shirt, which was all he was wearing, and slipped under the sheets beside me.

I found these classical touches, the bed, my own nudity, both moving and reassuring. All the weird stuff was over, at least for the time being.

Now he was kissing me and holding me, making funny, odd noises. He'd run his fingers through my hair, pushing it back off my face, and then he'd stop from time to time, to look at me. It was wonderful. I could feel his cold, hard skin, his bare chest – in spite of the common view, I've always found hairy men repulsive – and I sensed for the first time that it would all end up weighing upon me like a curse, that it was all nothing but the prelude to an endless, uninterrupted ceremony of possession.

I surprised myself with the depth of this thought while we rolled about the bed, now a warm comfortable refuge which brought me back down to earth, reminding me that outside in the street it must have been freezing, a most pleasing thought, while I was inside, safe and protected.

It really hadn't hurt all that much.

I made the most of a pause to enquire about something which had been obsessing me for quite a while.

'Did I bleed much?'

'You didn't bleed at all.' He seemed amused.

'Are you sure?' I was completely stunned by his answer.

'Yes.'

'Well I'll be damned!'

I hadn't bled at all. Not a drop. That really was a calamity. Something extremely important, something decisive had happened, something which would never happen again, and my body hadn't even deigned to commemorate the event with a few drops of blood, or even the most minimal of dramatic flourishes. I'd been cheated by my own body. I'd imagined something more horrific, more in keeping with the pathos of the situation, a real haemorrhage, a fainting fit, something, and all I'd had was an orgasm, a long, different kind of orgasm, in some ways even painful, but still, just one orgasm more.

He was laughing, laughing at me again, so I hid my face in his shoulder and gave up any idea of telling him what I'd been thinking. He reached down and picked up a packet of cigarettes off the floor.

'A little ciggie, like in French films?' His voice still sounded cheerful.

'Why do you say that?'

'I don't know . . . In Frog movies they always smoke after a fuck.'

'And why do you always say "fuck", instead of "making love", like everybody else?'

'And who told you that everybody says "making love"?'

'Well, I don't know . . . but that's what they say.' I'd taken one, of course. Smoking was an extra pleasure, yet another thing I shouldn't be doing.

'Saying "making love" is a gallicism and really pretentious.' He sounded almost like a schoolteacher. 'And anyway, although foreign in origin, in Spanish the expression "making love" has always meant to court, not to fuck. "Fucking" sounds good, it sounds strong, almost onomatopoeic . . . "Screwing" is OK too, even though it sounds a bit old-fashioned now.'

'Like "turned on".'

'Exactly, like "turned on", but I like that word.' He smiled at me, he'd probably heard me earlier. 'After all, sex, I mean fucking, fucking in itself, hasn't necessarily got anything to do with love, in fact, they're two completely different things . . .'

And so began my theory lesson, the first.

He spoke, on his own, for a long time. I hardly dared interrupt him, but I tried to remember every single word, to retain him in my memory, while he spoke of love, poetry, life and death, ideology, Spain and the Party, Marcelo, sex, age, pleasure, pain, solitude.

Then he stubbed out his last cigarette, and stared at me strangely, particularly intensely, then he smiled as if he wanted to replace his previous expression and said something like, pah, don't take any notice of me.

He lifted the sheet and started to run his hand over my body. I watched him, and I thought how beautiful he was, too beautiful, too old and wise for me. I would have caressed him, I would have kissed and bitten him, and scratched him. I don't know why, I felt I had to hurt him, to attack him, destroy him, but I was afraid even to touch him.

He penetrated me once more, but very differently, softly,

slowly, on top of me, moving carefully, as if trying not to hurt me.

A strange fuck, tender, almost conjugal, almost.

He kept on telling me to keep my eyes open and look at him, but I couldn't, especially when my sex started to swell, to grow spectacularly, and force me, stupidly, to be alone with it, so I could fully experience its grotesque metamorphosis. I tried, though, I tried to look at him, and I opened my eyes, and saw him there, his face above mine, his mouth half-open, and I could see my body, my long, erect nipples, and my trembling belly, and his; I could see his cock move, disappearing and reappearing beyond my few remaining hairs, but the mere fact of seeing, of watching what was happening, increased the demands my sex was making, forcing me once more to close my eyes. Then I'd hear his voice again, 'Look at me', and if I insisted on giving in, I'd also feel his thrusts, suddenly much more violent, painful again, because I wouldn't open my eyes. He would let the whole weight of his body fall on me, reawakening the pain, he'd move quickly and abruptly, until I obeyed him, and opened my eyes, and everything became wet, fluid once more, and my sex responded, it opened and closed, started to disintegrate. I was disintegrating, I was going, I could feel myself going, and unconsciously I let my eyelids drop, only to start all over again.

Until finally he allowed me to keep my eyes closed and I came, my legs stretched to infinity, my head suddenly heavy. I could hear myself in the distance, pronouncing unconnected words which I would afterwards not remember, and my whole body was reduced to one nerve, a single, tense but flexible nerve, like a guitar string, which went through me from my head to my belly, a nerve which trembled and twisted, absorbing everything into itself.

It was a tender fuck, almost conjugal, almost, but at the end, when I was exhausted and my body was threatening to become a body once more, vast and solid, around that single bristling, satiated nerve, he came out of me, moved forward a few paces on his knees, leant his left hand on the wall and put it in my mouth.

'Swallow it all.'

That's really all I had to do, endure five or six thrusts which I wouldn't have been able to avoid even if I'd wanted to, because he was holding me firmly between his legs, close my lips round the sticky flesh which tasted of him and of me too now, and then swallow, swallow the hot, viscous substance, both sweet and sour, with a slight aftertaste like the medicines which ruined many a happy childhood, swallow and hold back the urge to retch as the thick, revolting liquid flowed down my throat, a disgusting substance which I've never been able to get used to and never will, in spite of all the years of strict self-discipline which worthy resolutions entail.

He enjoyed it though. As I listened to his muffled groans and my head followed his movements to counteract the nausea which swept over me if I kept still, I tried to secrete as much saliva as possible so as to push down the last dose, like I did with Brussels sprouts, which taste putrid, and I was thinking that he was enjoying it, at least. I was reminded of one of the eternal invocations of Carmela, the nanny my mother brought with her when she got married, a pious, smelly old hag, riddled with sclerosis and completely senile, who went mumbling along the corridor like a ghost, *The Lord giveth and the Lord taketh away*, holding the *ABC* open at the Obituaries and 'Thanksgiving' page, *The Lord giveth and the Lord taketh away*; *he gives and he takes*; *it's all right*, *the circle is complete*, *everything begins and ends in the same place*; *he's enjoying it and that's fine by me*.

My first theory lesson had been a complete success.

Afterwards, I drank pints and pints of water. I always drink water afterwards, it makes no difference, but it's the only thing I can do, drink lots of water. I felt very tired, and very happy too. I turned over; I was sleepy. He covered me, and lay down close to me, put his arms round me, breathing against my hair, and said good night, although dawn was already breaking.

I sank into a pleasant, heavy sleep, like I do after a day in the mountains.

I don't remember anything else in particular.

I was woken by the sun and he wasn't there by my side.

I preferred not to think that he might have disappeared, dumping me there in his mother's workshop, which was certainly very quiet – nobody seemed to have come to work – and I tried to calculate the time.

It must've been very late. I'd probably missed at least three hours of classes.

Suddenly, I heard the sound of an old, creaking lock, somebody was opening the door. It might have been him, or it could have been anyone else. I put my head under the sheet and tried to keep still. I could hear the sound of footsteps – didn't seem like high heels, but you never knew – they were coming towards me, then I felt a weight on top of me. Somebody had thrown something at me.

'Cold *porras*[1] are uneatable . . .' It was his voice. I stuck my head out and saw him, leaning against the doorframe, smiling. 'What do you want for breakfast?'

'White coffee.' I smiled too; I'd never been so happy in all my life, ever.

He disappeared. I got dressed quickly; I was starving.

I didn't say another word until I'd devoured seven huge delicious *porras*, still warm, one of my favourite foods, while he watched, insisting he didn't want any more, he never usually ate more than one.

'You know it really bugs my mother that we like *porras* more than *churros*[2]. She says they make more of a mess, they're greasier, more uncouth, do you know what I mean?' I laughed to myself, remembering. 'She says you can eat a

[1]Elongated doughnut.
[2]Similar to *porras* but smaller.

churro with two little fingers – she always says it like that, two little fingers – so it's good, it's genteel, but eating *porras* in public, even with two little fingers . . .' I couldn't go on, I was choking, I had tears in my eyes I was laughing so much; he was laughing too.

'You're a sharp one, Lulu . . .'

'Thanks a lot,' but as I answered I realized that sometime I'd have to go back to the real world. 'What time is it?' I really would have preferred not to know.

'Twenty to one.'

'Twenty to one!' My legs were shaking; there'd be an almighty row over this. 'But . . . I had school today.'

'I decided to let you off, you were such a good girl last night.' He was smiling and I realized that for him, school, bunking off classes, one day more or less, none of it really mattered.

Maybe he was right, it wasn't such a big deal.

Anyway, Chelo would probably bail me out, she always did; she'd tell my mother that I woke up with an upset stomach and that her parents had decided to let me stay in bed. Dealing with the form mistress would be more of a problem. And in any case, there were more serious risks than that.

'Are you going to tell Marcelo?'

'No, he'd be green with envy.' He smiled to himself, strangely. 'And also, what we did last night won't fail to rock the foundations of the regime . . .'

We went out into the street. It was a beautiful day, cold but clear; the sun was warm for the time of year. I asked him to take me to the school gates. I had to see Chelo, so we could prepare my alibi before I went home.

He drove in silence the whole journey. I didn't feel like talking either, but when he stopped the car across from the school gates, he turned towards me.

'I want you to promise me something.' His voice suddenly sounded serious.

I nodded.

'I want you to promise that, whatever happens, you'll always remember two things. Tell me you will.'

I nodded again.

'The first is that sex and love are completely separate . . .'

'You already told me that last night.'

'All right. The second is that what we did last night was an act of love.' He looked into my eyes with particular intensity. 'All right?'

I stopped to think a few moments, but it was no use. I didn't know what it all meant.

'I don't understand.'

'It doesn't matter. Just promise me.'

'I promise.'

He smiled, gave me a kiss on the forehead, opened the car door and said goodbye.

'Goodbye Lulu, be good, and don't grow up.'

I didn't understand a thing and I felt bad again, like a little white lamb with a pink bow round its neck.

I didn't know what to say. In the end, I got out without saying anything. I walked quickly towards the gate, without looking back. I saw Chelo, and she saw me. She stood staring at me with a look of surprise. Pablo's car disappeared amongst hundreds of others.

I still felt bad.

'Where the hell have you been?' Chelo was astonished and then I thought that maybe it showed on my face, maybe my face had changed.

I took her by the arm and we started to walk towards home.

I told her, but only the half of it; I omitted most of the details. She looked at me in amazement and tried to interrupt, but I wouldn't let her. I ignored her constant exclamations, and went on talking, until I'd reached the end, and as I spoke the unpleasant feeling faded, I felt happy again, and pleased with myself.

She suddenly stopped dead. I tripped up on the root of a

tree and smashed my face against an acacia. That's typical of me; I don't have any reflexes.

She stood and stared at me. Her face took on a familiar expression. She was angry, angry with me, without any justification, I thought.

'Well, how did you do it then?'

'I've already told you, I was on all fours, I mean not exactly, because my hands weren't resting on the floor . . .'

'I don't want to know about that. I don't care about that, what I want to know is, how you did it.'

'I've already told you. I don't understand.'

'Are you taking the Pill?'

'No . . .' I was suddenly dumbfounded. I wasn't taking the Pill, of course not, it hadn't occurred to me, I hadn't given a thought to considerations of that kind while I was with him.

'Did he put a rubber on?' Her eyes shone with inquisitorial fury.

'No. I don't know, I didn't notice, I couldn't see him . . .'

'Don't you care?'

'No.'

'You're out of your mind!' She was working herself up into a fury, getting more and more angry without any prompting from me because I wasn't moving a single muscle in my face. It didn't bother me, I wouldn't let her get to me, and anyway I was really sick of her bouts of hysteria. 'You're . . . you're as bad as a bloke! You just go for what you want, without thinking about anything else. Don't you see you've been had? He's old, Lulu, an old guy who's taken you for a ride. See if he gives you the time of day now. You know what my mother says? Boys only have fun with . . .'

'Shut up!' Now it was my turn to be angry. 'I shouldn't have told you anything. You don't understand a thing.'

'Oh don't I?' She was screaming in the middle of the street; people were stopping to stare at us. 'You're the one who doesn't understand, you're the one who's acted like an idiot. You, Lulu, I'm sorry to have to tell you this, dear, but you just don't have a clue . . .'

It was me who phoned her, before leaving work. I called her because she's my friend, my best friend, and she means a lot to me.

She was still crying, hiccupping and sniffing.

I tried to cheer her up.

I said the examiner was a bastard and they had no right to change the date of the exam. I also told her I was sure she'd pass this time, even though I didn't mean it.

I felt lonely too that evening, and I didn't want to go on like that, I'd end up ringing Pablo; he'd have to turn the answerphone off sometime, the excuse was still valid.

In the end, I suggested a classic evening out.

If Patricia agreed to stay the night at my house – I'd pay her of course, she was a right little mercenary – and look after Ines, we could go out to eat, like two happy fat cows, and then we'd drink until we felt like laughing again, over nothing, like two madwomen, and if we were still up to it, we'd try to pick up some guys, in some trendy club, just for a laugh, like two old tarts, and tomorrow would be another day.

She said it sounded like a very good idea.

The evening was an absolute, total disaster.

As for eating, we certainly ate, a pile of sinful things, hundreds of thousands of calories, with bread, but it didn't manage to put us in a good mood.

As for drinking, we drank too, but it made us sad, drunk, miserable and tearful. Chelo didn't know what she was going to do with her life if she failed her exams yet again after so many years. I had left Pablo so I could run my own life, and now didn't know what to do with that either.

I had more freedom than I knew what to do with.

We drank in silence, each engrossed in our own thoughts. Chelo still looked tearful. The tears were welling up in my eyes too when I got up, my glass still half full, and said we were leaving, enough was enough.

I never cry in public if I can avoid it.

When I started the car, I'd decided to leave Chelo at her place and go back again. At that time, I spent my days divided between two basic preoccupations, deciding to go back and resolving not to go back, endlessly.

It was very late, but the streets were still full of people, laughing in small groups, walking up and down café terraces in search of a free table, bringing their drinks out onto the street, to see and be seen, ordinary people who looked like they were having a good time.

It was still very hot; it seemed like the summer was never going to end.

Chelo still lived in the same area as when we were children. We turned down a wide, elegant street we both knew very well. It seemed deserted, but they were there.

They were there, half hidden in doorways, done up to the nines and teetering on pointed heels, with tight shiny trousers, showy fake leopard skin over improbably smooth bodies, generous décolletés, perfect fabrics, enviably perfect, ruby red lips, false eyelashes thick with mascara, and childish hairdos – lions' manes must have gone out of fashion and now nearly all of them wore little pony-tails, with coloured hair bands and bows, their sweet little heads covered in clips with butterflies and apples.

Obeying an uncontrollable urge, I slowed down and drove close to the kerb. Chelo protested but I took no notice.

And then I saw him. He was right at the end of the street, almost on the corner with Almagro, dressed in a kind of orange jumpsuit, with a very wide black belt, decorated with chains and gold coins, in the midst of a little group, kissing them all, his lion's mane still intact; he was a classic.

I came up by his side, shouting his name out the window.

Ely turned, taking a while to recognize me – I tended not to drive, it was usually Pablo – and he came towards me with a great deal of fuss and excitement.

'Lulu, how lovely to see you!'

In the car parked next to mine, a well-dressed man not much older than me, who looked like an up-and-coming executive, a contented family man perhaps, was quietly negotiating with two transvestites, one tall and well-built, the other small and childlike.

Ely gave me a loud kiss on each cheek. He then greeted Chelo, equally effusively. He didn't look too good; he'd aged. We'd always been worried about him, Pablo and I; we had a feeling he'd end badly.

'What are you doing here?' He'd left for the South about a year before. 'I thought you were in Seville . . .'

'Aagh! Don't talk to me about it.' He flicked his hair back with his hand. His nails were painted pearly white. I'd never seen him use that colour before, maybe he thought it made him look younger. 'The Sevillians are too . . . Sevillian for me. I got bored with them very quickly, I missed the gang, the atmosphere, I don't know. And anyway, I'm in love again. I can't help it, you know what kind of girl I am . . .'

He'd lowered his voice to confess this – *I'm in love* – as if this were enough to explain his return – *I'm in love* – he said it in a sweet, shy, almost unctuous voice. *You're a sly little bitch*, I thought. When he spoke about love he forgot that he was really a man and he couldn't help thinking of himself in the feminine.

Chelo congratulated him loudly, adding that he should be careful, men were bad news. Ely answered to tell him about it, but that he still couldn't live without them. Chelo agreed with him there. I listened to their conversation, but kept an ear on the negotiations being concluded to my left. I thought I'd have to move my car to let them out, but then the three of them went and sat in the back of the car, the punter in the middle, and started to touch each other up.

'Hey!' Ely's strong Extremadura accent made me turn back to him. 'I saw your boyfriend on the telly a few months ago, in Seville! He's on quite a lot now . . .'

I nodded, smiling. Pablo was now forty-two, but for Ely he'd always be my boyfriend, just as for Milagros the insipid young thing was apparently Pablo's girl. Otherwise I wasn't surprised, he was suddenly fashionable.

'Why does he always come on and talk about that old priest?'

'What priest?' I didn't know what he was talking about. Anyway, lately I tried not to watch Pablo on TV. The other participants in the conference, debate, programme or whatever it might be, usually turned out to be such idiots that my husband's self-assurance, his knowledge, his scornful half-smile, hinting at the bolshiness underneath, all reminded me that I loved him, loved him terribly, in spite of everything, and it gave me an unbearable urge to go back to him, made me miss the pink bow and the soft, fluffy white fleece I'd worn for so many years.

'That priest, he died ages ago. Hell, I can't think of his name now. You know who I mean, the one who was involved with the little nun – she was all right that one, must have been a good person, that nun, and a clever little thing too.'

'What nun are you on about?'

'Which one do you think? The one with the sweets, the Saint, you know, the one from Avila . . .'

'Oh, San Juan . . .'

'That's it, San Juan of something, he's always talking about him. I don't know how he doesn't get bored. I mean, he was very good the other day – there was a Yank on with him, saying that when they beat themselves with a whip and all that, well really it was a turn on, it made them come, they were into pain, you know.' I nodded, I knew the cretin he was talking about. 'I thought he seemed really sweet, he was so amusing, but your boyfriend really lost his cool with him, he was very rude. I loved it, you know I love it when Pablo gets cross; he looks so handsome, and his grey hair gives him a certain something, I don't know what, but he looks really lovely.'

The man in the neighbouring car was very busy. He'd slipped his hands under the clothes of his two companions and pulled out their respective members, which he held for a moment in his palms, contemplating them appreciatively. One of them – the small, childish looking one – had quite a respectable-sized cock. The other one, the tall, showy one, with the dress sense of a musical revue star, feather boa and all, had a silly shrivelled little dick, which was by any reckoning the most feeble and wretched part of his anatomy. Just shows, you never can tell, which is what his client must have thought too, because he gave a little cry of surprise and amusement before beginning to caress them both equally, without discriminating – they're all God's creatures after all – one in each hand, while they did the same to him and kissed on the mouth the whole time. Ely asked me something, but I wasn't listening. He repeated the question, slightly louder.

'I said, where's Pablo?'

'To tell you the truth, I don't know. We're not living together any more.'

He couldn't have looked more surprised if I'd told him the world was going to end tomorrow. He was silent, looking into my eyes, not knowing what to say. Then I saw that curiosity had got the better of him and he discreetly moved his head closer to mine.

'He hasn't gone over to the other side, has he?' I smiled; yeah, and there he'd be, Ely, first in line; I was almost sorry to have to disappoint him.

'No, sorry, I don't think so; he's involved with a girl, a redhead, now.'

'Younger than you, of course.'

I was on the verge of telling him to piss off, but I restrained myself.

'Yes, she's younger than me.'

'So Pablo's left you for a little redhead . . .'

'No,' I tried to say it slowly, stressing every word. 'I left him, and then he got involved with the redhead.'

I'd been mistaken earlier. He was now looking more surprised than ever, his head tilted to one side, a sarcastic smile on his face.

'You left Pablo?' He emphasized each word too. 'You expect me to believe that? Who are you kidding, Lulu?'

'Up yours!' That was the only answer I could think of, *up yours*. I was furious, and I didn't want him to see me cry, the poof – Who are you kidding, Lulu? – *go to hell, up yours and I hope it fucking hurts*. He was looking at me as if I were mad; usually he answered with a 'Charming!' or 'May God be your witness!' and made me laugh, but that time he saw that I meant it, *up yours*. I drove off like a fury; we almost crashed into the car behind. Luckily he'd only just picked up the goods and was still driving slowly; to my left things were hotting up. The executive in the blue suit had got the little transvestite on top of him, he was going to stick it up him any minute, the other one was wanking. I was really sorry, I was going to miss the best bit.

Chelo was looking at me, terrified.

'What's the matter?' I didn't answer. 'What's got into you? I mean, Ely's always been in love with Pablo, hasn't he? That's what he's always said, isn't it? Please, Lulu, watch out! You'll get us both killed . . .'

I drove like a mad thing. I was completely off my head, jumping the lights, I didn't even see them. My eyes were filled with tears.

I hadn't been able to find my white blouse when I left the house.

Pablo had turned up with him one night, almost a year after we first met him. He'd been signing books at the book fair, an obligation he loathed, and he'd bumped into him there. Ely had come up to him holding one of his books and he'd stayed and kept him company all afternoon, because as usual almost no one came up to the stand. Pablo invited him to dinner as a thank you, and Ely cooked the dinner himself.

He was wearing a very pretty pale pink satin top, with fine straps and a low neck edged with lace.

'I love your top.'

'You can have it.' He looked very funny wearing one of my aprons and cooking ravioli. 'I mean it, Lulu, keep it, I've got lots more, in different colours.'

'It'll be too small for me, I've got much bigger tits than you . . .'

'Hey, don't you believe it.'

'. . . but you could tell me where you bought it, I really love it.'

So we arranged to go shopping together one afternoon.

We went to have cream cakes for tea first, I adore them too, he admitted, and then he took me to four places. Only one of them was a real shop, with a door onto the street and a brightly lit sign, shop assistants and all that. The others were just flats, all fairly near the Puerta del Sol; the last one was on the sixth floor with no lift.

When we got there I didn't really feel like going up at all.

I'd bought piles of underwear. Pablo had given me quite a bit of money, he knew I felt like buying some, and I really had a good time, trying on tiny little shiny aprons with matching caps, and corsets, the kind you do up at the back, and knickers up to your waist but completely open underneath. Ely helped me, giving his opinion, this doesn't suit you, this does, buy something in black leather, it gives really good results . . .

I took no notice of him; he must nave got fed up with me.

I didn't buy anything in black, or red. Really I would have quite liked to have one of those flashy suspender belts. They suited me, and they were so classic, but Pablo loathed those colours, so I stuck firmly to white, with some beige, pink, and yellow, and even a kind of indescribable thing, half-way between a nightdress and a swimsuit, covered in straps and with openings all over the place, terribly uncomfortable but so outrageous it was funny, in very pale green.

I really didn't feel like walking up to the sixth floor, but I forced myself, catching my breath as I climbed the old wooden steps which stank of bleach. I went up so Ely wouldn't feel disappointed, because, according to him, this place, which didn't even have a sign out on the balcony, or a brass plate on the front door, nothing, was the best; that was why he'd left it till last.

The owner looked as if she'd once been a flamenco dancer, her hair dyed a bluish black, scraped back and gathered in a flat bun, just above the nape. Her eyebrows were pencilled in pale grey and her eyeshadow was electric blue; her lipstick was very similar to Ely's, 'Scarlet Passion' or something. Matching rouge, very dark skin, a couple of gold teeth – her face looked like the map of a very rugged country.

She asked me if I was from Andalusia.

When I said no, she looked a bit disappointed. Then she wanted to know where I worked. I didn't know what to answer. At that time I was still battling with my translation of Martial, and I didn't think she'd be very interested in my struggles. Ely got me out of the fix by explaining that I was a decent woman, well, more or less. With that, the Flamenco dancer backed off, and drew her own conclusions, but she looked at me somewhat suspiciously.

For some reason, she didn't like me.

Even so, fat as a seal in her patterned dressing-gown, she led us down an endless corridor until we reached what seemed like the only outward facing room in the flat, a fairly large room with screens in the corners and some display cases where you could see clothes, together with all kinds of contraptions for providing pleasure.

I saw it immediately, up on a hanger.

It was tiny, white, almost transparent; the batiste was so fine it looked like gauze.

The collar, closed at the top, had two tiny lapels edged with ruffles. Just beneath them, two butterflies held a garland of very small flowers, embroidered in satin thread and little pearls. On either side of the embroidery, there were some very very fine gathers. And that was all. It had short ruched sleeves, ending in a ribbon which fastened with a little mother of pearl button. The blouse too was very short. It fastened up at the back with pink buttons, and the end one, at the waist, was hidden by a little bow on a ribbon, like the one on the sleeves but wider.

It was a little newborn baby's blouse, but made to fit a child of eleven or twelve.

When I turned round, holding it in my hand, Ely looked at me, surprised. Not the Flamenco dancer, though. That one must have seen it all, at her age.

'Do you like it?'

'Yes, I really like it, but I can't take it, it's too small. Do you have one in a bigger size?'

'No, it was made to order and nobody ever came to collect it.'

'Who ordered it?' I was suddenly seized by ridiculous suspicions.

'Oh, I don't know his name. A man of about forty-five, had a Catalan accent, that's it.'

'Did he bring the little girl with him?' By then I was only curious. The Flamenco dancer was starting to look uncomfortable.

'What little girl?'

'Well, judging by the size, this blouse is for a little girl, isn't it?'

'He had the measurements written down on a piece of paper, I never ask questions. Look, I don't care who the blouse was for, all I know is I've still got it, and I'm not going to find it easy to get it off my hands . . .' She was looking at me with a frightened expression and then she turned to Ely. 'Hey . . . she's not a copper, is she? You haven't brought me a bloody copper, have you, you bastard?'

Ely shook his head, I broke in.

'No, look, I'm sorry, I was just curious.'

'All right . . .' She seemed to calm down. 'I could get one made for you if you want.'

I nodded and she went out, apparently reassured that my intentions were honest, saying she was going to get a tape-measure.

Ely came up to me, and took hold of the blouse. He looked at it closely.

'Do you really like it?'

'Yes, and Pablo'll love it, I'm sure, more than anything else we've seen today.'

'This?' He was genuinely puzzled. 'Are you sure? I never would have thought it. Your boyfriend must be much more of a pervert than he looks . . .'

The Flamenco dancer, tape-measure at the ready, was listening to our conversation from the door. I ordered three blouses, all the same, in white – that surprised her even more. After demanding an exorbitant deposit, she told me I could come and collect them in a fortnight. Ely offered to pick up the blouses as he'd ordered a kind of short kimono, in black covered with brightly coloured dragons, horrendous, but which he thought terribly elegant. When I held out my hand to the lady of the house to say goodbye, she took me by the shoulders, gave me two kisses and addressed me unexpectedly informally.

'If you need to go back to work any time, come and see me. You could make a mint, now, dark girls are back in fashion, especially in the summer, all the foreigners, you know, Scandinavians, Belgians, Germans, and the French – you wouldn't think so, being so near to us, but they're really keen on girls like you, the French are. You'd have to say you were from Andalusia, but even so . . .' She paused and smiled at me. She thought she'd understood the expression on my face. I wasn't angry or offended, I just couldn't believe my ears. 'Don't kid yourself. He'll leave you pretty soon, with tastes like his . . . You really are very pretty, and I expect he's not all that old yet, but as time goes by he'll want them younger and younger, slim little blondes, and in the end he'll go for little girls, like the Catalan, who was having it away with his own daughter, the pig. A lovely child, it was a crying shame . . . To tell you the truth, I don't understand why he's gone for you. I mean, I don't know him, but I don't understand; there are so many grown women around who look like little girls, but you, you must be quite young, and you look older than you actually are. I simply don't understand.' She sounded friendly now, like an old lady genuinely concerned for my future. 'Anyway, come and see me if you ever need to go back to work . . .'

Those thoughts had already crossed my mind lots of times, but I'd never attached much importance to them. I mentioned it to Ely when we got outside. After all, Pablo had known me since I was a baby, it was different; he'd often played with me as a little girl, and he'd go on thinking of me as a little girl, if he wanted, it couldn't have been too difficult for him. I didn't think I did anything special to encourage him, really.

Ely was looking at me without really understanding what I was saying.

Despite his angry protests – *How old do you think I am, I'm not an old granny, I'm not into that sort of thing yet* – I dragged him off to have a cup of broth, thinking all the while that for someone who'd spent so many years as a prostitute, he really was incredibly slow sometimes.

Those thoughts had already crossed my mind lots of times, and I hadn't attached much importance to them, but that night, as I drove like a maniac, the Flamenco dancer's words, and Ely's too – *much younger than you, of course* – had stuck in my brain like needles, long, sharp needles.

My white blouse hadn't turned up. It was the last one; the others had gradually fallen to bits and this one wouldn't last much longer. It had lasted over five years, nearly six, not bad. At first I took it to be a good omen that it hadn't turned up. Pablo must have hidden it because he wanted to keep it, so it seemed I wasn't leaving for good. I didn't know if this was the case or not – in fact I didn't really know why I was leaving and that was the truth; but then maybe she was wearing it now, my little newborn baby's blouse. It probably suited her better; she was younger than me.

When we got to her place, Chelo forced me to come upstairs – you can't go home like this. She was even a bit scared. I've always suspected she thinks I'm mad, slightly unbalanced, as she'd say.

The video was in its box, on top of the television; I saw it as soon as I came in. Chelo said she was going to have a shower and she asked me if I wanted to join her. I said no, that was the last thing I needed that night, for Chelo to get silly on me. I said yes the last time we went out to dinner together, and then I had a hell of a time getting her off me.

'It's funny . . .' she'd said, 'you've got hairs on your cunt again, after all these years.'

I poured myself a drink, the umpteenth that night, and picked up the box. The cover showed three magnificent tanned, healthy specimens. On the left of the picture there was a very beautiful man, standing with a white towel round his waist and another one over his shoulder. It was Lester, but I hadn't met him yet. By his side, another bloke, taller and even more beautiful, with dark hair and a smile on his face, in a pair of faded old jeans. He was amazing; I thought he was the most beautiful man I'd ever seen in my life. A small, blonde woman with a cheeky expression, sitting totally naked on a chair, completed the picture, on the right. More or less above her head there was a symbol I'd never seen before, three linked circles, the first two with a little arrow, the third with a little cross, all pointing upwards.

'Chelo, sweetie, what's this?'

'What?' She came across the room naked towards me. 'Oh! it's a film – Sergio brought it over yesterday. We didn't watch it though, because, well, anyway, I don't know what it's about . . .' She sounded slightly apologetic.

I looked at her more closely.

There was a long scratch over her left breast. Although she'd purposely stood against the light, I could see other marks distributed all over her body. They were recent.

She looked me straight in the eyes and put her hand on my shoulder.

She knew what I was thinking and she also knew that I wouldn't comment on it. It was no use, after so many years. She'd assure me it had been an accident, that it would never happen again, like all the other times.

Pablo had never hit me.

'Look, Chelo, I'll just finish this drink and go home, if that's all right with you. I'm very tired and it's already late . . .'

'Fine, do what you want,' she interrupted me before I'd had time to finish my sentence. She was offended; that's what she was like, I was used to the way her mind worked, to her soft, ambiguous, tearful concept of friendship. The waiter she'd picked up this time had given her a good beating the night before, and now what she needed was comfort and affection, something soft and delicate, pleasure of a purely sensitive kind, as she put it. It was obviously all part of the game, pretending to be helpless and tender, bathing her bruised flesh in tears and sighs which would move any unwary young girl to act as the exact antithesis of the brute who'd savaged her obediently a few hours earlier – because that was how she did it, I'd witnessed the preludes before: she provoked them and insulted them, gradually loosening the reins until they took the bait, and they always did, because she made sure they were always innocent enough. She always chose the same type, waiters, bikers, bellboys, recently arrived in Madrid, innocents still, just like the girls had to be, to swallow that story about the rapes and the painful scars. She didn't even try to foist it off on me any more, not even when she miscalculated and he turned out to be less malleable than she'd thought; and some of them were like that, with ideas of their own.

She tried to get her revenge for my unswerving indifference to her tricks by reminding me how insensitive I was, but that too no longer bothered me, after all those years.

I heard the door slam, and the sound of running water in the shower. I was still holding the video, and continued to be intrigued by the unfamiliar symbol, the chain of little circles, two the same and one different.

I stood outside the bathroom door and shouted.

'Do you mind if I take it? The video, I mean.'

She didn't answer. I repeated the question twice more.

'Do what you like!' Yes, she was angry with me.

I put the tape in my bag and left quietly. I was beginning to think that maybe I wasn't behaving like a very good friend; and she was perfectly capable of suddenly launching one final, desperate attack.

They were so moving, so utterly moving, moving rather than beautiful. Their delectable flesh moved me, their tanned skin, their hard flat stomachs, and very short hair, their beauty conquered inch by inch, sweat and more sweat, trying to prolong adolescence beyond the age of twenty, or even thirty. They were grown-up teenagers, big children, a little gang of bored youngsters. *They're all alone*. I thought, *they must be bored*, poor things, and they keep themselves amused the only way they know how, with their huge, erect penises, the only toys they have; they massage one another and kiss, but never on the mouth; they caress one another but don't embrace, they look at one another and they like what they see; they can't help feeling attracted. I'd already caught them feeling one another's muscles, rubbing their arms, comparing themselves, watching each other out of the corners of their eyes as they played. They were delightful and moving, I would have liked to console them, to put my arms around them and hold them tight; they inspired a kind of maternal passion in me, they moved me deeply. They looked so young, and they were so beautiful, so perfect, but they'd probably reject me; they'd refuse my embraces and my affection. 'Leave us alone,' they'd say. 'We're grown up; we know how to have fun on our own, exactly as we please.' They'd be selfish and arrogant like all youngsters, the silly things, and they'd go back to their games, mounting one another. It was moving to watch them play, a gang of eternal teenagers, swapping roles, and smiling, and provoking, even rejecting one another sometimes. 'Hey, leave me alone; I mean it, go away; I don't want to, it's not right.' One of them was a born actor. He looked at his little friends with timid, frightened eyes – he didn't want to, and they licked their lips at the sight of him. They were delightful, so amusing, the two of them, as they caressed each other; they looked so funny, standing there so formal, one arm hanging down at the side, the other held out towards their friend's body, running their fingers through each other's hair. They touched and stimulated each other with their sweet little hands, and they warned the little coward curled up on the sofa, covering his eyes with his hand and peeking through his fingers: 'Little cheat, we're going to do it to you; yes we are, it's no use resisting,' and they laughed out loud. A girl, a little blonde, was joyously clapping her hands; she was young and beautiful too, but they took no notice of her. That was the right attitude, of course; I approved energetically from afar. *Ignore her*. What was she doing meddling in boys' games? 'I'm going to pee.' *Ugh! how horrible, how could she be so vulgar*? 'I'm going to pee,' she said again, and they looked at her with interest. *Yes, it's natural*, I thought, *they're still so young; they're curious about the opposite sex*. She was vulgar, decidedly vulgar. The actor took his hand away from his face, a charming, moving reaction. He wanted to know what was going on too, and she repeated, 'I'm going to pee.' The other two were standing and watching her. One of them had rested his head on his companion's shoulder and was stroking his back with his free hand – what an affectionate boy. The other one was acting tough; he was the gang's little fighting cock. He had an idea. 'Come and stand in front of me.' She obeyed. How extraordinary – he had the makings of a leader, so young and already so decisive, he was moving, and so sure of himself. He smiled at his companion. 'Leave me now for a while; we'll carry on playing later. Wait and see, I've had a brilliant idea.' She was standing in front of him, slim and fragile. *It's strange*, I thought, *how in Anglo-Saxon countries the boys mature earlier than the girls*. He picked her up effortlessly – she was light as a feather. Holding her by the thighs, he separated his arms and kept her up in the air. *You bad, bad boy, now I know what you're up to*; but the girl was slow to catch on. I guessed before she did. 'Now I know. You want me to piss myself, here, now.' The little lamb on the sofa tried to escape, but the leader's pal stopped him. *You see, you shouldn't have put up a fight, silly*. She said she could hold it for a bit longer. 'It's more of a relief afterwards.' *Isn't it incredible how this girl needs to be the centre of attention*? In the end she didn't manage to keep her promise. She pressed her tummy with one hand and she pissed, generously spraying the unfortunate soul who'd been watching her so intently. He deserved it for having cheated. The others were laughing – it was just a joke of course, a joke typical of their young age. What fun they had, it was wonderful, seeing them laugh. Then they stood next to each other again and she rubbed shamelessly against both of them. They were rubbing against each other, then the little lamb tried to escape again – what an innocent. The leader grabbed him by the waist. 'No, remember, we're going to do it to you right now.' His little body trembled, but it was all an act. He was pretending he didn't want to; he let them stroke his chest, caress his penis, looking resigned. His innocence was truly touching. The leader of the gang lifted him up in the air and threw him on the sofa. His pal congratulated him, of course – he admired the leader, it was understandable. He rubbed his hands together; he was going to have fun too, you bet he was, that was why he'd wagered on the winner. The rebel looked like he'd put up a good fight, though, so he crouched on the floor, on all fours. 'All right, I've lost, I'll pay a forfeit.' He was dignified, a good boy too. The little fighting cock was holding his chin in his hands, he was thinking. His friend flung himself on the floor. He clenched his fist and held it out towards the loser, then he let him feel the knuckles against his arse. He pressed them against his buttocks, leaving faint marks, and then moved back to the boy on the sofa. The object of these attentions was whimpering and pleading, 'No, no, please, not that; do anything you like, I mean it, but not that. The leader looked at his friend, who was still on the floor, and smiled. I realized that the business with the first hadn't been serious – of course it hadn't; it was just a joke. The torture was cut short. 'Turn round.' 'What?' He didn't understand; he was bewildered by fear, poor thing, it was touching. 'Turn round. Sit on the sofa and part your legs.' He obeyed straight away. 'That's better. Play well or don't play at all. You,' he said to the girl, who was still hanging around making a nuisance of herself, flirting with them all the time, 'you,' he said again, and gestured with his head. She crouched on the floor, on her heels, and began doing strange things with her hands. She plunged her fingers inside herself and pulled them out for a moment, before pushing them inside the pathetic young thing who was waiting on the sofa, holding his legs up in the air with his hands. *Aren't these kids clever? What a lot of things they know*. The little lamb's skin was glistening by now. 'That's enough, stop.' The eldest, the one who was acting as leader, took a few steps forward, bent his legs and made several attempts to plough through the body curled up on the sofa, but it didn't seem possible – the unruly youngster was tensing his muscles unpredictably, or maybe it just wasn't big enough. Poor things, what a setback; but no, there we go, he managed it, thank goodness. Now he can even rest his knees on the sofa. That's good; he must be tired, poor angel, after all that *pushing*. He goes in and out of his little friend. How amusing, look, the soft little cushion of flesh is lifting its head to see what's going on – what a rascal. Now he's smiling with his mouth hanging open, a dopey look on his face. He's enjoying it, though he occasionally grimaces with pain. *Well, nothing's free in this life, my boy*;

you have to suffer – and he is suffering, but he shuts his eyes and saliva dribbles out of the corner of his mouth. How moving; he's enjoying it too. His resistance was all an act; now he means it. He's put his hand down towards his penis and taken it in his fingers. The third youngster is watching the scene. He puts his thumb out towards the mouth of the victim, who sucks it, how amusing. Is he going to give the poor little lamb a good time now after having made him suffer so much with his threats? No, he stands behind the leader, pushes him forward against the body of their common victim, and bends his knees too. Good, they're going to do some acrobatics now, but no, it can't be, it just doesn't seem possible, and yet he manages it first go and cleanly penetrates him. A good lesson in humility for the little fighting cock, I thought. You've got to be on your guard the whole time, boy. Anyone can seize power from you in an instant, although really it's him, the leader, who's in the best place. He's not even moving any more; the one at the back is doing it for both of them, and he's sandwiched between his two little friends. They're so touching, totally adorable, so young, so perfect, they're having such fun all on their own . . .

When the room started to fill with the faint milky light filtering through the balcony railings, I decided to try to sleep for a while.

It was cold.

I got into bed with great ceremony, plumping up the pillows and smoothing out the sheets. I lay on my back, very stiffly, shut my eyes tight and conjured up in my imagination all kinds of delicious foods: almond ice-cream, crème caramel, lemon meringue pie. It usually worked but that night it was useless.

When I got fed up with tossing and turning, I jumped out of bed, resigned to a night of insomnia, wrapped myself in a blanket and went to the kitchen in search of something to eat. My failed attempt at getting to sleep had made me ravenously hungry. In the larder I found a box of puff pastries which Carmela had brought back from her village. The cakes she occasionally brings me are the only good thing about her. I love these country cakes – good, stodgy, greasy pastries – I just love them. I shouldn't, I thought, but this is a special occasion, and I took the whole box with me back to my observation point in the sitting room.

I bit off the corner of a cake covered in pine kernels – I always eat them very slowly so they last longer – and I found them again. There they were, at a distance, dancing for me. They no longer seemed able to surprise me. I'd immersed myself in their world earlier, and now I could watch them with a certain cold objectivity, although their sincerity – the sincerity distorting their faces bathed in sweat, the sincerity which escaped from between their lips in uneven, muffled panting – was still deeply moving to me.

Their arrogance didn't impress me. They inspired me with a strange feeling of compassion, tinged with envy and violence, an obscure, heavy feeling. And once my initial frenzy had passed, my awareness of their youth and inexperience persisted. Silly little things. I felt very superior, and much older than them. I couldn't get the idea out of my head that they were just a lot of big children having fun. If any one of them so much as brushed my face with the back of his hand he'd send me flying and not disturb a hair on his head, I thought, but that didn't change a thing.

Their arrogance didn't impress me. A good spanking and a week without TV would take them down a peg or two. Same as with Ines.

Somewhere I heard the faint bleeping of my alarm clock. I'd fallen asleep. I was watching them through the spy-hole of a thick wooden door – I'd locked them in there – and now one of them, picked earlier at random, was showing the others his scars, his rump scored with white stripes against the reddened skin, and they all cried and caressed him. They behaved like animals, incapable of repenting and changing their behaviour. I'd have to be more strict with them in future. I was absorbed in these thoughts when the alarm went off. The television screen was a confused blur of black and white stripes. I've got to wake Ines, get her washed and dressed, make her have breakfast and take her to school. The daily ritual finally prevailed and I managed to get up, but it was then that the blood started to pour. My face filled with imaginary wounds; the skin on my cheeks became stretched, tense and burning.

I felt ashamed, and frightened too, an indefinable feeling, unfamiliar and unpleasant, but as I became more fully awake, everything seemed to fall back into place. The blood was leaving my face and flowing normally through my body again.

I've got to wake Ines, I thought. It's a shame I had a row with Ely last night, because I'd love to go to a boxing match, and I'm sure he knows where you can get tickets for that sort of thing . . .

At one time transvestite hunting was one of my favourite games.

I knew that it was an absurd pastime, a ridiculous, even cruel thing to do, but I hid behind my solidarity, a vague gender-based solidarity with classic whores – real women with drooping tits and bad teeth, who now had an increasingly hard time of it, what with all that unfair competition, poor things.

Pablo indulged this habit – he's always indulged all my whims – and he stuck to the kerb, driving very slowly, while I sat hunched in my seat, so as not to attract too much attention, and only he could be seen. Then they came out of their dens. We could see them in the lamplight: they planted themselves, hands on hips, only a few yards in front of the car. Pablo slowed down almost to a standstill. They opened their clothes, parted their lips, and waggled their tongues, and when we were just the right distance from them, wham, we'd slam on the accelerator. We'd give them the fright of their lives, or almost, because we'd never get so close that they thought they were actually going to be run over. No, what we wanted, well, what *I* wanted, because it was me who'd invented the game and its rules, was to see them jump and scuttle off, with all their accessories – necklaces, broad-brimmed hats and shawls – floating in the wind. They were really funny. They'd trip over on their high heels and fall flat on their arses. Big, and heavy, they still weren't really used to their clothes and they ran picking up their skirts – when they wore them – holding their handbags, running with their little fingers sticking out. It was so funny. Some of them, with looks of hatred in their eyes, insulted us and shook their fist, and we'd laugh like mad. We've always had a good laugh together, always, and with him I never felt guilty afterwards.

In the end, they must have got to know our faces, or maybe our number plate, and one night, just as we were starting off and were moving very slowly along the kerb, one of them came up from the left and gave Pablo the bash in the face we'd been deserving for a long time.

I barely had time to see him: his terrifying clenched fist, topped off by a huge crimson nail, coming through the car window. Pablo lurched forward, hitting the brake and putting his hands up to his face.

I just had to hit back, I still don't understand why – I just had to.

I got out of the car and started to yell furiously at the hazy figure moving away quickly down the road. 'Come back here, you bastard, let's see if you dare.'

The witnesses to the scene, all colleagues of the attacker, stood round in a circle on the pavement. I was still screaming. 'I'll kill you, you pig, I'll get you, coward, you queer, I'll kill you!'

He stopped and turned round slowly. In the surrounding houses lights were beginning to come on. 'Hey, that's enough! It's the same every bloody night!' The locals didn't seem too keen on these emotional scenes.

Pablo, a hand still over his cheek, was laughing loudly.

The transvestite came back up the street towards me. The onlookers were disconcerted. I was furious. Completely drunk and absolutely furious. 'You bloody bastard, how dare you hit my boyfriend!' I couldn't call him my husband, even though that's what he was. We'd been married almost three years, but I just couldn't bring myself to say the word.

'I'm warning you, if you so much as touch another hair on his head, I'll poke your eyes out with my bare hands, you little shit.'

He was now standing in front of me. He looked as disconcerted as his companions had earlier. Pablo was shouting at me to get back in the car and leave it.

I looked at him closely for a moment. He wasn't very tall for a man, but he was for a woman – he was about the same build as me. He was very young, or at least he looked it, one of the youngest transvestites I'd ever seen. I was then twenty-three and he looked about the same age. He had a round face, a moon face, with no angles at all, in spite of the thick layer of blusher with which he'd tried to create the illusion of prominent cheekbones. She was pretty, but he wasn't. Before changing camps he must have been a strikingly ugly man, with that innocent little girl's face.

He didn't scare me.

We grabbed each other by the hair. It was really funny. We actually grabbed each other by the hair. He smelt of Opium. I didn't smell of anything, I assume. I never wear perfume.

We struggled for quite a while, clutching at each other. The spectators were egging him on to kill me. I could hear their shouting, full of violence and hatred. They called me everything under the sun, but he didn't want to hurt me. I could tell he didn't want to hit me hard, so I gave up the idea of kicking him in the balls. In the end, it was all over with a couple of slaps.

Pablo separated us. He looked serious. He grabbed me by the elbows and held me against him, so I couldn't move. I went on kicking for a few seconds more, out of stubbornness.

Then my opponent said something, precisely the last thing I expected, but I didn't know then that he was into John Wayne phrases. He was fascinated by the sheriffs in Westerns.

'Take care of her. You're a lucky guy. She's no ordinary woman.'

His unexpected words calmed me down. Pablo was very good at handling this kind of situation and characters like these.

'Yes, I know.' He was trying to sound calm. 'I'm sorry, the whole thing is our fault, but she's just like a little girl – she likes playing cruel games.'

'You're telling me it's your fault, more than your fault. That's a really dirty trick you go around playing . . .' He was looking at us with curiosity; he didn't seem angry. The little group was already dispersing, disappointed. 'My name's Ely, with a y.'

He held out his hand and Pablo took it, smiling. I was sure he'd liked that bit about the y.

'My name's Pablo and this is Lulu.'

'Brilliant! I'd love my boyfriend to call me that . . .'

It was a common mistake. Most of the people who'd met me with Pablo thought that Lulu was a recently acquired name, that he'd been the one to call me that. Nobody seemed prepared to believe that it was in fact a family nickname, derived from my own name, and imposed on me as a child.

I shook his hand too and said sorry. It was all very amusing.

Pablo said we were going out to eat. In fact we'd gone out that evening to celebrate one of my father-in-law's infrequent but generous donations, and he invited Ely to join us. He hesitated a moment, really he was working, he said, but in the end he accepted our offer.

We had a good time, the three of us, we had a really good laugh. We went to a pretty swanky restaurant – that was typical of Pablo – where everybody stared at us. Ely was delighted too. He loves shocking people. He was wearing an electric blue plastic mini skirt, extremely high-heeled sandals with thongs, and a crêpe blouse with a pattern in white, purple and blue, with a matching scarf round his neck.

He sat very upright, smoking with a cigarette holder and he kept touching his mane of long, backcombed hair, puffy as candyfloss, the ends flicked back as if he'd just had an electric shock. He had blond highlights, but they needed redoing – his dark roots were showing.

I couldn't take my eyes off him. You could see his nipples through his blouse. He realized what I was looking at.

'Do you want me to show them to you?'

'What?'

'My tits.'

'Yes!'

He pulled open his blouse and I stuck my nose down his décolleté. I saw two perfect, small, firm breasts, which ended in points. They must have been recent acquisitions. I felt like touching them, but I didn't dare.

'Amazing,' I said, 'lots of women would want . . .'

'I'm sure. Want a look?' He was talking to Pablo.

He shook his head; he was laughing and looking at me.

Ely began to tell us about his life, though he wouldn't reveal his age, or the name he was baptised with. He would have preferred the name Vanessa, or something similar, but it was a bit old-hat so he'd gone instead for a diminutive, which sounded chic. He looked like an Andalusian, but was in fact from a village in Extremadura, near Medellín. Land of the conquistadors, he said, winking at me.

Once he got the menu, he stopped talking and read through it carefully. Then in a different voice, sweet and winsome, and extremely feminine, he looked at Pablo and asked, 'Can I order baby eels?'

Yes, he could, so he did.

He ate like a pig, ordering three courses and two desserts. He was obviously starving, though he tried to hide it. He claimed he didn't eat much because he was watching his figure, and saved up for special occasions like that evening, but men had really changed. That was why he liked old black and white films. Things were different now; there were fewer and fewer gentlemen prepared to buy a girl a decent dinner. He talked and ate without a pause.

A pink mark was starting to appear on Pablo's cheek, which later turned purple, with yellow edges and greenish tints.

He'd given him a good punch.

'This is terrible, I'm really sorry!' He stroked Pablo's face. 'That's one thing I couldn't get fixed, with hormones, I mean . . .'

'Don't worry.' Pablo let Ely stroke him. He didn't want to appear to be rejecting him. He was always like that with the strange creatures he picked up on the streets.

Then Ely gave a start. It had occurred to him that maybe we could celebrate by rounding off the evening in bed, the three of us, free of charge, of course.

Pablo said no. Ely insisted, and Pablo again refused.

'All right, well then at least let me give you a blow job . . . We can do it in the car – not very romantic, but I'm used to that . . .'

I was laughing my head off. Pablo wasn't; he was just shaking his head. Ely was smiling.

'This boy's so conventional.' He was speaking to me.

'Yes, what are we to do with him . . .' I decided to go over to the enemy's side. 'Come on, Pablo, have a go! You've got to try everything once in this life.' I turned to Ely. 'I tell you, it's a real shame, he's got a good one . . .'

'Oh my God!'

He flung his whole body backwards, fluffing up his mane of hair with his hand, exaggerating all his gestures. Now he was acting the mad thing, deliberately. He was very funny.

'Please, let me give you one!' He was feigning desperation, although he too was laughing loudly. 'What's it to you? I'm not going to do anything weird to you, I swear. All I've got is a tongue and teeth inside my mouth, just like everybody else. Go on, let me have a go! What a country! Come on, I'll pay for the meal, and you'll enjoy it; I'm very good . . .'

We were shouting, making quite a racket. They brought us the bill without us asking for it. Pablo paid and we left.

He told us to drop him off where we'd found him. It was early; he could still do business, he said, but he carried on pestering Pablo the whole way. He'd had quite a bit to drink. So had we. I felt unsure.

I wondered if I'd be allowed to do it or not. I didn't want to cross the line. In fact, I didn't know where the line was. He seemed to be amused by everything I did, but there had to be a limit, a line, somewhere.

In the end, I asked him to stop the car and I moved into the back seat. I preferred not to look him in the face. Ely moved up. He was surprised. I flung myself at him and stuck both my hands down his blouse. I looked up and my eyes met Pablo's, riveted to the rear-view mirror. He was watching me. He seemed calm, and, I supposed, repeating it to myself, this meant that the line was still some distance away.

The flesh was so hard that you could almost feel the implants, the two implants that he must have had in there. I squeezed and kneaded his tits, pulling at his nipples and regretting, deep down, that I didn't have long nails to dig into his flesh and leave him smeared with his own blood.

This surgically-produced hybrid being inspired surprising feelings of violence in me.

He gave me a kiss on the cheek but I turned my face away. I've never been as considerate as Pablo, and I didn't want his kisses. I put my hand in his crotch. He had a hard-on. It didn't seem logical. Pablo remained motionless, watching us in the mirror in the pale light of the street lamps. I touched him again. He definitely had a hard-on. Then I lifted his blouse and put one of his tits in my mouth without taking my hand away. It was freakish.

I hung onto his tit, kissing, sucking, biting it, and rubbed him with my hand, on top of the blue plastic, which was rolled up so high over his thighs that my wrist was touching the hem, and I could feel him grow.

He took my hand and tried to put it under his skirt, but I didn't let him. I didn't feel like it.

'You're a woman who knows what she wants, aren't you?'

I bit his nipple so hard he screamed. I felt wild.

He started to feel my own tits, which were much bigger than his, over my t-shirt, and he told Pablo to drive on – we could go and have one last drink in a bar he knew, and he gave him the address.

Pablo drove off. Ely carried on behaving strangely. He was stroking my thighs. I was wearing a skirt too, a long, white summer skirt. He put his hand under it, right to the end, and I felt his nails, and first two, then three fingers, inside me, pushing hard, moving backwards and forwards, slowly at first, then faster and faster. He made me catch my breath with his fingers, and I could hear him, talking to Pablo – *She's a cunning bitch, this one* – he was laughing – *You'll ruin your health if you stay with her* – while I still hung onto his tit. Staying in that uncomfortable position so long was making my neck hurt, but I held on, rocking against his hand, and he was digging his fingernails into me, speaking quite calmly, as if he were at the hairdresser – *You should try it with one of us, seriously, we're much less demanding* – until I came.

We must have been stationary quite a while. When I opened my eyes, I met Pablo's gaze. He was turned towards me, watching me. Then he opened the door and got out.

We walked in single file, Pablo in front, Ely behind and me in the middle. We were in an expensive, modern, elegant area, which in the evening filled up with expensive, modern, elegant tarts. It was hard to imagine a street transvestite hanging around there too often.

He knocked on an old Castillian style wood-panelled door. A little window opened and a man's face appeared. They started talking. I couldn't see what was going on because Pablo had put his arms around me and was kissing me in the middle of the pavement.

Ely asked if he had any money left. The meal had cost us a fortune with all he'd eaten. Pablo nodded, without taking his tongue out of my mouth, yes, he had money. At times like that he always had money.

The door was opened and we went in. It wasn't really a bar. There was a kind of small vestibule, a small counter, like in some Chinese restaurants, and a glass door opening onto a long corridor, carpeted in a relaxing green, with doors on either side, a corridor which came to an abrupt end and led nowhere.

'What are we going to drink?' Ely had regained his composure, although his blouse was still undone. His tone was that of an elegant hostess.

'Gin.'

'Oh no, not gin, how ghastly, let's have champagne.'

'I don't like champagne.' It was true, he didn't and nor did I – I'd got used to drinking neat gin, like him. 'But you have some if you want.'

'Yes, yes, yes!' He moved his eyes and lips at the same time. 'Two bottles then, one of each . . .'

Pablo was huddling behind me; he often held me like that. He put his left arm round my waist and stroked my breasts with his other hand and rubbed his nose against the back of my neck, whispering in my ear one of my mother's favourite expressions, the fulminating, definitive pronouncement with which she concluded all our rows in those days:

'You'll end up in the gutter . . .'

The man who'd talked to Ely placed two bottles and three glasses on a metal tray, and walked on ahead of us. He opened the third door on the right, put the drinks down on a small, low glass table, and disappeared.

We were in a fairly small room with no windows. A very wide padded bench, covered in electric-blue velvet which clashed aggressively with the green carpet, ran along one of the walls. Around the table, four stools upholstered in the same velvet, were all the furniture in the room, together with a rather ugly wooden bureau with a sliding door, standing in a corner, completely empty – I conscientiously checked all the drawers – and totally out of place there. There wasn't a single chair.

We sat down all three of us on the bench, with Pablo in the middle. Ely went all serious and stopped talking. There was a large mirror facing us, and our reflection in it struck me as rather comical. Ely was looking down; Pablo was smoking, watching the smoke as it curled away; and I was staring straight ahead. I suddenly felt anxious. I wondered how it was all going to end; then I suddenly started to laugh, to roar with laughter all on my own, uncontrollably. Pablo asked me what had got into me and I had trouble answering him.

'We look as if we're in a dentist's waiting-room . . .'

This remark temporarily eased the tension, and the two of them laughed with me. Ely started to chatter away again and uncorked the champagne with lots of oohs and aahs. He poured himself a glass, drank it and fell silent again. Pablo was silent too. He was watching me with a look of amusement, a faint smile on his lips, but not uttering a word.

The truth is, I'd assumed from the start that he'd take the initiative – he was always the one to take the lead in situations like these – but this time he didn't seem prepared to lift a finger, and soon we were once again, all three of us, sitting silent and motionless, like in a dentist's waiting-room, me feeling increasingly tense, Ely nonplussed and, I assumed, angry – he must have been thinking that we, or rather I, had taken him all the way there for nothing – and Pablo imperturbable, as if it had nothing to do with him at all.

When the silence became unbearable, I leaned over and whispered in his ear that he had to do something, anything.

He responded with a loud laugh.

'No, my dear, you're the one who has to do something. You set this whole thing up, all on your little own.

All I did was invite your girlfriend to have dinner with us . . .'

Ely looked at me. He was perplexed.

But I wasn't. I'd understood perfectly.

I looked at him a moment. He didn't look cross with me, just a little surprised.

I knelt in front of him, keeping my legs very close together, and, sitting back on my heels, I undid his belt. I looked at him. He smiled. He was giving me his permission. I continued and looked at Ely, who'd leaned towards me, but he wasn't looking at me; he had his eyes fixed on the movement of my hands.

Meanwhile, I tried to analyze Pablo's impassivity. Earlier, during the meal, he'd rejected Ely several times, flatly. I'd even felt a little embarrassed by his harshness, his cutting little macho refusals, leaning back in his chair, merely shaking his head, not one joke, not one witty comment, a simple, wordless *no, I don't want to*.

Now, instead, he wasn't offering any resistance.

True, it was me doing it all – Ely hadn't budged from his seat – but still, there were three of us there.

Maybe this wasn't the first time. Maybe he'd been to bed with a man before. Maybe lots of times. Perhaps, and worst of all, with my brother.

Marcelo and Pablo in a double bed, naked, kissing on the mouth . . .

It was funny. I suppose it should have seemed horrible but I found it funny. I smiled inwardly and decided not to give another thought to such rubbish.

When I turned to look at him again, Pablo's cock now in my hand, Ely hadn't moved an inch.

I threw back my shoulders and straightened up as much as I could, lifting my head and letting my left hand drop onto my white skirt which was spread out over the floor. I was trying to adopt a pose which looked both submissive and dignified, looking Ely straight in the eyes, Pablo's penis in my hand. The disturbing images had faded. I was sure that he had never been attracted to men; it was me he was attracted to. *Look, he's mine, he does what I want, and I want him*. I was talking to him in silence but he refused to look at me. Pablo was no longer there – this happened sometimes. He never disappeared entirely – a single word from him would have been enough to turn everything upside down – but he was no longer there. I went on looking at Ely and repeating to him, silently, *Look at me, he does what I want*. I knew it wasn't quite like that; it wasn't true, but the truth had disappeared too, so I went on thinking it. It was a pleasant thought. At times like that, I really felt like someone, sure of myself. It was strange, but I only felt aware of the true nature of my relationship with him when there was someone else present. Then he always singled me out, and I understood that he was in love with me and it seemed right, and logical – something which almost never happened when we were alone together, even though he behaved just the same. I always felt unsure; I still found him too beautiful, too big and wise, too much for me.

I loved him too much. I've always loved him too much, I suppose.

I put his cock in my mouth and began undressing him. He's never liked fucking with his clothes on. I took off his shoes, one with each hand, and his socks, while I moved my lips with great application, my eyes closed. I put my hands on his hips and he lifted himself up slightly, just enough for me to pull his trousers down. Then, my hands free again, I threw myself on top of him, having given up any idea of trying to appear like the statue of a graceful young girl, something which was beyond me anyway – I've never been very graceful – and I concentrated on giving him a brilliant blow job. It had to be brilliant because I wanted Ely to see me.

When I considered that I had displayed skills worthy of respect, when I'd sucked it, bitten it, kissed and rubbed it against my lips, my cheeks, my whole face, I swallowed the whole thing and kept it there for quite a while. That was something that had cost me a huge effort, learning to gulp the whole thing down, to keep it there inside my mouth, pressing against my palate, swelling against my tongue. When at last I took it out, it was purple, swollen, sticky and hard, and I heard Pablo, his adorable sighs, his light breathing, and I looked at Ely, and saw that he was at last returning my glance. He was looking straight into my eyes, his mouth hanging open, so I gestured with my head and suggested he join the party.

He could have thrown himself at Pablo without getting up from his seat, but he chose instead to kneel by my side.

He's always been an aesthete.

I hadn't let go of Pablo's cock. I held onto it firmly with my right hand and I wouldn't allow my new companion even to touch it. I would be the one to decide when he'd be allowed to enter the game. So I ran my tongue over it once more, from top to bottom – it was mine – and I turned my head, passing it over my mouth, moving my lips faster and faster, as if I were brushing my teeth with it, until my neck was hurting, and my ear was burning, pressed as it was against my shoulder. Only then did I move it up close to his mouth, next to me. I guided it with my hand and placed it against his lips, and he kissed it, but he'd hardly touched it when I took it away, then moved it up close to him again, and saw how he licked it, with his whole tongue out, and I stuck my own tongue out, and licked it too, and then I passed it back to him. We carried on like that for quite a while, until he caught it between his lips and I didn't dare pull it away. I moved closer and we both started to suck it, each of us on one side, each doing his own thing. It was impossible to follow Ely. He was a mad thing even in that, constantly changing the rhythm, so in the end I decided to swallow it, to have it to myself for a bit. Then I offered it to him, holding it in my hand while he sucked. I loved watching him, his dyed hair, his scarlet lipstick smeared all over his face, his Adam's apple moving in his throat. *Eat, my son, take nourishment, but don't be greedy*. I pushed my hand up until he was forced to stop, and I swallowed it again, keeping it inside for a time and then put it back into his mouth. I no longer passed it over to him but put it straight into his mouth. I wanted to see him, to see how he sucked in his cheeks, how he gave head to another man.

I leaned back slightly, without letting go of my prize, and watched him. I looked at Pablo too, but he couldn't see me. His gaze was directed at some fixed point on the ceiling. The expression on his face made me think that Ely's self-publicizing must have been justified, he – or rather she, as he would have had it – seemed very good at it. I decided to let him have free rein, after all. I gradually loosened my grip until I had let go of it completely. I lay down on the floor, leaning on my elbow and nibbled at Pablo's balls. Before starting, I glanced over to my left.

Ely was masturbating.

Under his blue skirt, in his left hand, he was clutching a small, soft, whitish penis. I was wondering whether his tits had something to do with the pitiful appearance of this sickly looking appendage, when Pablo's thighs shook.

I got up immediately. I wanted to watch him come in Ely's mouth. I stood by his side, one knee dug into the bench, the other foot on the floor. I could see myself in the mirror, from the side, his head showing between my breasts and my chin. I took his face in my hand and leaned toward him. I kissed him, moving my tongue in his mouth while savouring in advance the moment when I would turn towards Ely, down there, on the floor, and start giving orders, shouting at him, *Swallow it all, dog, swallow it*, but that moment never came. I would have slapped him if he'd let one single drop spill out of his mouth, but I never got the chance, because Pablo took me by surprise. He suddenly grabbed me by my left knee, making me turn abruptly until I was facing him. He let go of me for a moment to rip my knickers, pulling the elastic with his hands, and made me mount him.

I put my arms around his neck and started to move up and down on top of him.

Whenever we did it like that it reminded me of how, years ago, when I was five, seven, nine, after I'd pestered him about it for hours on end, he'd sit me on his knees, and holding me by the wrists, first pull me towards him, then let me fall back until my head touched the floor, see-saw, chop-chop, down come the King's trees, down come, the Queen's on top. The last time we did it I was nearly fourteen, and he was twenty-five. We were alone in Marcelo's room. He was sitting on the bed, and I asked him to do it, and he said no, I was too big for games like that, and I pleaded, one last time, please, just once more, and he agreed. You're pretty heavy now, see-saw, chop-chop, and it went on for a very long time, and when we'd finished I was wet and he had something hard, unfamiliar, under his jeans. It should have been the last time, but it was really the first.

I repeated it to him under my breath, see-saw, chop-chop, down come the King's trees, in his ear, as I moved up and down on top of him. He lifted my skirt up completely at the back and put it over my head, the hem brushing my forehead. He grasped me firmly by the waist and sucked my nipples over my cotton t-shirt, until there was a big wet mark around each nipple.

Just then, everything around me started to sway. Pablo was taking over my body; his penis was becoming part of me, the most important part, the only one I could feel. He entered me, going a little deeper every time, opening and closing me up around him, piercing me. I could feel his thrusts right up against the back of my skull, as if my entrails were tearing as he moved, and everything else became blurred, my body, and his, and everything else. That was why I took so long to notice the humid caresses which brushed my thighs from time to time as if inadvertently, light, brief touches which, after a few seconds of doubt and a moment of astonishment, reminded me that Ely was still down there, kneeling on the floor, licking at whatever I wasn't making use of, jerking his white, soft, miserable little dick, while I fucked my eyes out, indifferent to the grotesque street animal behind me, feasting on the left-overs from my private banquet, so indifferent that I had managed to forget his existence.

I would have liked to see him down there. That was my last coherent thought before letting myself go. I was starting to feel the full effect of my impacts against Pablo, as they became increasingly urgent, and seemed to move gradually nearer my head, and I could no longer control myself. I let myself go, so that after three or four more agonizingly brutal thrusts, the last ones, he finally crashed against my skull, shattering it into thousands of small soft pieces, before he too let himself be caught between the elastic walls of my sex, now suddenly autonomous, which were strangling his penis, beyond my control.

Afterwards, I knew that I wasn't capable of doing anything other than just staying there, completely still, trying to regain control of myself, so I didn't move for quite a while, my arms around Pablo, holding him very tightly, missing my home. I wanted to be at home, with a bed nearby, but it was still pleasant, the warmth, the touch of his still-burning skin.

He came to much quicker than me. His body was more obedient than mine, and we weren't at home, so he kissed me on the lips, lifted me up for a moment to slip his penis out from inside me, and pushed me gently to one side, leaving me lying on the bench.

I stayed like that for quite a while, curled up, my knees pressed against my breasts, my eyes closed, while he dressed, and I remembered Ely – I'd forgotten him again.

They exchanged a few words in whispers; a voice which wasn't Pablo's mumbled a goodbye, and I heard the sound of a door closing.

I sat up. He was leaning against the wall, his arms crossed, smiling. I stood up to get dressed and realized that I was already dressed. My torn knickers were lying on the floor. I picked them up – I don't know why, it just isn't done to go leaving torn knickers around the place – and I stuffed them in my bag. When I passed the table I saw that the bottle of gin was still there, untouched. We hadn't even taken the cap off. I grabbed that too, and put it in my bag. I don't believe in leaving behind full bottles of booze you've paid good money for. Pablo burst out laughing, transparent, unambiguous laughter. He wasn't angry, and that made me feel good, so I laughed too, and we went out laughing into the street.

When we got in the car, I remembered Ely and felt curious.

'Did you give him some money?'

'Yes.'

'And he took it?'

He burst out laughing again.

'Of course he took it!' He looked at me as if to say, *You idiot*, and I knew that's exactly what he wanted to say, but coming from him it wasn't an insult, rather the opposite. As long as he was still amused by my silly remarks, like that one, everything would be all right. 'Why wouldn't he have taken it? That's how he earns his living, isn't it? Hey, do you know where there's a petrol station?'

'Somewhere round here. There's one near Jumbo, but I don't know if it'll be open at this time of night.'

We drove along wide, empty streets, lined with tall buildings with bodies of concrete and steel, and glass faces, all alike, all spotlessly clean, as if they'd just been unwrapped. From a small island of greenery, surrounded by a neatly trimmed hedge, ran a little cement path leading to a glass door.

My mother had always wanted to live in a block like that, with that kind of entrance, an enormous, bare hall in pale marble. I hate them – they've always reminded me of the reception areas in the new Social Security clinics, the same impersonal, antiseptic atmosphere, but without the marble or the porter's desk in dark polished wood. Entrance halls are terribly important to Madrid ladies of a certain age, it seems. My mother always loathed ours, a long, narrow, dark area without a desk for the porter, Eugenio. He was a real sweetie. At sixty he was still carrying the butane gas bottles up the stairs two at a time. He didn't have a desk, just a little cubby-hole behind the door, and to cap it all he always wore blue overalls. I've always been very fond of Eugenio. When I was little he used to give me sweets, and when I got married he gave me a hideous jewellery box, handmade out of seashells dyed all different colours, and 'Souvenir of El Grove' written in italics on the lid. His wife was from Galicia and had ordered it from there specially for the occasion. It's one of my favourite objects. Poor Eugenio, he was always so friendly and helpful to Mummy, carrying her shopping bags up to the third floor, while she cursed his blue overalls, but she's been punished for her sins. Poor Mummy, she'll be stuck in Chamberi for the rest of her life; she'll never have a marble entrance, a porter in blue livery and mains gas.

We drove along wide, empty streets. The only thing moving as we passed were the embassy flags, ridiculous little rags set against the monolithic power of those large glass façades. They're not Madrid – the thought struck me every time I drove through there – they don't fit in with this city which isn't a city, but a chaotic hybrid, a disaster both in theory and in practice; an urban disaster, with disastrous roads and traffic; a disaster in education, politics, sanitation; an ecclesiastical disaster – there's no cathedral – a pornographic disaster – there's no red-light district either – all in all, a total disaster. The only place where you can live as you please is right in the middle of the disaster, where nobody asks any questions, because nobody is anybody, and you can go out and buy bread in your slippers and quilted dressing gown and nobody stares at you, and they'll give you a couple of pickled anchovies with your beer, in noisy bars with the floor covered in crumpled paper napkins. The patios of the houses always smell of chick-pea stew, and the women of the neighbourhood sing '*Ay Campanera*' as they hang out the washing, even though people don't like it in the courtyards of Madrid, not here, in these village houses, a ghost village full of nosy porters – What floor are you going to? And what the fuck do you care? – a boring, pretentious, provincial village in the middle of the city, a huge city which everybody calls a village.

A few streets further on you come to Tetuan, 'Tetuan de las Victorias', pretty name, Bravo Murillo, with all the chaos, grilled prawns and shops-signs yellowed with age, sale due to change of proprietor. They never change proprietor, but there's always some mug who gets taken in by the lure of these constant, illusory sales. We drove on along the other side and crossed La Castellana, passing the Bernabeu stadium. Pablo stuck his hand out the window: two fingers to the enemy's stadium. It was like a ritual which he never forgot to perform, and we drove on, little houses to left and right, and then I remembered Ely again. He was probably a Real Madrid supporter, like all new arrivals to the city. Could a Spanish man suppress his passion for football when he changed into a woman? 'But poofs don't like football on the whole, or do they?' I asked Pablo. 'Hey, do poofs like football, how the fuck should I know?' He didn't know either. Some of our friends didn't like football but I suspected it was just a pose, a passé, trendy leftie pose – that's what we'd been for a long time, armchair lefties, and we used to do a lot of things just because of that, because it was the trendy leftie thing to do . . .

The thought was still there, at the back of my mind, banging against my temples. I thought about approaching it in a roundabout way, but in the end I asked him straight out.

'Pablo, have you ever gone to bed with a man?'

He gave a small laugh, then it grew louder, until in the end, he was roaring with laughter.

But I wasn't laughing. I didn't find it at all funny.

'The problem with playing sorcerer's apprentice is that in the end you lose control . . .'

That was all. But I had no intention of leaving it at that.

'You haven't answered me.' He had a mischievous look in his eyes. He's taking the piss out of me, I thought, and I didn't like it much, because that meant it might take hours, days, even weeks, before I got an answer.

But I was wrong. That night, he felt like talking.

'If what you want to know is whether I've ever desired a man enough to get into bed with him, then the answer is no, never. I've never been attracted to men.'

'But . . .' I'd come to understand even the slightest nuance in his voice, at least when he was telling the truth, and I felt there was something left unsaid.

'Do you mean it, you really want to know everything? Aren't you scared you might hear something you don't like?'

Yes, I was definitely a bit scared, but I still wanted to know. Pablo now looked serious, but that meant nothing – he could lie to me for hours on end if he wanted to, so I shook my head. I wanted to know everything.

'Where did it happen?'

'Inside, a long time ago.'

Prison. I could remember it all very clearly, one Sunday at seven in the evening, hot chocolate and toast and a quiz show on TV. The phone, my mother in hysterics, weeping, shouting, comings and goings; 'Marcelo's been arrested again, Pablo was with him, Pablo's been arrested too, and loads of others.' Arrested, tried and condemned, four years, four years each. The first time it happened, the charges had been fairly light, possession of subversive propaganda, or some such thing, and my father had stepped in. He'd called on all his father's old acquaintances, like a valiant knight on a crusade, and he'd managed to get lots of promises and an individual cell. Eight months. It wasn't the first time for Pablo either. He'd served eight months too, always eight months, before Marcelo. Now at least they'd both been nabbed together.

This time, in the spring of '69, I was eleven and my father had refused to intervene in spite of the pleas of my mother, who, in extreme circumstances, always sided with the right camp, like all mothers. It was like the whole house had caved in on top of me. Marcelo in prison, for four years. That meant total solitude, or worse, I'd be an orphan, a cruel fate to be suddenly thrust upon me in a house full of people. But my father proved intractable. They'll straighten him out in that prison, the little bastard, that's all the thanks I've got for all I've done to give him good education, a career, a . . .' and at that point his speech always ground to a halt. He was stumped; he couldn't think of anything else to say. 'And on top of that, he won't get a penny, not a single penny from me,' he'd say over and over. 'He won't be needing money in Carabanchel[1]; he'll be fed and clothed in there – what else does he need?'

Pablo touched my shoulder. We'd got to the petrol station and there was a queue. Twenty past five in the morning and there were three cars in front of us. I was surprised. He never spoke about his time in prison, even though they'd done thirty months in there. In the end, they had their sentences reduced on account of I don't know what, and they came out on parole after a stretch of two and a half years. They'd had thirty months of their lives stolen from them, thirty-eight months in all, from each of them. Marcelo came home. I could never understand why he lived at home when he paid rent on a flat which he used for fucking and little else. Years later I found out that his staying at home was tied up with all the political stuff. Pablo shook me. 'Hey, what's up?'

Nothing was up, so I told him, 'Nothing's up.'

'Well, you played a big part in all this . . .' He was still in a good mood.

[1]Large prison in Madrid.

'Me?'

'Yes, you. You'd write to us every week, first just to Marcelo, then a letter each, and in the end one, very long letter for the two of us . . . Don't you remember?'

Yes, I remembered. I also remembered how worried I'd been. The stories people told, I believed it all: the beatings, the torture, the rapes, my brother, who was both a father and a mother to me, and my boyfriend, because I liked to think of him as my boyfriend, there, in prison, at the mercy of that lot of bastards, with bloody noses and mouths, writhing under the blows of a wet towel. Yes, I remembered. I'd write to them and tell them everything that was happening to me, to give them a laugh, so that they'd think of me. They'd answer, from time to time.

Pablo went on talking; he talked without stopping.

'When you were twelve, you sent a letter announcing the arrival of a postal order. You always seemed very concerned about money . . .'

'Well yeah, Daddy told everyone about how he wasn't sending Marcelo a penny.'

'It wasn't true.'

'Yeah, but I only found out about it afterwards . . .'

'We had money, but you were going to send us all the money you'd got for your birthday, so that we could eat properly. You loved being Mummy to us.'

He stroked my face. I didn't look at him – it was embarrassing to remember all this. I'd told my mother I was going to do charity work that year. I asked everybody to give me money instead of presents. I said the nuns at school had suggested we make up food parcels and take them to the slums, out beyond Vallecas. Mummy had been surprised – food parcels in April, it was the kind of thing you did at Christmas, but still, it was charity, and she couldn't refuse. I lied convincingly and they all believed me. I got 1575 pesetas – 1575 pesetas in '69 was a lot of cash, and I sent it to Carabanchel, so that they could eat properly, it was true.

'I tell you, at first we froze in our tracks. We were really touched; Marcelo was nearly in tears, but then he had a brainwave, one of those fucking brilliant schemes your brother has from time to time, and he dragged me off to a quiet corner and said, "How about we spend Lulu's money on having a go with the Portuguese guy, what do you think?" I laughed, but he was serious, and I thought maybe after all it wasn't such a bad idea. We'd been in there eleven months already; I was starting to get a callous on my hand from all the . . .'

The car in front moved.

'Who was the Portuguese guy?'

'He was a poof, in there for having stabbed his boyfriend in a row – jealousy, I think. He hadn't killed him and the boyfriend went in to see him whenever he could; he'd forgiven him. The Portuguese guy always said he'd done it out of love.'

'But you two were politicals . . .'

'So what? The homosexuals were in our wing, and we'd see all the others, in the yard, or in the refectory. To be honest they were much more interesting than the other prisoners from the Party. That's where I met Gus, and a couple of others you know.'

'Gus? Was he already a dealer?'

'No, he was into nicking cars. He was just a lout then, and very young. He started to take drugs in there, in Carabanchel.'

'So what happened?' I wasn't worried any more, just curious.

'Nothing. The Portuguese guy was a girlfriend to all the prisoners, and to more than one of the warders. He was very versatile. He'd do hand jobs, blow jobs, put it in or have it put in, depending on what you were willing to pay. He made a mint. He was saving up to buy his boyfriend a flat, as compensation, I suppose. He wasn't the only one. There were others like him, but he was young, and not bad looking, and his mouth was healthy. He had a huge dick too, according to rumour, and he was the most popular one.'

Pablo was looking at me and smiling, as if his time in prison had been a holiday, a little break. I was disconcerted.

'So you spent my money on the Portuguese guy . . .' It wasn't a question, I was just repeating it to make it sink in once and for all.

'Yes, nearly all of it, in your honour, as Marcelo put it. We spent quite a long time discussing the procedure. A hand job wasn't enough, so we opted for a blow job, a Portuguese blow job, very exotic, but I nearly fucked it all up, because when we went to sick bay, to negotiate terms, you might say . . .'

'Why sick bay?'

'Because that's where he worked. It was one of the cushiest jobs – he always got the best. He had lots of lovers, all over the place. Anyway, I asked him if he'd give us a discount for giving us both a blow job at the same time, and he got livid.'

He suddenly looked serious. He was silent a moment, then looked at me.

'You don't know what it was like in there, you can't imagine.'

A sad place, I thought, above all, sad.

We got to the petrol pump, filled up the tank and went home. Pablo was silent the whole journey. Then, when I was already in bed, he came and lay down beside me.

'Do you want to hear the end of the story?'

I didn't dare admit that I did, but he told me anyway.

My money had been enough for ten blow jobs, not one more or less, at 150 pesetas a go, five each. He'd enjoyed it, and Marcelo had too, so they carried on paying for it themselves, out of their own money, rationing their pleasure, because they were scared of getting hooked. They'd go to the sick bay once, maybe twice a month, each of them separately, until one day, the Portuguese guy suggested that my brother say he had flu, or something, and he'd get him a bed, and take good care of him, no charge. Seemed he was quite taken with Marcelo, but Marcelo said he didn't feel like it; he got scared, and he gave it up. Pablo didn't, though, he carried on until the end. He even thought about fucking him – he said it without batting an eyelid – for quite a while he'd considered the possibility of buggering him. So what, it couldn't be all that different from buggering a woman, and that was enjoyable, but then one day, when he'd almost made up his mind, he had a flash of lucidity – that's what he called it, a flash of lucidity – seeing him bare from the waist up, his hairy chest, flirting with a couple of old guys out in the yard, so he reminded himself he was in prison for being a Communist, as if Communism were a sure sign of virtue that gave him strength and he dropped the idea.

'Anyway, we already knew we wouldn't have to serve our whole sentence; we'd be getting out soon. If I'd thought I had another ten or twenty years in there, like some of them, I would have probably done it, and I expect I would've enjoyed it. What you do, say or think outside, isn't valid in prison, it's a different world in there.'

He was silent for a moment. Then he started talking again. He seemed to want to empty himself, to tell me everything, after having spent years without referring once to that time. He didn't like talking about it. He could have played the martyr, years ago, when everybody was boasting and lying about how they'd once been arrested at the Puerta del Sol, and put in gaol. He could have boasted too, and cried, but he hadn't ever; he'd never said a word about it to me until that day.

'Promise me you'll never tell Marcelo that you know about this. When I told him I was involved with you, that was the first thing he asked me.'

I nodded that I promised. I was very moved by it all. I didn't love them any less; if anything I loved them more than before, and I no longer cared what they'd spent my money on.

'I think it was in there I started to fall in love with you.'

'With me? But I was only a kid.'

'You were eleven, then twelve, thirteen, yes, by the time I came out you were thirteen, but your letters were very grown up. You sounded so worried about us – they were the most sincere letters I received in there – and your handwriting was very clear, that cheered me up too. The ones from Mercedes and the others were almost illegible, but yours weren't, and also, they had your smell.'

'What do you mean, my smell?'

'Don't tell me you never found out about it!' He smiled at me, astonished.

'Found out about what?'

'We called it the Surrealist episode, Marcelo and I . . .' He leaned back against the headboard of the bed and lit a cigarette. He handed it to me, and lit another one for himself: this was going to take quite a while. 'One fine day, your brother's lawyer, who was also acting for me and about ten or twelve others in there, announced that your mother would be coming to visit him the following week. She wanted to discuss some family matter – the lawyer didn't know what it was all about, something private, he said. Marcelo got a bit worried. Your mother hadn't been in to see him since his first week inside; your father had forbidden her to go. Lola would come in, and Isabel sometimes, but you never did.'

'They didn't let me.'

'It doesn't matter, we've forgiven you.' He turned for a moment to look at me, kissed me lightly on the cheek, then went back to staring intently at the ceiling, and started talking again. 'Your mother finally turned up, but she didn't stay very long. I was in the cell – nobody had come to visit me that day – and Marcelo came back up pretty soon, pissing himself, tears running down his cheeks he was laughing so much. The serious and private family matter she wanted to discuss was that she had caught you one morning, sitting naked on your bed, holding your nightdress up to your nose, saying over and over again, "I smell different," and you held out your nightdress, and stuck it under your poor mother's nose, saying, "Look Mummy, smell it, I smell different." He was laughing his head off – so was I, it was such a funny story. Don't you remember it?'

Yes, I remembered, although I hadn't thought about it for ages, it was so long ago. One day, about three weeks before my first period, I noticed that I smelt completely different. It was a really strange feeling. I smelt totally different. I felt like a different person and I concentrated on fully investigating this strange phenomenon. I didn't just smell my nightdress; I also smelt my sweat, my clothes, my sheets, my sisters' sheets . . . Patricia's things didn't smell at all, Amelia's smelt a bit like mine, but different. Since then I've always tried to remember exactly how people smell, especially Pablo. He already knew about it; I could recognize his smell almost anywhere.

'Yes, I do remember,' I said, 'but I don't understand why Mummy went to see Marcelo about it. She didn't mention it to me. She refused to smell my nightdress, told me to stop being silly and left the room. That was it.'

'Well, apparently she was very worried.' Every so often Pablo would laugh, stifling his laughter so that it was difficult to understand what he was saying. 'She wanted Marcelo to write to you and tell you not to do it ever again, because it was dangerous, or something like that.'

'But why?' I just couldn't understand.

'You were only eleven, and she thought it was a sign of some murky sexual disturbance, she couldn't say exactly what. She didn't have the imagination to think of a precise explanation, but she was absolutely horrified. According to your brother, she was scared it might degenerate into a real perversion, and you'd end up completely depraved, and anyway, on top of that, it wasn't right.' He couldn't restrain himself any longer and burst out laughing. I waited a while, smiling too, until he stopped. 'Carmela had caught you sniffing your parents' bed, your own parents' bed . . .'

'Yes, though it turned out to be less interesting than I'd hoped . . .' My dispassionate, almost clinical tone of voice made him laugh again. 'Marcelo refused, didn't he?'

'Of course he refused; he never did anything your mother asked, on principle, and anyway the whole thing seemed so ridiculous . . .' His expression gradually softened, his laughter fading into a melancholy smile. 'There he was in prison, in a bloody terrible state, serving this absurd sentence, in this crazy country, and your mother was worried because you went around smelling everything in sight . . . "She smells different," he said, "all right, so what, Everybody's smell changes, either before or after, and anyway her smell is her business; she can do what she likes with it," then he turned round with the utmost dignity, and went back upstairs, shaking with laughter.' Pablo fell silent for a few moments. I didn't dare say anything. 'I laughed too, at first, but then I came round to your mother's view. I began to think you probably were a perverted little girl, a lost cause. It stuck in my mind, that image of you, naked, smelling your nightdress and whispering over and over again, "I smell different." That night I masturbated with that image in my mind. I constructed a wild fantasy, which seemed very real, around it, night after night. I was obsessed with the vision of you hiding in corners, giving your brothers and sisters the slip, undressing and smelling yourself, sniffing over your parents' bed and then touching yourself. You were enchanting. Of course, I pictured you as older. When I got out and saw you again, I was amazed that you were still so young, but I'd already decided it would be worth the wait, to have a hand in your undoing, so I waited . . .'

My eyes had filled with tears.

I didn't want him to see, so I turned over and curled up under the sheets, trying not to make a sound.

It was no good.

He understood, and moved closer. He put his arms around me, kissed my forehead and then he turned out the light so I could cry in peace.

My legs no longer ached.

I didn't know whether to feel happy or sad. I felt a bit of both, I suppose, when at last I managed to sit down on a chair without the usual sharp stab of pain, the only tangible consequence of the night in Moreto. I'd never kept my legs so wide apart for so long before.

My legs no longer ached. Sixteen days had passed; I remember it clearly because I'd been counting them, until that afternoon, which was number seventeen.

When I got back from school, I found Amelia in a state of collapse, weeping inconsolably in the flabby arms of my mother. Being fairly used to pathetic scenes of this kind, I went to the kitchen, made myself a sandwich of sliced onion and tomato sprinkled with olive oil and salt, my favourite sandwich, and went to my room intending to do a bit of work. I had a philosophy test the following day.

They hadn't moved. My mother was the one to speak, with the cold, clinical tone she tended to use when giving unexpected news.

'I expect this will also interest you, Marisa; after all, he's always saying how you're his favourite girl . . .' Amelia's sobs drowned out the rest of the sentence.

'What will?' Ockham was all right, not as entertaining as the Sophists but definitely much more bearable than Saint Augustine; I'd start with Ockham.

'Pablo's leaving, he's going to live abroad.'

'Pablo who?'

'Who do you think?' My mother looked at me, perplexed. 'Pablo Martínez Castro, Marcelo's friend. I don't know what's the matter with you, Marisa, you've been acting like a dim-wit lately, dear . . .'

I didn't answer, or move, I didn't want anyone to see my face.

I stuck my nose in my book and tried to think fast. It must be Paris, he was probably going to Paris – not very fashionable these days, but then neither is mysticism, or going to live outside Spain, now that the old bastard's on his last legs, about to kick the bucket . . . You can get to Paris by train, on the Puerta del Sol, I know; it can't be all that expensive to get a ticket in third or fourth class, or whatever, it can't be, it's not so far, Paris . . .

'He's going to some American university, I don't know the name, in Philadelphia, or near Philadelphia; I can't remember where your brother said . . .'

Somewhere a glass object shattered. I heard a sound like the ringing of a bell and then the tinkling of fragments on the floor.

I didn't have the strength left to ask myself how much a plane ticket to Philadelphia might cost.

I looked up from my book and resolved to stay calm. There was no reason for anyone to suspect anything, and least of all those two. I still couldn't help uttering a kind of general reproach, though.

'He can't be, I mean he's not even thirty yet . . .'

'So?' My words roused my sister from her pained silence. Up till then she'd kept in character. 'What's that got to do with it?'

'Well, I mean, I know they all go off to American universities, but not until they're much older . . .'

'And how would you know?'

'You just have to read the papers . . .'

I repeated it to myself, *They all leave*, *he is too*. *Why shouldn't he*? The pieces fitted together perfectly, all the details made up an entirely credible story, it must be true.

It was true. Pablo was leaving. Going to Philadelphia, the other side of the world.

'I suppose he'll be teaching Spanish literature?'

My mother nodded. 'The Golden Age, I think . . .'

'How original!'

This set Amelia crying again and my mother turned back to her. I just stood there in the middle of the room, my mind a complete blank. The sandwich I'd nibbled at was making me feel sick. I was still holding my book. I didn't understand what was happening; I didn't really have a clue about what was going to hit me.

'Is Marcelo in, Mummy?'

'No, I haven't clapped eyes on him for two days, and that's another thing – your brother treats this place like a hotel, he brings me his dirty washing and then off he goes again. He'll be the death of me . . .'

'Right, well, I'm going to his room to work then. I've got a philosophy test tomorrow.'

As I was going out of the door, I heard them whispering. Amelia was urging, 'go on, Mummy, ask her', and my mother was reassuring her, 'don't worry'.

'Marisa . . . you don't mind if Amelia wears your yellow dress this afternoon, do you, the one your grandmother gave you?'

'Yes, I do mind, I haven't worn it yet.'

'But darling, you never go out together, you don't have the same friends, why should it bother you?'

Any other day I might have fought, protested, screamed and threatened, maybe even cried, and it wouldn't have been any use. That day I gave in immediately. All I wanted was to be alone, to shut myself in Marcelo's room so I could be entirely alone, but hardly ten minutes later she came into the room.

She generally never bothered to knock.

'Marisa, dear, I need to talk to you.' I instantly recognized that I'm-not-just-your-mother-I'm-also-your-best-friend tone which she had recently acquired at those religious retreats for parents of large families.

'Not now, Mummy, I really don't feel like talking.' I blinked rapidly so as to keep back the tears. 'I've got to study, and anyway, I don't mind if Amelia wears my dress, if that's what you're worried about, I swear I don't . . .'

'Don't swear, Marisa.'

'Sorry, Mummy, I mean I don't mind, really, as long as she doesn't split it . . .'

'Yes, Amelia is much plumper than you, and she's much uglier too . . .' She was almost whispering. 'Look at me, darling; put down your book.'

I looked at her. I was intrigued. She realized from my reddened eyes that I'd been crying. She sat down on Marcelo's bed. She'd just had her fifty-first birthday, but she looked about fifteen years older. She was wearing a woollen dress with a pattern in navy blue and black, and thick tan coloured tights, the kind they sell in chemists for varicose veins. Her legs were ruined, the blood forming an intricate pattern of reddish and purple blotches beneath the pale, transparent skin. Nine children and eleven pregnancies, eleven in seventeen years. She no longer had a body, just a distended stooping sack, filled with exhausted, worn-out entrails. And still she wept for the children she hadn't had, one who was stillborn between Vicente and Amelia, and the two miscarriages, in only four years, two miscarriages, between the twins and me. I felt sorry for her, but also, in moments of extreme clarity, moments like the one that afternoon, looking at her closely, I felt something close to disgust. Years ago I thought I hated her. Not now, though; now I realized that I'd never stopped loving her, but that I couldn't stand her.

'Of course you mind about the dress!' She gave me a sympathetic smile. 'You're fifteen, it's normal for it to bother you . . . I think about you a lot, even though you might not think so. I love you very much. Marisa, come over here.'

'No, if you don't mind, I think I'd rather stay here.' It had been about five months, I thought, since her last maternal outburst.

'You have a lot of things to thank God for, dear,' she whispered. 'You're pretty, and clever, you enjoy your studies, you get good marks, you've got strength of character, and you know how to deal with problems and setbacks . . . I'm not worried about you, which doesn't mean I don't love you.'

She was silent a moment. So I intervened, trying to speed up her confession.

'Yeah, I . . .' It was pretty obvious she didn't worry about me.

'I mean that you don't need me. You'll get on in life without anyone's help – you'll go to university, get a good degree, and you'll be successful; you'll marry a good-looking, rich young man; you'll have lots of healthy children, and you won't get fat. You'll be a great comfort to me in my old age . . .' She smiled at me, but I didn't smile back. She had a nerve, I thought. 'Amelia, on the other hand, has so many complexes, she needs me to help her still; so does Vicente, he doesn't have much strength of character, he's very weak; and José, who's so impulsive; and the little ones too, of course. Marcelo doesn't, he's like you, strong and intelligent, although he's turned into a Communist, I can't understand why. I don't know what he's seen in this house that's so bad.' At this point she was about to burst into tears. 'And a lout, stays out till all hours, a real troublemaker . . .' She checked herself for my benefit; it must have terrified her to think that I might ask what exactly she meant. 'All this political business really worries me. Isabel used to be such a good girl, and now she's getting herself into more and more trouble . . . Well, God gave me nine children, and every day I thank him for it, but I can't see to all of you at once, and you're so intelligent and responsible, and quite tough too. I don't mean that you're not sensitive, but you seem so sure of yourself – you don't let anything bother you; you give me so little trouble . . . Marisa, dear, do you understand what I'm saying?'

I nodded. I would have liked to answer, to scream that my looks and my good marks at school didn't mean that I didn't need a mother; I would have liked to shake her and scream that I couldn't go on like this all my life, with a brother as my only family; I would have liked to hug her, hide in her arms and cry like Amelia earlier and tell her that I loved her, that I needed her, that I needed her to love me, to know that she loved me, but all I did was nod because it was no good – it was too late now.

She came over and kissed me and said that she had to go to the kitchen to pod beans. Before she went out, I asked her why Amelia had been grizzling.

She looked at me for a moment, hesitating.

'Do you promise that you'll never tease her about it?'

'Yes, Mummy.'

'Amelia is in love with Pablo, she has been for years. He's never taken any notice of her, but the poor girl can't get him out of her head.'

Great, I thought. In this house you can't even cry alone.

The persona of the headmistress of the boarding school underwent several transformations before settling as an attractive woman of about thirty-five, a Nordic type, with glasses, the stereotypical nymphomaniac librarian that I'd seen in Marcelo's magazines. I systematically ransacked his shelves in those days, devouring all the books in brown paper covers. He must have noticed, I suppose, but he never said anything.

Her hair scraped back in a little high bun, severe-looking in a white blouse and dark skirt, sitting very stiffly behind a huge desk covered with papers, it was always she, the headmistress, who spoke first.

'I'm very sorry, but you'll have to take charge of her. We can't keep her here any longer.'

Pablo looked at her. He wasn't angry; he seemed to find the matter amusing, and this annoyed the headmistress even more. He was forty years old, but strange enough he still looked the same as when he was twenty-seven. Yet his character had also been changed quite a lot. At first, he'd been my guardian, the executor of my parents' will, or something similar. Then, it seemed, he'd bought me somewhere and for some unknown reason he spent his money on making me study. In the end, he was simply my father, and this was to be his role for the greater part of my adolescence.

'Would you mind telling me the whole story again in more detail? I haven't quite understood what the exact problem is. It's a long time since I've seen my daughter . . .'

'Well, Lulu . . . is a very dirty little girl.' The headmistress leaned forward and looked at my father over her glasses. She was very excited – she always became very excited when she was talking about me. 'Do you understand what I mean?'

'No.' Pablo smiled at her.

'Well . . . she's very precocious. She's obsessed with sex. She doesn't wear anything under her skirt, you see – she says the fabric bothers her, and she always sits with her legs very wide apart in class. She caresses herself constantly, and she forces the others to caress her. She stirs up her classmates, and, well, I'm ashamed to admit it, but she became involved with the maths mistress – I myself caught them – and you won't believe this but it was always she, Lulu, who took the lead . . .'

'So you watched them for a time did you?' Pablo interrupted her, a malevolent smile on his lips.

'Yes, I . . . had to be sure before making any decision, and I saw them. Your daughter was lying on the bed, naked. She was pinching her nipples with her fingers – she has long nails, you know, painted red, it's forbidden but there's no way of making your daughter obey the rules – and Pilar, the mistress, had her head hidden between her thighs. She was licking her cunt, until at one point, she stopped, lifted up her head and said something like, "I can't go on, darling. I mean it, my tongue hurts, you've already come three times", so then Lulu sat up and slapped her. That's when I intervened.'

At this stage the headmistress would fall silent. She was very aroused and was rubbing herself with her hand. Here there was an alternative. In the classic version, nothing happened. In the quicker version, when I felt that I couldn't stop myself coming before it was even my turn to appear on the scene, Pablo would joke about the headmistress's last sentence, in which she said she'd 'intervened'. 'Do you mean you got into bed with them?' and she answered in the affirmative, and would tell him the story, slowly lifting her skirt so that my father could see the awful bruises that I'd left on her skin.

But this almost never happened.

The headmistress would make a telephone call, and shortly after, I would appear through the door. Pablo turned to look at me. My character had also undergone numerous modifications, in particular with regard to my age. At first I was quite grown up, fifteen, my real age. This didn't fit in very well with certain parts of the story, so I took it down to fourteen. I was scared to go on reducing it until one day I thought, this is stupid, it's all a fantasy anyway, and I decided to stick at twelve, but with a body much too well-developed for a girl of that age. I wore a uniform very different from mine, from my real uniform, an extremely short navy-blue pleated skirt, with straps in the form of an H at the front.

Pablo looked at me closely.

'You've really grown, Lulu!'

I would come up to him, kiss his face, and sit on the arm of his chair. He discreetly slipped a hand round the back, under my skirt, to make sure that I really wasn't wearing anything underneath.

The headmistress would ask him what he intended to do.

'I'd thought of taking her home with me for a while.' Pablo seemed wonderful. 'We've been apart for a long time . . . What do you think, Lulu?'

I would answer, 'I want to go home with you.' We'd say goodbye to the headmistress and climb into a huge dark car, driven by a chauffeur who was sometimes black, sometimes blond, but always very handsome.

'So your little cunt doesn't give you any peace, eh?'

And then I understood that he desired me, even though he was my father, and I desired him, terribly, and above all I didn't want to study. I didn't want to go back to any boarding school. I had no shame, and I always felt like it. I would explain it to him in a little innocent voice, twisting a section of my skirt between my fingers, pulling the waist forward and lifting the fabric slightly so he could see my bare stomach.

'It's not my fault, Daddy, it was always them. They wouldn't leave me alone – the headmistress too, she was one of the worst. She'd hit me with a cane when I refused to eat her pussy, the woman's a bitch, but she did it to me really well when she was in a good mood, and I can't help it, it itches so much, here.' I'd take his hand and pull it towards me until it touched my sex. I'd choose one of his fingers and rub it against me. 'I'm a big girl now, I need it, Daddy . . .'

'I can see that.' Pablo would look at me with shining eyes; he'd lean over and kiss me, joking with the chauffeur. 'What do you think of my daughter?' He'd unbuttoned my blouse and was stroking my breasts, which were held by the strip of fabric joining the braces on my skirt. 'She's lovely, Sir. It will be wonderful to have her among us, she'll make us very happy.' And then we'd go through a very tall black gate, topped with gold spheres. We'd arrive at a huge house and Pablo would take me in his arms and show me round. It was empty, full of empty rooms, with hardly any furniture. Everything was very big, and I lived there with no brothers or sisters, only my father, and the servants, lots of them, and there were always oysters for dinner – I could have a whole tray of them all to myself, and nobody said anything.

Everybody knew that I slept with my father, and they didn't think it strange. He would take me into town, from time to time, and buy me clothes, lots of the clothes I liked, and chocolate. He pampered me and I was spoilt rotten. That amused him: he liked spoiling me. I was happy. I walked around the house half-naked. I loved him so much and I fucked him all the time.

At this point, nearly always very close to orgasm, an infinite number of alternatives might unfold.

We were sitting at a grand dinner table, three or four middle-aged men, he and I. I was wearing a diaphanous white dress. Occasionally I lifted up my skirt and crouched on the chair, with my legs very wide apart, so that he might dip each mouthful inside my sex before putting it into his mouth. Sometimes he sat me on his knee and lifted up my skirt, showing me to his friends. They all agreed, *She's lovely, your daughter*. He'd kiss me on the cheek – he couldn't live without me – I'd slowly stroke myself with my little slender finger for all those gentlemen to see. Pablo would lift me up and sit me on the table, and with a sweep of his hand he'd clear away glasses, plates and flowers, throw me back and fuck me there and then, in front of everyone. I'd come, and when he'd finished he'd invite his friends, *You can continue, if you wish, I'm not a jealous man*, and they'd come up to me and all of them would penetrate me, one after the other, but none of them gave me as much pleasure as he did.

Sometimes he'd be angry. I'd done something wrong, it didn't matter what, and he'd punish me. He'd put me over his knee, lift up my skirt and smack my bottom. They were humiliating, those slaps. He'd hit me hard, I'd cry and writhe about. I promised I'd never do it again, but he'd be implacable; he'd tie me up somewhere and leave me there alone for hours, even days. Sometimes a maid came in, or a manservant. They'd bring me food but I couldn't eat because my hands were tied. Sometimes they'd hit me too, at others they'd make me do things for them, or they'd do things for me, and later Pablo would return. He always came back. He'd put his cock in my mouth and I'd take it in my mouth without a fuss, until he relented and untied me and fucked me on the stone floor. They were wonderful, those reconciliations.

We'd wake up together, in a huge bed. He'd caress me for a while, then uncover me, *You carry on by yourself, I want to watch you.* Then we'd go down a huge staircase to breakfast. *I've got a surprise for you. I'm very pleased with you. I've bought you a toy – you'll see it in a minute – but first, finish your breakfast.* He'd take me by the hand and lead me to the library, where a boy in blue overalls was waiting. *He's yours, you can do what you like with him.* I'd go up to the apprentice gardener and unzip his trousers. He had a magnificent shaft. I was naked. He'd put his arms around me, clumsily – he was like a bear. He'd suck my tits and bite me; he didn't know how to do it. He hurt me. We'd lie on the floor and he'd move on top of me like an animal. He was brutal. At first it was amusing, but then it became boring. *Get off me.* Pablo was sitting in his armchair, watching us. *I don't like it, Daddy, I don't like him.* I'd take hold of his penis and mount him. He'd give me instant pleasure, he knew how to move so slowly. *You're delightful, Lulu,* he'd whisper to me, *delightful, I love you so much . . .*

My Greek teacher was leaning against one of the thick columns in the entrance hall and looking at me with an ironic expression.

'Where are you off to, looking like that?'

I smiled at him while I searched for an innocuous excuse for my appearance, but I couldn't find one. I could feel my hands trembling, I put them in my pockets. My lips were trembling too, so I decided to say something.

'Come on, Felix, buy me a coffee . . .'

'You're entirely mistaken if you think I'm going to risk my hard-earned reputation at this establishment by being seen with a girl dressed like that.'

'What reputation are you talking about? Come on, buy me a coffee.' I took his arm and dragged him off to the coffee bar in the basement.

Felix was an excellent Greek teacher, a highly intelligent man, with a particularly subtle sense of humour, and an old friend of mine. I'd been to bed with him three or four times and enjoyed it. But he had one big defect. He was a terrible gossip, so he was the last person I wanted to bump into there, that particular afternoon.

Things weren't working out too well.

I'd got so nervous waiting at home on my own that in the end I decided to leave half an hour earlier than planned. In my calculations I'd already allowed for arriving at the faculty half an hour early, to get a seat in the middle of the front row, so when I bumped into Felix I still had almost a whole hour to wait – too long to go on hanging around the doors to the lecture hall, which were firmly locked.

It hadn't occurred to me that the doors might be locked. I hadn't thought to check, even though I passed by them every bloody morning.

The best thing would be to go down to the coffee bar, sit at a slightly secluded table and chat for a while.

I was so desperate for good omens that I persuaded myself that my meeting with Felix was auspicious after all.

'Are you wearing anything under that coat?' He was examining me with genuine interest.

'Of course I'm wearing something! Clothes. I'm fully dressed.' I tried to look offended. 'I really don't know why you're so interested in my appearance. It's not as if I was disguised as . . .'

'Yes, you are. Unfortunately, I don't know what as, but you're definitely in disguise.' I wasn't going to be able to fool him so I just changed the subject.

When I went up to the bar to get the coffees, the occupants of one of the front tables, a small group of first year students, let out muffled giggles and nudged each other as I went by.

I wondered if I hadn't gone a bit over the top.

I wasn't too worried about the coat, a white wool coat was always going to be showy, but that's exactly why I'd borrowed it. I needed to attract attention.

The worst bit was the stockings, in an indefinite shade of beige, which kept on falling down round my ankles. The elastic had shown truly remarkable tenacity, but in the end, after having boiled them three times and wrapped them tightly round the base of a couple of champagne bottles for a few days, I managed to get them to slip down my legs convincingly, even though they were brand new.

Maybe it wasn't the stockings – they weren't all that ridiculous in themselves – maybe it was the combination with the shoes which was so bad. I remembered the crowd of shop assistants which gathered round me when I asked for a size 6 in the style with the highest heel, in brown, and took one of the stockings from my handbag, rolled it round my ankle, and tried on loads of shoes, carefully examining the effect in the mirrors leaning against the columns, before settling for a very simple classic style, which made me a good four inches taller than my actual height.

And yet, the day I went to the shoe shop I was wearing normal nylon stockings. That afternoon I had bare legs, in February. My coat, on the other hand, was buttoned right up.

Maybe I'd gone a bit over the top, but it was too late to do anything about it now, so I sat with Felix, and waited. One of the porters had told me that the doors to the lecture hall were opened about ten minutes before the hour given in the timetable.

Five minutes before the ten minutes, I sneaked away, saying I had to go to the toilet. I walked slowly towards the stairs, reached the entrance hall and slipped in through the now open doors, and sat in the very middle of the front row.

For quite a while I was the only person in the hall.

I'd found out about the event quite by chance. The Department of Hispanic Philology was always organizing jamborees of this kind and I'd never paid too much attention to the leaflets and notices pinned up on the board. But I'd been trying to find some private pupils. I needed the money; I was determined to go to Sicily by whatever means, the following summer, and I'd been told about a couple of new ads, two moronic sixth-formers, probably struggling with the uses of the dative.

And then I saw his name, in tiny letters, in amongst lots of other names.

Panic, fear of confronting reality, of being irrevocably disappointed, because afterwards I wouldn't be able to rescue him; I wouldn't be able to return him to the large empty house where we loved each other, fear of losing him for ever.

It had all been a long time ago.

I'd found it very easy to keep him intact in my memory, because I led a life of laborious monotony. I was alone, especially since Marcelo had left home. My days were all the same dull grey, with the constant struggle to win some living space in a packed house; the constant loneliness in the midst of so many people; the endless arguments – *No, I'm not going to do law, Daddy, whatever you say* – the endless interrogations about the strength of my faith, or the nature of my political beliefs – I'd become a member of the Party, more for sentimental reasons than anything else, even though they'd both left it; Marcelo had smiled strangely when I told him – the endless invitations to bring my successive boyfriends round for dinner – my mother insisted on believing that all the blokes I went to bed with during those years were my boyfriends – the endless solitary practice of a despondent, futile love, every day the same.

Who knows, I might have been happy if he hadn't stepped into my life, but it was done. He'd left his mark on me twenty-three days before leaving for Philadelphia, and all the time that had elapsed since then didn't count – it was just an interlude, a meaningless twist of fate, a substitute for real time, for the life which would begin when he came back.

And now he had returned.

I'd seen his name up on the board, in tiny letters, and since then my body had felt completely hollow.

Inside, I was writhing with desire.

My ambitions had diminished at an alarming rate, day by day, as I went about staging my plan. I went to see Chelo to ask her for the plastic bag which she'd kept for me in her wardrobe for the last three years, since the afternoon when my mother remarked that the yellow dress Patricia was wearing was the one worn for the first time by Amelia, the one my grandmother had given me: *Hasn't this child grown? She's almost as tall as you now.* I didn't wait for her to come and ask for my old uniform. I whipped it out of the way a few months before it was due to be discarded, and then I spent the whole summer going round looking amazed, repeating that it must have been magic, my uniform disappearing so mysteriously.

I made the mistake of asking Chelo if she'd be prepared to do me a really big favour. Of course I would, you know that. 'Shave my cunt.' 'What?' 'Well I'm a bit scared of doing it myself.' 'What?' 'Shave my cunt, it'll be easier if someone helps me.' She refused, of course. I was expecting her to, because I'd told her about the business with Pablo. She knew it was for him, and she was really offended by my suggestion. She'd never, ever forgive him his negligence with contraception. She'd always thought him doubly guilty – in those days Chelo hadn't yet discovered the pleasures of mortified flesh, and she only liked very leftie guys. She saw *coitus interruptus* as both a courtesy and a statement in favour of sexual equality, so in the end I had to do it myself, furtively, in the bathroom. I took down the mirror without making any noise, at three in the morning, so that nobody'd come and bash on the door. It took me nearly two hours because I went very slowly, knowing how clumsy I am, but the end result was quite satisfactory. I could feel my skin, naked and smooth once more, as I sat there, in the middle of the front row, praying to all my adored dead gods that they intercede in my favour, so that he would accept me, and not reject me. That was all I dared ask for: that he shouldn't reject me, that he should take me once, at least, before leaving again.

The hall gradually filled with people.

A small, bald man with sideburns was the first to come and take his place on the rostrum. Pablo, who arrived talking to a Biblical-looking bearded guy who'd greeted him effusively at the bottom of the stairs leading up to the platform, sat down last, at the end of the row.

It was five years, two months and eleven days since I'd

last seen him. His face, with its large nose and square jaw, had hardly changed. The grey hadn't gained much ground either, his hair was still mostly black. He was quite a bit thinner, though. This surprised me – Marcelo always said the food was quite good in Philadelphia – but he'd got thinner, and it made him look even taller and more gangling. That was one of the things I'd always liked most about him – he'd always looked as if he was about to come apart, not enough flesh for all those bones.

His age suited him.

While the guy with the sideburns introduced the speakers in an exasperatingly ponderous manner, he lit a cigarette and glanced round the hall. He was looking in every direction except mine.

The hollow inside was devouring me.

I felt very hot. And very scared.

I didn't look at him straight on but I noticed that he'd gone very still.

He was staring at me intently, his eyes half closed, a strange look on his face. Then he smiled, and only then did he move his lips, silently, two syllables, as if pronouncing my name.

He recognized me.

I acted according to my plan. I slowly unbuttoned my coat, uncovering my horrendous, brown school uniform. I tried to look sure of myself, but inside I felt like a bad old magician, only just keeping up appearances but expecting the eight wooden skittles he's juggling to come crashing down on top of him. Pablo put his hand over his face, and stayed like that for a few seconds, before looking at me again. He was still smiling.

He spoke very little that afternoon, and very badly. He went blank a couple of times and stammered; he seemed to be unable to construct a sentence of more than three words. He didn't take his eyes off me, and my neighbours were looking at me curiously.

When the old guy with the sideburns kicked off the question-and-answer session, I got up from my seat.

To my surprise, my legs still held me up.

I walked the length of the row, very slowly, without tripping, and left the lecture theatre. I crossed the hall without looking back, went through the glass doors at the entrance and only had time to take about eight or nine steps before he stopped me. He put his arm on mine, took me by the elbow, made me turn round and, after looking at me closely for a few seconds, he touched me with his magic wand.

'I'm so pleased, Lulu, you haven't grown up at all.'

He accepted all I offered him with exquisite elegance. He read all the signs without making any comment. He spoke little, just enough. He willingly fell into my traps. He let me find out all I wanted to know.

He took me to his place, a very large but furniture-packed loft in the centre of town.

'What's happened to the workshop in Moreto?'

'My mother sold it a couple of years ago.' He seemed sorry. 'She's bought herself a truly ghastly little house in Majadahonda.'

Then, in silence, he ran his eyes over me, slowly, from my head to my toes. He held my arms above my head and I kept them there while he pulled my jumper off. He undid my blouse, removed it and looked into my face, smiling. I wasn't wearing a bra and he still remembered everything. He leaned forward, seized me by the ankles and pulled them suddenly upwards, making me fall on the sofa. He drew my legs towards him until they were on top of his. I was now lying down. He undid the clasps on my skirt. Before removing it, he took one of my hands, held it up to his face and looked at it closely, lingering over the round, blunt fingertips. That was one detail I'd overlooked. Even though I knew I shouldn't, I broke the silence.

'Do you like long nails, painted red?'

My hand still in his, he gave me an ironic smile.

'Does it matter?'

I couldn't answer that it did, it mattered a lot, so I gave a vague shrug.

'No, I don't like them,' he admitted at last. That's lucky, I thought.

He finished undressing me, slowly. He took off my shoes, my stockings and then put my shoes back on. He looked at me a moment, without moving. Then he stretched out his open hand and slid it softly over me, from the instep of my foot to my neck, several times. He seemed so calm, his gestures so steady and light that for a moment I thought he didn't really desire me, that this was only an echo of his former desire, now long gone. Maybe I'd grown too much, after all.

He slipped his arm under me and sat me up. I was now sitting on his knees. He put his arms around me and kissed me. The mere contact with his tongue reverberated throughout my body, sending shivers down my spine. He is the meaning of my life, I thought. It was an old thought, that I'd endlessly repeated to myself during his absence, and violently pushed aside in recent months, for being mean and pathetic, and useless. There were still so many great causes to fight for in the world, but at that moment, as he kissed me and rocked me in his arms, it was the only truth, the plain and simple truth: he was the only thing that gave meaning to my life.

I caught his hand and covered my face with it. I held it still a moment, feeling the pressure of his fingertips, and gave his palm a long, moist kiss, then I bent his fingers, one by one, hiding the thumb under the other four, put my hand round his fist and pressed my cheeks and lips against his knuckles.

I was trying to make him see that I loved him.

'I've got something for you . . .'

He put me aside very gently, stood up and crossed the room. He took out a long narrow box from one of the desk drawers.

'I bought it for you about three years ago, in a moment of weakness . . .' He smiled at me. 'Don't tell anyone about it. I think I find it embarrassing now, but at the time I'd get these crazy urges every so often, especially when I was on my own. I'd get in the car and head off to New York, to Fourteenth Street and Eighth Avenue. It's a really lively place – how can I explain what it's like . . .' He was silent for a moment, thinking it over. Then his face lit up. 'Yeah, that's it, Fourteenth Street is like a kind of Bravo Murillo but wilder; it's full of people, and bars and shops. It would take me over four hours there and back, just to go and eat tuna *empanadas* and sing 'Asturias, Beloved Homeland' in a bar owned by a guy from Langreo. I'd get blind drunk, and then I'd feel better. In one of those stupid fits of nostalgia, I bought you this.' He sat down next to me and handed me the box. 'At the risk of sounding vulgar, I'll tell you, it was very expensive, and I was broke at the time, but I bought it for you anyway, because I owed it to you. I've felt strangely responsible for you all these years. I never dared send it to you, though. The truth is, I expected to find you all grown up, and grown women don't always appreciate toys . . .'

The box, carefully wrapped in cellophane, contained a dozen plastic objects in white, beige and red – an electric vibrator with a grooved surface, surrounded by a set of detachable covers and accessories. There were also two small batteries, in a bag.

I had no problem showing I was satisfied. I was very pleased, and not just because he'd remembered me.

'Thanks a lot, I love it.' I gave him a big smile. 'You should have sent it to me, I could have really done with it. I suppose it's my size . . .' He was watching me and laughing. 'If you like, I could try it out . . . now.'

I tore off the cellophane and carefully examined the contents. I found the slot for the batteries without too much trouble and loaded the vibrator. I turned the little switch at its base and it started to tremble. I increased the power until it was dancing in the palm of my hand. It was funny, just like on Christmas morning as a child, when after fitting two batteries into its back, an ordinary, inert doll, would start to talk or move its head. I realized that I was smiling.

I looked at Pablo, he was smiling too.

'Which do you think is the best?'

He didn't answer, he just stood up and went to sit in an armchair leaning against the wall opposite, about seven feet away, exactly facing me.

Now I'll show you, I thought, I'll show you if I've grown up or not. I felt good, very sure of myself. I had a feeling that this was my only winning card. I'd thought about it often in the last few days and I hadn't been able to come up with a concrete plan, or any definite tactics, but he'd made it all very easy for me. He was attracted to me, and I remembered that he liked dirty little girls – all right then, I'd show him just how dirty I could be, really dirty. I remembered the headmistress's words and I urged myself on. The only thing I was worried about was that my performance might be a little too theatrical, even slightly hysterical, and not convincing enough. I didn't care about anything else. I have a strange sense of propriety. A lady exclaiming 'Isn't he sweet!' at a handicapped child in a wheelchair; a parvenu kicking up a fuss when the fifteen-year-old waiter at a little bar on the beach says they don't have wholemeal bread; or a pair of rich, fat cats in swanky clothes who won't give beggars more than five pesetas – that's the sort of thing that makes me feel ashamed. The other kind of propriety, the conventional kind, is something I've never had.

I slowly opened my legs and slid my finger along my pussy, just once, before starting to chatter.

'I think I'll begin with this one.' I extracted from the box a flesh-coloured plastic cover, which was a pretty faithful reproduction of the real thing, veins and all. 'Do you know something? I don't like being so tall any more. I used to be really proud of it but now I'd like to be about ten inches shorter, like Susana – do you remember Susana?'

'The one with the recorder?' His expression, both thoughtful and amused, was the one I had made an effort to retain in my mind's eye all these years.

'That's right, the one with the recorder. You've got a good memory . . .' I was looking straight into his eyes the whole time, trying to affect the cold, calculating expression which characterizes expertly lascivious women, but my sex, as yet empty, was throbbing and swelling all the time, and I've never been able to stay calm when I felt like that. 'There we are, but it's huge! I suppose you won't be embarrassed if I put it in right now, will you?' He shook his head. I rubbed myself a couple of times with the new toy before unhurriedly sinking it inside me. I became distracted and wasn't able to observe his reaction, although this had been my main purpose. It was the first time I'd used one of these things and my own reactions absorbed me entirely.

'Do you like it?' His question upset my concentration.

'Yes, I do . . .' I was silent a moment and looked at him, before going on. 'But it's not really like a man's cock, like I'd imagined, first because it's not hot, and then, I've got to move it myself, so there's not that element of surprise – do you know what I mean? There's no change of rhythm, like when it stops, and then suddenly speeds up, that's what I like best, when it speeds up . . .'

'You've fucked a lot all these years, haven't you?'

'I haven't done too badly . . .' Now I was moving my hand more quickly. I was vigorously pumping the fake penis against the walls of my vagina, and it felt good. It was starting to feel a bit too good, so I stopped suddenly and decided to change the cover; I didn't want to precipitate things. 'Is this one with the spikes meant to hurt?'

'I don't know, I don't think so.'

'Well, we'll see . . . I was telling you something, ah yes, the thing about Susana. Because she's five feet tall, all blokes seem huge to her – it's brilliant. Every time I ask her she always says the same: "it was this big,"' I spread my hands wide apart, '"enormous", but like, complaining.

I can't understand her, she's always complaining. I'd love it, but because I'm so big, well, they never quite fill me up, so it's a disadvantage really, being so tall, you're too long all over . . .'

'Yeah . . .' He was laughing loudly and watching me. I knew he was enjoying it all so I decided to link this story with another one from a completely different source. I'd never have believed I could tell him about it, but at that moment it didn't seem important.

'Hey, you know what? The spikes don't hurt. Now I'm going to put this on, let's see what happens.' I took out a kind of red cap, covered in little bumps, and fitted it onto the tip. 'Yeah, and a funny thing, talking of Susana, a couple of months ago I dreamt about you one night, and dildoes played a big part in the dream.' I stopped for a moment. I wanted to examine his face, but I couldn't detect anything special. 'Well, it turns out, Susana's become a little goody-goody recently. She used to be the sluttiest in the class, at school, but a couple of years ago she got a fiancé, terribly serious, a real old square, he's about twenty-nine . . .'

'I'm thirty-two . . .' At first he looked at me with the same expression as my mother when she caught me poking around in the larder, then he burst out laughing.

'Yeah, but you're not a square.'

'Why not?'

'Because you're not, like Marcelo – he isn't square either, even though he's got a kid and everything. Well, anyway, the thing is Susana's fiancé is really loaded. He's got an ad agency but not an ounce of humour. The other night we went out for dinner – the two of them, Chelo, who brought quite an amusing guy, and me. I didn't have anybody to take, seriously, look, if I'd had this then, maybe I could have worn it.' I took the vibrator out from inside me and started to remove the accessories. I wanted to try it with nothing on – it would probably be less effective like that. The spikes were starting to excite me too much. 'The fact is we got drunk, including Susana, and we told him the story about the recorder. Chelo's bloke laughed a lot, he thought it was really funny, but Susana's got furious. He said it wasn't funny at all, he definitely didn't find that kind of stupidity funny. I told them I thought that was a bit odd and that when you'd found out, it really turned you on. Didn't it?' He nodded. 'Did you bring me a recorder back from New York too?'

'No.'

'What a pity!' At that I couldn't help laughing, but I managed to get a grip on myself after a few seconds, and went on. 'Well, the fact is, that night I dreamt we were both driving along in a really big, flash car, with a really handsome black chauffeur, who called you Sir and had a really big cock. I don't know how, but I knew he had a really big one.' His smile, different now, made me worry that he suspected what kind of dream this really was, so I started to improvise, to try and make the whole thing seem more likely. 'I was wearing a long, sixteenth-century style, dove-grey dress with a huge décolleté, a white ruff and hoop skirt with a tulle bustle over my bottom and loads of jewellery all over the place, but you were just dressed in ordinary trousers and a thick red jumper, and we stopped in Fuencarral Street, which was really Berlin, even though all the street signs were in Spanish. Everything was the same as it is in real life, and we went into a shoe shop, with loads of shoes in the windows, of course . . . Hey, you don't mind if I carry on with my finger, do you, just for a little bit? I need a rest.'

'Please, feel free.'

'Thank you, so kind, right, where was I, ah yes. In the shoe shop there was an assistant dressed up as an old-fashioned page, but his clothes weren't really like mine. His costume looked French, like Louis XIV, lots of lace and a powdered wig, you know the kind of thing, and then I sat down very nicely on a seat. You remained standing by my side and the assistant came up to you and said, "What can I do for you, Sir?" because the funniest thing is, you can't imagine what the relationship was between you and me, you'll never guess . . .'

'Father and daughter?'

'Yes . . .' I stammered. 'How did you guess?'

'Pah, I said the first thing that came into my head.'

'Don't you find it incredible?' My amazement, tinged with embarrassment, genuine embarrassment, despite my proverbial lack of shame, threatened to paralyze me at any moment.

'No. It's charming.' His words dispelled my doubts. 'Then what happened? I wasn't getting you kitted out for school, was I?'

'No way.' I laughed. The unpleasant feeling had completely disappeared, and I was feeling better and better, and more convincing. I went back to stroking myself so he could see me, moving slowly on the carpet, arousing him from a distance. That really excited me, but I also felt a terrible urge to go over and touch him. 'You told the shop assistant that you were going off to Philadelphia for a couple of weeks, to give a course on Saint John of the Cross to those poor savages – the Indians, I mean – and that you were worried about leaving me all alone like that, because I was a shameless little hussy and there was no knowing what I might do, so you'd thought of inserting a dildo inside me to comfort me and keep me company while you were away. The assistant agreed it was a good idea. "These young girls nowadays," he said, "you can never be too careful." Then the man went into the back room and came back with these two stands. I don't know what to call them – a pair of metal poles with rings at the top – and he put them in front of me, one on either side. I knew what I had to do. I lifted up my skirts, spread my legs and put a heel in the ring at the top of each stand, like when you go to the gynaecologist. I was wearing long white bloomers down to my knees, but all open underneath, with a buttonhole embroidered with little flowers, and the shop assistant put his finger inside me. He looked at you and said, "I can't try any of them out, she's completely dry. If you like, I can try to do something about it," and you agreed, so then he kneeled in front of me and started to lick my cunt. He did it really well and it felt good, but when I was about to come you said, "That's enough," and he stopped . . .'

'That was rather disagreeable of me, wasn't it?' He was smiling, drumming his fingers on his flies.

'Yes,' I answered, 'you were definitely very rude. Well, then the man started to fit me with big golden dildoes, longer and bigger ones, and as I was already quite aroused, well, I came right in the middle of the fitting. You liked that. The shop assistant wasn't very pleased, but he didn't say anything. In the end he put a horrible one inside me, it really hurt, but you loved it and you said, "Yes, that one, that one," so he pushed a little bit more and it went right inside me, the whole thing, and I couldn't get it out. I cried and complained, "I don't want this one," I told you, but you went to the till and paid. You helped me up and led me out, saying you'd miss the plane, because you were going to Philadelphia by plane, from Paris, oh, I mean Berlin, but I couldn't walk, I just couldn't. I had to keep my legs wide apart and I could feel it inside, that great big rod. When we got in the car, the chauffeur asked what was the matter, and you lifted my skirt for him to see. He put the tip of his finger inside me and exclaimed, "Size 56, wonderful, that's the best one," and I said to you, whimpering, "How are we going to be able to say goodbye if I've got this inside?" and you said, "Don't worry, there are other ways," and you forced me to kneel on top of the back seat. You lifted up my skirt, and put a finger in my bottom . . . and then I woke up. I was soaking, and I thought about you.' I looked at him, for a long time. He didn't say anything but just smiled, then I spoke again. 'Did you like my dream?'

'Yes, very much. I'd be very happy if I had a daughter like you.'

'Listen, Pablo . . .' From his words and his eyes I could

tell that it had been a success. Now he knew, he knew just how dirty I could be, and he probably knew a few things more, but it still wasn't enough, I had to go all the way. 'I'd love to suck your cock. Will you let me?'

He undid his flies, pulled out his penis with his right hand and started to stroke it.

'I'm waiting . . .'

I crossed the distance separating me from him on my knees, leaned over his cock and put it in my mouth. This was turning out to be a real reunion.

'Lulu . . .'

'Hmmm,' I didn't feel like talking.

'I'd like to sodomize you.'

I didn't open my eyes. I didn't want to hear what he said, but his words stayed jangling inside my head for a few seconds.

'I'd like to sodomize you,' he said again. 'Can I?'

I removed my lips from their absorbing occupation and looked up at him, still rubbing his penis gently against my hand.

'Look, you don't have to take things so literally . . .' I was just trying to impress him, I thought, that was it, I'd wanted to impress him, but not that much. 'It's not rational to believe in dreams, and anyway, I've already told you I'm used to never being filled right up. You don't have to take so much trouble . . .'

'It's no trouble.' He looked at me. He'd got me there, well and truly got me. I felt I'd never manage to be a *femme fatale*, a proper *femme fatale*. My plan had backfired, and now I couldn't think of anything dirty or original to say. 'Anyway, from what I could see, and hear, it doesn't seem like it would be the first time . . .'

'Well, as it happens, I think it would . . .' Then I fell silent. I looked at him a moment and decided the best thing would be to go back to how things were before, so I again closed my mouth around his penis and displayed the whole range of my skills, one after the other, very fast.

I thought maybe that way he wouldn't feel like it any more, but scarcely a few minutes later the pressure of his hand forced me to stop.

'Well?' He insisted politely.

'I don't know, Pablo, the thing is . . .' I was trying to awaken his compassion, looking at him with the expression of a lamb being led to the slaughter. It wasn't too much of an effort – I felt really bewildered, because I couldn't say no to him, not to him, but I didn't want to let him do it. I knew I definitely didn't want to. 'Why do you ask me things like that?'

'Would you have preferred me not to ask?'

'No, it's not that. I'm not saying I think it was a bad thing you asked, it's just that, I don't know, I . . .'

'Never mind, it doesn't matter, it was just an idea.' He slid his arm under mine, indicating that I should get up. Once I was standing up in front of him, he sunk his tongue into my navel, for an instant, and then he stood up too, put his arms round me and kissed me on the mouth, at length. He slid his hands slowly from my waist, up my back, and then rested them firmly on my shoulders. Then he turned me round abruptly, tripped me up with his right foot, knocked me down onto the carpet and threw himself on top of me. He locked my thighs between his knees so that I couldn't move and let all his weight fall on his left hand, with which he was pressing down between my shoulder blades, pinning me to the floor. I felt a cold, soft blob, and then a finger, alarmingly clearly, going in and out of my body, finally distributing the remainder of the cream around the orifice.

'You bastard . . .'

He clicked his tongue several times.

'Now, now, Lulu, you know I don't like you using that kind of language.'

I flung my legs up and managed to hit him on the back a couple of times. I was also trying to free my arms when I felt the tip of his penis, probing me.

'Keep still, Lulu, it won't do you any good, I mean it . . . All you'll get, if you carry on being silly, is a slap.' He wasn't angry with me. His tone was warm, even soothing, despite his threatening words. 'Now be a good girl. It'll only take a minute, and it's not such a big deal anyway.' He opened me up with his right hand. I could feel the pressure of his thumb, stretching my skin, pulling the flesh apart. 'Anyway, it's really all your fault – you're always the one to start. You stare at me with those big hungry eyes; I can't help it if I find you so attractive . . .'

His right hand, which, I imagined, was closed round his cock, pressed against what felt like a tiny, fragile orifice.

'You bastard, you bloody bastard . . .'

After that I couldn't speak. The pain left me speechless, blind, motionless, it paralyzed me completely. I'd never experienced such agony in all my life. I started to scream. I screamed like an animal being led to the slaughter, emitting long, piercing shrieks, until my tears drowned out the sound, depriving me even of the consolation of being able to scream, reducing me to feeble, intermittent sobs which seemed even more humiliating, underlining my weakness, my total powerlessness against the brute writhing on top of me, panting and sighing against my neck, succumbing to an essentially iniquitous, insulting pleasure. He was using me, just as I had earlier used the white plastic toy, using me, taking from me by force a pleasure to which he denied me all access.

I would never have imagined it possible, but the pain suddenly intensified. His thrusts became increasingly violent and he let his whole weight fall on top of me. He penetrated me with all his might, then moved away and I felt as if half my entrails were going with him. My head started to spin. I thought I was going to faint, I felt I couldn't bear it a moment longer, when he started to groan. I guessed he was coming, but I couldn't feel anything. The pain had desensitized me to the point where all I could feel was pain.

Then he remained motionless on top of me, still inside me. He bit the tip of my ear and said my name. I was still crying, silently.

I felt him leave me, slowly, but it was as if he were still inside. The hole he'd opened up refused to close.

He turned me round, moving me gently. I didn't help him at all – my body was a completely dead weight. I didn't move. I kept my eyes closed, still crying.

He wiped the tears from my eyes, stroking my face with his hand. He leaned over me and kissed me on the lips. I didn't respond. He kissed me again.

'I love you.'

He moved his lips over my chin, then down my throat, closed them round my nipples. He slid his tongue down my body, across my navel and down my stomach. He bent my legs and then pulled them open.

I felt ashamed and deeply unhappy. My pussy was moist.

His fingers rested on the lips and pressed them together. He relaxed the pressure for an instant and then pressed again, moving gradually higher, producing a muffled sound, like a gurgle. When he reached the end, his hands parted the lips, completely baring my sex and exposing the tight, pink skin, which was still stinging like an open wound.

He ran his tongue over me slowly, from front to back, soothing me, and then concentrated on the insignificant ridge of flesh to which my whole body was now reduced, sliding, pressing, stroking it. I could feel the hard tip of his tongue, rubbing against it, and my flesh swelling, swelling outrageously, and throbbing, then he caught it between his lips and sucked it, let go and sucked it again. He took it in his mouth and licked it, and I had to move, arching and pushing my body towards him, offering myself to him, so as to enjoy fully the pleasure he was giving me.

He inserted two fingers inside my sex and started to move them following the same rhythm as my body against his tongue. A little later, he slipped two fingers into me lower down, into the channel which he himself had earlier opened.

The memory of his violence added an irresistible note to the pleasure taking hold of me, setting off an exquisitely brutal climax.

His tongue stayed firmly in place until my very last spasm had subsided. His fingers were still inside me when he rested his head on my navel.

We're quits, I thought. We've swapped individual pleasures, he's given me back what he earlier snatched away.

I found the thought comforting.

It was definitely a debatable point of view, but still a point of view.

'I love you.'

Then I remembered that he'd said it to me before, *I love you*, and I wondered what exactly this might mean.

He lay down beside me, kissed me and turned over onto his front. I climbed laboriously on top of him. My whole body ached. I placed my legs on top of his, covered his arms with mine and rested my head in the hollow of his shoulder.

He greeted me with a grunt of pleasure.

'Do you know what, Pablo? You're becoming a highly dangerous individual.' I smiled to myself. 'Lately, every time I see you, I go a whole week without being able to sit down . . .'

His body shook beneath me. It felt good. He hadn't finished laughing when he called my name.

'Lulu . . .'

I made a vague sound in reply. I was too absorbed in my own sensations. I'd never done it before, lain on top of a man, like that, but it was a delicious feeling. His skin was cool and the shape of his body beneath mine, the flipside of the one I usually came into contact with, was full of surprises.

'Lulu . . .' I saw he was now being serious. I felt no surprise – I even expected it, in spite of my elaborate performance. I was quite prepared for another farewell, it was inevitable.

In spite of this, I moved my mouth close to his ear. I wasn't sure that my voice wouldn't let me down.

'Yes?'

'Will you marry me?'

We'd played cards as a team lots of times, in years gone by. He was the best liar I'd ever known. I was sure, almost certain, that he was kidding, but I accepted his offer anyway.

I found somewhere to park straight away, really surprising for a Friday. As I was locking the car door, one of them bumped into me.

'Sorry.' His voice was gentle and affected, it was unmistakable.

I watched them closely as they walked on down the hill.

There were two of them. The one who'd said sorry had very short brown hair, shaved over his ears. A long, lank fringe, dyed blond, completely covered one eye. The other one, whose face I couldn't see, was dark. His curly hair was tied back in a small pony-tail, at the nape of his neck.

They walked in step down the middle of the paved street. The shorter one was constantly flicking his fringe off his face. He was wearing a very pretty shirt, in a shiny fabric, and a pair of very tight black trousers. His friend, who looked much more interesting, at least from the back, was very tanned. An orange scarf tied round his waist brightened up his otherwise sober outfit, a very low-cut black vest, and a pair of very wide trousers, also black and elasticated at the ankles.

I followed them at a distance. I had plenty of time.

Two blocks further on, a guy leaning on a car, under a street lamp, greeted them with a wave of his arm. He was dressed from top to toe in white, from his espadrilles to his hair band. He was very good-looking and very young.

He still had the fragile air of an adolescent about him.

I stopped in front of a shop window and watched them in the reflection. The shorter one got there first and gave a light kiss on the lips to the young guy who then stood up and went up to the one in black, now standing with his arms crossed, in the middle of the pavement. He clung to his neck and kissed him on the mouth. I could see their tongues intertwining as they kissed passionately.

They walked on down the hill, the three of them, the one with the fringe on his own, to one side, the other two with their arms round each other's waist, the dark one stroking the backside of the one in white from time to time, and giving him little pats.

I followed them, without any specific aim. I was delighted to have found them; I'd been lucky.

They turned down a side-street. I watched them from the corner and saw them go into a bar which I used to go to quite a lot in my student days. It was funny to think of that leftie hang-out turning into a gay bar.

I walked past the door but couldn't see them. A pair of fortyish-looking women, with a look of progressive civil servants, who in the past might have been referred to as emancipated women, were perched on stools at the bar. Next to them, a couple of youngsters, a boy and a girl, were flirting away peaceably.

I went in to make a phone call.

They were standing in a corner. I glanced round the place. There were all sorts in there, people of every variety, so I decided to stay. I leaned on the bar and asked for a drink.

'Hello?' I heard my brother's voice at the other end of the line.

'Marcelo? Hi, it's me. Look, I'm really sorry but I'm not going to be able to make it for dinner.' I made my voice sound slurry. 'I've been drinking all evening with a friend who's recently split up with her bloke and I feel pretty bad.

I think I'd better go home and sleep it off. Tell Mercedes I'm really sorry, maybe next week . . .'

'Duckling,' he sounded worried. I knew what he was going to ask. 'Duckling, are you all right?'

'Yeah, of course I am, I'm pissed but I'm fine.' Since I'd left Pablo, Marcelo seemed obsessed with my well-being.

'Sure?' He didn't believe me.

'Look, I'm fine, Marcelo, I've just had a bit too much to drink, that's all.'

'Do you want me to come and pick you up?'

'Look, I'm thirty. I think I'm capable of getting home all on my own.'

'That's true, I always forget, sorry.' He'd never stopped treating me like a child. He was just like Pablo, but it didn't bother me – I've always really adored my brother too. 'Call me tomorrow, OK?'

'OK.'

As I sipped my drink, I wondered why I'd gone in there, why I'd cancelled dinner at Marcelo's, what I was expecting from all of this. A moment later I told myself that I wasn't expecting anything. I'd gone in there to watch them, so I concentrated on that.

They were still standing at one end of the bar. I could watch them in peace. They probably couldn't see me, half hidden as I was at the other end of the bar.

The very young guy and the one in black were going out together, I was almost certain. They made a very good couple. About the same height, both slightly over six feet, they had the same healthy, relaxed look about them. The dark one had a wonderful body, like a Greek god, with huge shoulders, a powerful torso, long, strong limbs, not an ounce of fat, and just the right amount of muscle. He must work hard at it, I thought, like my little Californians. He had a long, angular face; very large, dark eyes. He definitely wasn't ugly, but taken as a whole his face was too hard. It didn't really go with the pony-tail, or with his status as a sodomite. Whether he liked it or not, he looked like the typical Mediterranean macho type, the kind who take a strap to their women, and no amount of weight-training in a gym would alter that.

His boyfriend looked divine, and totally ambiguous. He was very slim, with a slightly languid air, like the young men of ancient Greece, although he was really too big, too solid, all in all too masculine to compare with the classical model. That was what I most liked about him. I can't stand effeminate boyish youths, they really don't do anything for me. He had a perfect bottom, hard and round, its contour clearly defined beneath the light fabric of his tight trousers, which were exactly like those of his companion. His face was a perfect oval with lightly pink cheeks, long curly eyelashes framing brown, almond-shaped eyes with a gentle expression. His lips, by contrast, were thin and cruel. A small nose, a long, delicate neck . . . He must drive them wild, I thought.

They were talking amongst themselves, facing each other. At first they smiled affectionately, but then the tone seemed to change. The one with the dyed fringe joined in. I didn't like the look of him at all – he looked too much like a typical queen, even though he wasn't sporting any of the traditional attire, long nails, make-up, etc . . . The young guy then became extremely submissive. He caressed his friend's arms, sliding his hands over his muscles, rested his head on his shoulder and kissed him on the neck. He seemed to want to show him how much he loved him. There could be no doubt that he did, but the dark-haired one was playing hard to get. He acted distant, then his gestures became abrupt and they seemed to be arguing. The young one seemed prepared to do anything to mollify him. He seemed to be pleading for forgiveness with his face, his hands, all his gestures, but it was no use, there came a point when he was rejected and the athlete pushed him away. The one with the fringe couldn't help showing how pleased he was – he was delighted – but he got an earful too; the dark one shouted at him and shook him without hesitation. He seemed fed up with both of them. The younger one turned his back on him, leaned against the wall and hid his head in his arms, obviously in despair. Moved by this, his companion finally went up to him and put his arms round him from behind, stroking his naturally blond hair. In the end, the young guy turned round and they kissed as passionately as when they'd met. Soon, it looked as if nothing had happened.

I was having great fun. I asked for another drink, without taking my eyes off them.

'Homosexuals are only human beings like any others.' I turned round, really surprised, as much by the peculiar construction of the sentence as by the unknown identity of the speaker.

Behind the bar, a young man who looked very like the guy with the fringe was directing a furious glance at me.

'Absolutely no doubt about that,' I answered, as I turned towards him.

'In that case I don't know why you're staring at Jimmy so much.' This one was really ugly, poor thing.

'I don't know who Jimmy is.'

'Seriously?' My answer seemed to have totally disconcerted him.

'Seriously.'

'He's the one in black, but I don't understand. If you don't know him . . . why are you staring at him so much?'

'Because I find him attractive.'

'You find him attractive?' He burst out laughing. 'Well, you haven't got a hope, sweetheart. He's gay, you know, through and through – the little blond guy there's his trick.'

'I've already realized that.' I looked at him seriously and paused. 'I may be a woman, but I'm not stupid, you know.' I went on before he could say anything. 'And anyway, I find him attractive *because* he's gay, just because of that, got it?'

'No.' He was so utterly disconcerted that it made me smile.

'I simply find homosexuals attractive. I like them, they really excite me.'

'Sexually, do you mean?'

'Yes.' He stood petrified, a glass in his hand, astounded. 'I don't see why it's so earth-shattering. Men, I mean heterosexual men, like lesbians, good-looking lesbians anyway, and nobody finds that unusual.'

'Well, it's the first time I've ever heard of it . . .'

'You can't have been around much then.' I didn't have any evidence but I refused to believe my desire was unprecedented.

Unprecedented desires don't exist.

'The first time . . .' he repeated, astounded, shaking his head, as he served my drink.

A few minutes later, he brought it up again.

'Do you mean you'd like to go to bed with them . . . even if they didn't do anything to you, just to watch, say?' His expression was still one of shock and disbelief. He was looking at me as if I was a real freak.

'Yes,' I answered, 'I'd love that.'

'Do you want me to speak to them?' I covertly examined his face. He seemed solicitous, but devoid of financial motives, at least for the time being.

'Please do,' I answered, and only then did I realize what a mess I'd landed myself in, all on my little own, without anybody's help.

He disappeared through the door at the back of the bar. He reappeared a few seconds later, talking to Jimmy and his boyfriend, or whatever he was.

The barman was telling them about it as if it was a big joke, laughing loudly the whole time. The blond guy also found it funny. Jimmy didn't. He just looked at me. I met his gaze and wondered what I'd do if they wanted money. It was shameful, paying to go to bed with a man, definitely much more shameful than being paid. On the other hand, they weren't men, I mean they didn't really count in that sense.

They deliberated for a while, the two of them, the barman keeping on the sidelines. Then Jimmy called the one with the fringe, and he joined in the discussion, staring at me the whole time, his eyes like saucers. They took a long time to reach an agreement. Then the blond guy exchanged a few words with the waiter and both of them came over.

Jimmy's boyfriend came up to me and gave me a kiss on each cheek.

'Hi, my name's Pablo.'

'Oh, bloody brilliant.'

'Why do you say that?' My not terribly polite response had offended him.

'No reason, just a little obsession of mine, really . . . it's not important.' His face remained stony, so I explained. 'Look, the thing is my husband's called Pablo too, and as I've just left him . . .'

'Yeah, right,' he smiled. 'What a coincidence!'

'Yes . . .' I didn't know what to say.

'Could you stand up?' he asked. 'My friend wants to take a look at you.'

That was one thing I hadn't been expecting.

I stood up and gave a complete turn, revolving slowly on my heels. Then I sat down again and looked in Jimmy's direction. His boyfriend was looking at him too. He gave the thumbs up. The bloke with the fringe was still by his side.

'All right.' The blond guy looked at me. 'Any cash in it for us?'

'Maybe . . .' I think I've never uttered a word with so little conviction in all my life.

'Thirty thousand each.'

'You must be kidding!' I was aware of my inexperience. I could understand them making the most of the situation to rip me off, but not to that extent. 'Twenty, or you can go to hell.'

'Twenty-five . . .'

'Twenty.' I looked him straight in the face, but couldn't

guess anything from it. 'Twenty thousand. That's my last offer. I mean, all I'm going to do is watch . . .'

'OK,' he answered quickly, obviously not unhappy with the deal.

Well done, Lulu, I thought. You sucker.

'Twenty each,' he said again.

He would have accepted fifteen, twelve even, I thought.

'Forty . . .' I said it two or three times, thoughtfully, as if the figure really meant anything to me. It seemed exorbitantly expensive, a real stupidity on my part, still, I could allow myself the luxury, not very often that was for sure, but just this once . . . In fact I didn't have a clue what the going rate was for a tart, and this lot must be more expensive, or maybe not, perhaps they put the price up if the punter was a woman – or maybe they didn't, how could I tell? Pablo would no doubt have known what to do, but he'd never even told me how much he'd given Ely, that night. Ely was a transvestite, but this lot didn't even look like professionals . . . I was in a right muddle.

'No. Sixty.' The blond guy's surprising correction brought my speculations to an abrupt end.

'What do you mean, sixty?' I looked at him indignantly. 'We agreed twenty each. Two times twenty makes forty.'

'But there's three of us.'

'Who's the third?'

'Mario, the one over there with Jimmy . . .'

'The one with the fringe?' He nodded. 'No way, he's not included, I don't like him at all.'

'The thing is . . .' He was giving me a pleading look; he seemed to be in a bit of a fix. 'If he doesn't come, Jimmy won't want to.'

'Why not?'

'Well, the thing is . . .' He was going red. 'Mario's his trick.'

'But isn't Jimmy going out with you?'

'Yes . . .' he said, 'but he's going out with Mario too.'

'You're a threesome?' It was a possibility, but he

quickly shook his head. 'Oh, I've got it . . .' I suddenly understood; their argument earlier gave me the answer. 'You're two couples with an interchangeable member, in both senses . . .' I scanned his face. Close up he was even more beautiful. 'What I can't understand is . . . how you could be so bloody stupid. You shouldn't have to share a bloke with anyone, ever. You must have them queuing up by the hundred . . .'

'It's none of your business.'

'That's true,' I admitted. 'Well, anyway, I don't want that one with the fringe. He can come along if he has to, but I'm giving you forty thousand, not a penny more. Afterwards, if you want to, you can sort it out amongst yourselves, but I'm not having anything to do with it.'

He stared at me a moment, in silence. Then he turned round, and went off looking sheepish to inform the committee. The other two started to argue with him; it can't have seemed a good deal. The blond guy was shrugging. In the end they reached an agreement and he came back over to talk to me.

'All right, it's a deal, but I told them it was forty-five, fifteen each.' He looked at me apologetically. 'Look, I didn't have any choice . . . You give me the money afterwards, I'll keep ten, and that's that.'

'You're an idiot.' I was really indignant. It was a crying shame, he was so beautiful.

He stood there without saying a word. But I had to sort out a few more things.

'Where are we going to do it?'

'Your place . . .' He looked at me, surprised. 'Or not?'

I had to think about it a while. Ines was spending the weekend at Pablo's so that was no problem, but I wasn't too sure if I wanted them in my flat. Going to a decent hotel would cost me much more – I'd be the one who had to pay for it, of course – and what with the forty thousand this little jaunt was going to cost, that was more than enough. I couldn't let them choose, God knows what kind of dive they might take me to. So in the end, I thought the best thing would be to take them back to my place.

'OK,' I said. 'You don't have a car, do you?'

'No, but Jimmy's got a motorbike. He can go and get it. I'll go with you, if that's all right, and please don't start insulting me again.'

I wrote down my address on a paper napkin which he took to his friend. He gave him a long farewell kiss on the mouth. I found them disgusting, I found Jimmy disgusting all of a sudden. I was on the point of regretting the whole thing and running out, when the blond guy came back and took my arm.

We went out into the street. We walked to my car, in silence at first, then I found a banal subject of conversation, the charm of old Madrid or something similar, and he livened up.

We walked along chatting, and he told me his life story, as they always do.

'I'm a really strange guy, you know,' he confessed. 'For instance, I don't love my old woman.'

'I don't love mine either,' I answered, 'so there you are, that's something we've got in common.'

He told me he was twenty-four, but I didn't believe him – he didn't even look twenty. He was very much in love with Jimmy, who was his first man. He told me their story, and it just confirmed my impression that his boyfriend was nothing but a revolting pimp.

'Sometimes I'd give anything to like women, I mean it, anything.'

He was just a kid, a delightful, clumsy kid. He reminded me a lot of Ely.

He had a really gutsy approach to life.

I stopped at a bank with a cash machine and took out thirty thousand pesetas. I wanted to keep ten for the shopping the following day, and I hardly had any money left at home.

* * *

I remember fragments, images, startlingly vivid details of that night.

He was their favourite, I was sure, in spite of the constant humiliations.

They didn't let him join in at first. He had to watch it all, sitting by my side. Jimmy spent a long time arousing Mario. He whispered to him tenderly, words of love and desire. He put his arms round him gently, then he gripped him more firmly, and finally he turned him round abruptly, forcing him to lurch forward a couple of steps until they were both standing in front of us. Then, with one hand he squeezed his friend's penis, and Mario parted his legs. He slid his other hand along his rump, and then set both hands in motion, rubbing the flesh through the fabric, the tips of his fingers touching between his thighs and then returning to their initial position. His palms were moving over the trousers as if he wanted to polish them, more and more quickly. The penis was growing, becoming harder, it was clearly outlined beneath the fabric, now stretched tight and about to burst, to give under the pressure of the stiffened flesh. His thighs were trembling, his tongue pointed out between his lips, his face was distorted into a bestial expression – the face of someone mentally retarded who pants and groans, unable to speak, to keep his eyes open, his head upright.

They're like animals, I thought. Just like animals, beautiful little beasts wallowing in the slime of a pleasure that was immediate, absolute, self-contained.

It took him only a couple of seconds to get rid of any hindrances, then he firmly grasped his lover's penis in one hand, plunged the index of his other hand into the cleft in his rump, slid it slowly downwards and then sank it inside him, starting simultaneously to masturbate him, and looking me straight in the eyes.

Mario jerked forward. My eyes closed for an instant and then I looked at Pablito, who was watching them with reddened eyes, biting his bottom lip, which was already turning purple. He was definitely their favourite, but he didn't know it – he was too young to understand. I would have liked to talk to him and tell him: *Older men sometimes have strange ways of loving. I know how you feel*; *I've been through this too*, but my compassion did nothing to diminish my desire even for a moment, so I just held his hand, and he squeezed mine without looking at me. Jimmy saw what was going on. He called out to Pablito and gave me a defiant look which I returned. I agreed, I wouldn't interfere in his complicated love life again: he'd give the orders; I'd just watch. Then he began the foreseeable ritual of humiliating Pablo, their little puppet, a pitiful object. I remember fragments, images, startlingly vivid details of that night. The other two were looking into each other's eyes, languidly caressing each other, while he satisfied them both, his fine, cruel lips distorted into a grotesque grimace, until a foot kicked him, pushing him violently well away from them. He fell at my feet, moaning, and waited until he was required again, and returned to pleasure them in return for blows and insults. Jimmy threatened him as he opened up the arse of his lover, Mario, who was crouching on all fours on the sofa. Pablito moved his head closer, stuck out his tongue and sank it obediently into the detested flesh. He licked his rival, who was whimpering like a fretful baby. Jimmy didn't let go of Mario – he was still gripping his rump – but this didn't prevent him changing position. He contorted himself so his mouth reached the erect, purple, stiff penis. He sighed to announce his arrival and then sucked it, slowly, for a long time, noisily, so Pablito would hear even if he couldn't see, and know just why the one between them was fainting with pleasure. He was almost fainting, and then finally there came the supreme humiliation, when I could no longer restrain myself. I'd decided not to touch myself until they left, it seemed contemptible to writhe there in front of them, so isolated, and so separate from them, it would seem both comical and sad, but I just couldn't stand it any more. I rubbed my nipples with the tips of my fingers and stroked my thighs. I was still dressed. I felt that my whole body was tense. Jimmy asked me if I was going to get undressed. His question sounded like an invitation – so I did. I got completely undressed, and I heard him say, 'Look, that's a woman for you, and she's not bad either.' Pablito was watching me, uneasily. Mario was laughing out loud – 'Don't you find her attractive?' – Pablito didn't answer. I felt infinitely dirty, because Jimmy was a revolting pimp, the worst kind of scum, but at that moment I would have licked the soles of his shoes clean if he'd told me to. I simply would have done it.

I went up to him, then lay on the table, a low table, on my back, following his instructions. He went on talking: 'You've never fucked a woman, have you?' Pablito protested, said he had, of course he had, but he was lying, even I realized that. 'Well, it's about time you tried, you're a big boy now.' Mario was choking with laughter. 'Don't worry, I'll give you a hand.' I leaned on my elbows and watched them. Pablito was crying, begging, pleading: he didn't want to do it. Jimmy was holding him, a sinister smile on his face. I was wondering how he thought he was going to force him to fuck me with that flaccid penis dangling between his thighs. 'Kneel on the table.' He came towards me and obeyed, his shoulders hunched, arms hanging down by his sides, head bowed. He was looking at me and crying. I no longer felt any compassion for him, not any more. Now he was just an animal, a beaten, mistreated dog, infinitely desirable.

'And now I'm going to ram it up your ass, my love.' He moved up behind him, stroked his chest, pinched his nipples with his nails – 'I'm going to ram it up your ass and you're going to die of pleasure' – then caught Pablito's penis in both hands and began to caress it and massage it expertly, but it still refused to grow. Jimmy's voice matched his body, a magnificent man's voice: 'It'll get hard, you know it will, you won't be able to help it. When I put mine inside you yours'll get hard, for sure, and then all you'll have to do is put it in the girl's cunt, that little hole there. Come on, you might even enjoy it.' Mario started to laugh again. Pablo closed his eyes. He wasn't crying any more but he was in torment, which didn't stop his penis growing. Jimmy leaned over him and whispered in his ear. I didn't hear what he said, but I saw the results, a spectacular erection, then he pushed him forward. He forced him to crouch on all fours over me and he penetrated him, tearing from him an inhuman scream. He was still holding his friend's penis, masturbating him at the same time as he bored into him, until he decided that that was enough. 'You, lift up your bottom.' I placed my clenched fists under my lower back and lifted myself up as high as I could. My legs were trembling, my sex was trembling. He guided his boyfriend himself, and it was his hand that held Pablito's cock as it entered me, and then, almost immediately, I felt something pressing against my head. I looked up and realized that it was Mario's thighs. He'd moved up to the other side of the table and was now holding his penis in his hand, stroking it under Pablito's nose. Pablito looked at it for a second and then, with a kind of sigh of resignation, he put it in his mouth. We stayed like that for quite a while, him filled up, squeezed, every last corner of him used, giving all three of us pleasure, transmitting to me by force, against his will, the thrusts he received from his lover. The knowledge that he wasn't taking any pleasure from me didn't diminish in the slightest the intense pleasure I was taking from him. On the contrary, I felt satisfied. All my expectations had been fulfilled: they were like animals, delicious, brutal, sincere, violent, slaves to their greedy flesh, as wilful as small children, incapable of restraining the least desire, and now I too couldn't restrain myself. I was dying of pleasure under Pablito, at the same time watching him pay his final forfeit, with Mario's cock moving in and out of his mouth. Then came the definitive tremor and I set off a chain reaction. I couldn't bear it any longer, so I abandoned myself to a furious orgasm. A chorus of groans joined mine, and everything around me began to shake, everything was moving. A drop of semen slid down my cheek at the very moment that Pablito's late, enforced initiation reached a satisfactory conclusion and he emptied himself at last inside my body.

I'll think about all this tomorrow.

I was nibbling at a cake, I didn't have any with pine kernels left, when I heard the doorbell ring.

I'll think about all this tomorrow, about the terrible hangover that came over me, the deep feeling of shame which chilled me at the end, when they'd left me alone, naked, on top of the table, and my only thought was that I had to pay them. I felt so bad, so desolate. They were talking amongst themselves. They meant nothing to me: I didn't know them, they didn't know me, but I had to pay them so I did, then said goodbye, clumsily. I left Pablito counting the notes and shut myself in the bathroom, thinking I'd been lucky – they could have stripped the place, or anything. Trust me to think of letting them in the house. I turned on the shower and waited until I heard the door slam. I came out to make sure I was alone and then went back and stood under the steaming hot stream of water, to wash off the drops of semen that might still be on my skin. *I'll think about all this tomorrow*, I repeated to myself, *tomorrow*, as I went to open the door.

Pablito was crying, his face hidden in his arm, leaning against the doorframe.

After a few minutes of silence, broken only by the uncontrollable sobs which seemed about to burst his chest, I searched for something to say. All I could think of was a totally inane question, but I blurted it out anyway.

'Did you leave something behind?'

He moved his arm away from his face, looked at me and shook his head. Just as he seemed to be calming down, he burst out crying again, and the volume of his sobbing increased, until it was truly deafening. So I made him come in. If he carried on crying like that, he'd wake all the neighbours.

I put an arm round his shoulders. I was moved – I'd never seen anyone cry like that, I'd never witnessed such utter dejection. He's unhappy, really unhappy, I thought, so I put my arm round him but he closed both his arms round my neck and clung to me, still crying. As he was a lot heavier than me, particularly in that state of desperation, I realized that we were going to fall, we were falling, but I didn't feel I could tell him to let go of me, so I quickly swivelled and we fell on the sofa at least.

I stroked his hair, still held back in a tiny pony-tail, for nearly twenty minutes, until he was in a fit state to talk.

'Can I sleep here?' His question surprised me almost more than his weeping fit. 'I don't have anywhere to go . . .'

'Of course you can, but I don't understand.' I looked at him a while. I searched for scars or needle marks, something which I might have missed earlier, but I didn't discover anything new – nothing which might explain his situation. He didn't look like a vagrant. 'Don't you have a home?'

'Yes, I live with Jimmy, but we've had a row . . . he told me he's not going to put up with my fits of jealousy any more, that I'm hysterical . . . he's going to sleep at Mario's . . . tonight . . . after what he forced me to do . . . now he doesn't even let me sleep with him . . .' His speech was barely comprehensible, more a confused succession of disconnected words, choked and distorted by sobs. 'I can't go there, I'd die . . . if I went home I'd die, I couldn't bear it, and anyway, he's taken all my money, what you gave me, oh yeah, by the way . . .' He looked up at me and made an effort to speak more clearly. 'Thanks a lot, for the five thousand extra. He took them too, and another three thousand I had on me – I haven't got a penny, please, let me stay here . . .'

'That's a real gem of a boyfriend you've got there.' I

knew that my words would depress him even more but I felt obliged to say it. 'Of course you can stay.'

He nodded in thanks, and carried on crying, until he had no tears left.

Once I thought him calm enough to speak coherently again, I asked him where he'd rather sleep.

'You can sleep with me in a double bed or in my daughter's room – she's not here at the moment – whichever you'd prefer . . .'

'You've got a child?' He seemed very surprised at this news.

'Yes, I've got a daughter of four and a half, Ines.' He looked even more amazed. 'Are you surprised?'

'Yes, I'd never have thought you were a mother, you really don't look the type . . .'

'Thanks a lot, I love people telling me that.'

'Why?' Now he was smiling. 'I don't understand. You're the same age whether you've got kids or not.'

'I'm sure you can't understand it, you're a million miles away from all of that.' This was my last comment on the subject. 'Right, where do you want to sleep?'

'Mm, don't know . . . I suppose it'd be better if I slept with you. I don't know, I think I'd feel funny about sleeping in a four-year-old child's bed . . .' He finished his sentence with a laugh.

'Fine, let's go to bed then. I'm exhausted and you must be tired too, today's been a special day,' I tried to give a hint of irony to my smile, 'first times are always exhausting . . .'

He laughed again. His laughter did me good, I found it comforting. I felt very close to him. We're definitely both lambs from the same flock, I thought, white and fluffy, with a little bow round our necks, mine pink and unbearably comfortable, his pink too, I suppose, but much more painful.

When I came back after brushing my teeth I found him curled up on my side of the bed.

'Do you mind moving over to the right?' I took off my bathrobe and slippers. 'This is my side . . .'

'Aren't you going to put anything on, to sleep?'

'No, I've always slept in the nude.' This wasn't true – until I was twenty, I wore nightdresses which came down below the knee, but Pablo didn't like nightdresses. He didn't like any clothes other than those which were absolutely necessary, and you didn't need any to sleep in, that was one of the first things I learnt. 'Why? Do I disgust you?'

'No, it's not that . . .' I got the impression he was even slightly scared. 'It's just that I've never slept with a woman before . . .'

'Don't worry,' I wanted to reassure him, but I couldn't help laughing, 'I'm not going to attack you from the back, promise.'

I got into bed. He was watching me, smiling. He kissed me gently on the lips but still curled up as far away from me as he could.

When I woke up, he was attacking me from the back.

I could feel his arms round my waist, squeezing me, and his erect penis, bumping me between the buttocks. His whole body was moving rhythmically against mine, and he was sound asleep.

I took his hand and put it on top of one of my breasts. He let it drop as soon as I let go, although touching one of the unequivocally feminine parts of my body didn't seem to have put him off. That's a good one, I thought. Maybe he thinks I'm a transvestite. I tried it again, with the same results, and let out a giggle. I was delighted with my little experiment. Until then it had been as inexorable as a law of physics: the first thing a bloke does when he wakes up close to a woman is put out a hand and hang onto her breasts. It had never failed, until then. This one was refusing to do it and it was funny.

Just as I was about to put one of his hands between my thighs to see if he lost his hard-on, the doorbell rang.

I suddenly realized that I'd already heard it earlier, that was what had woken me up. This was the second time it was being rung. I looked at the clock, nearly noon, and quickly threw on my bathrobe. I thought it might be Marcelo, he hadn't sounded too convinced by my excuses on the phone, but all that ringing, that deafening avalanche of piercing, short, repeated rings, could only be Ines.

It was Ines.

Pablo was carrying her, wrapped in a wet raincoat. He himself was completely soaked, water was streaming down his face.

'Hello.' From the tone of his voice we might have last seen each other a couple of hours before at most. 'Did we wake you up?' I nodded. 'Sorry, but it's suddenly got freezing. It started to rain, and there were only summer clothes in Ines's bag. We've come to get a raincoat, and a couple of jumpers . . .'

I was expecting a kiss, but didn't get one.

'Hello, darling.' Ines, on the other hand, flung herself at me to give me a kiss, and Pablo took off her raincoat before transferring her from his arms to mine. Then he came into my flat as if he owned the place.

'This is Cristina.' He looked at me a moment with a stony expression. 'Cristina, this is my wife . . .'

Then I realized that there were three of them. The redhead, not as colourless as Chelo had described, was half hidden behind the door. She took a couple of steps forward and then threatened to advance further, but I held out my hand before she had time to get her lips any nearer to my cheek. She shook it, confused. Pablo came to her rescue.

'Marisa can't bear kisses which are only given out of politeness . . .'

'Please don't call me Marisa.' Lately he'd been pursuing with assiduous cruelty a policy of petty revenge, which was extremely effective. Something inside me broke every time he called me that.

'Why not? It's an affectionate diminutive.' He turned to

his girlfriend. 'She doesn't let just anyone kiss her, you know, she's very choosy. She's not very well brought up. Of course, that's my fault rather than hers . . .'

Ines started to laugh her head off. She had an unfortunate habit of suddenly bursting out laughing for no reason. This time, however, her explosion came just at the right moment.

Signs of the night's fray were preserved intact in the sitting room. A spurt of semen had dried in a strange S shape on the glass table. He made no comment, however.

'I'm going to make myself a coffee.' I put Ines down on the floor. Pablo sat on the sofa. The redhead flopped down at his side and tried to take his arm, but he stopped her. 'Do you want anything?'

They both wanted coffee.

She was pretty, very pretty, and obviously very young, twenty or twenty-one – she could have been his daughter. I would never have passed for his daughter even if I'd tried, which I never had, but she was slim and supple, elastic, agile. Her legs were unattractive though, too thin, and that cheered me up, but her greenish eyes were huge, and her red hair was thick and shiny. She was very pretty and had pert tits. You could see the shape of her nipples through her jumper – she still had the breasts of a teenager.

Ines dragged Pablo off to her room to show him the folder where we kept her drawings from school. Cristina followed me to the kitchen and stood in the doorway, watching me.

'You know, I really admire you.' She looked calm and sure of herself.

'No, look, please . . .' I wasn't going to stand for it, not that. 'I'm a hysteric, as you know, and if there's one thing that makes me bloody furious it's these heart-to-hearts between women, so I'd be grateful if you'd spare me.'

'I wasn't talking about any of that stuff,' her voice was still steady, 'I've read your book.'

'That seems unlikely,' I answered. 'I haven't written a book.'

'Of course you have,' she insisted, looking surprised. 'Pablo lent it to me, the book of epigraphs. I really liked it.'

'Epigrams.'

'What?' She gave the impression that nothing much really bothered her.

'Epigrams, not epigraphs.'

'Oh, right.' She giggled. 'Same thing.'

'No it isn't,' I shouted, 'of course it's not the same thing.'

She was silent and looked down. She was a perfect target, now.

'It's not my book.' The coffee was spilling everywhere, the coffee-pot was ruined. 'I only translated it, and wrote the notes and an introduction, that's all. It was written by Martial,' she looked at me, surprised, 'Marcus Valerius Martial, a guy from Catalayud, and you didn't really like it or really hate it because you haven't read it, and I really don't feel like continuing this conversation. You don't admire me, you're just curious about me, but the feeling isn't mutual. To be honest, you look like a rather common young lady, so we have nothing more to say to each other. Get out and fucking well leave me alone.'

I had the upper hand now.

All she had was her pert tits.

I was thirty and married to him.

She looked at me a moment, red as a tomato, then she turned round and disappeared.

Martial. My golden years, a wonderful piece of work, financially disastrous, but over a year of small personal triumphs, I was so proud of myself when the book finally came out, Pablo was so proud of me . . .

I closed the coffee-pot and put it on the hob. She's pretty, very pretty, I thought. And very young. She's still got the fragile air of an adolescent about her.

I thought for a moment, trying to remember who'd given me the same impression, just recently.

The coffee-pot was whistling. I turned off the heat and ran out. When I got to my room, it was already too late.

Pablito was still asleep, naked, with a spectacular hard-on under the sheets. His penis looked like the central post of a circus tent.

Ines was sitting on the edge of the bed and pointing at it.

'What's that, Daddy?'

Pablo, kneeling by her side, was smiling.

'Oh that . . . he's missing Mummy.'

'Is she an orphan, poor thing?' She sounded truly sorry.

'No, Ines,' Pablo laughed. 'He's not a little orphan, he's missing Mummy, your Mummy, Lulu, do you understand?'

'You don't have a thing like that when I sleep with you, and you say you miss Mummy too . . .' She turned to him, she seemed intrigued.

'Well I'm much older than him.'

'But it's a girl, silly!' She turned round, overjoyed. She loved catching us out, either one of us. 'She's got a pony-tail, like me . . .' She touched her hair. I liked watching her, she looked a lot like me. Pablo would say to me, 'I want to have a daughter like you.' I'd touch my belly and laugh, but he got his way in the end, and we had a daughter just like me.

'No, Ines.' He spoke very quietly, his voice was steady, calming, the one he used to explain important things. That voice fascinated her, me too. 'That has nothing to do with it. I could have a pony-tail too, if I stopped cutting my hair. He's a boy. Look at him closely, he's got a little bobble in his throat . . .'

'Elisa's got a bobble too and she's a girl.' Ines had always called Ely 'Elisa'. She was very fond of him. She found him very funny with his mannerisms, his accent, the way he walked, and above all, his Adam's apple.

'But Elisa's got tits and he hasn't, look.' Pablo pointed to Pablito's smooth chest and Ines stared at it, nodding her head in agreement – this last point had convinced her.

I'd often wondered if this was the right way to bring up a child. I'd asked Pablo too, one night when Ely was at our house. He'd come to watch *How To Marry A Millionaire* on TV. 'I'd just love to be Marilyn!' he'd announced as soon as he came in the door, then a friend phoned, a Frenchman from Pablo's Philadelphia days. He was passing through Madrid and wanted to see us. We couldn't find a babysitter, so in the end we accepted Ely's offer and he stayed to look after her. Ines was just two, so I asked Pablo if this was the right way to bring up a child, and he answered that he thought it was better than bringing her up like I'd been brought up and ending up with a bloke like him. 'But we're depriving her of the pleasure of being depraved later on,' I objected, but he insisted, 'I still think it's better.' He was smiling.

'What's his name?' Ines blindly believed that her father knew everything; she had much less faith in me.

'Pablo.' They both turned round to look at me. 'His name's Pablo, like Daddy, and he's very tired, so we're going to let him carry on sleeping. Anyway,' I said to Ines, 'Cristina was looking for you just now. She told me she wants to play hide and seek with you . . .'

'But she never feels like it . . .' she stammered. I'm not surprised, I thought. It was utter torture playing hide and seek with Ines: she never got tired of it and cheated all the time.

'Well today she's dying to play.' Pablo burst out laughing. 'I'd make the most of it if I were you . . .'

She got up and ran out. He stood up too and we left the room.

'Well, well!' His voice was cruel again. 'Where did you pick up that piece of meat?'

All my hopes vanished instantly.

'I could ask you the same question . . .' I mumbled.

'Cristina?' He looked at me, surprised. 'Good God, it's much less obvious in her case and you know it.'

'But she's very young. That's what you like, isn't it?' His expression grew even more stony. Then he seemed to calm down. He was getting ready to hurt me.

'She's seventeen, but she's growing up fast.'

'We all grow up.' I gave him a look of triumph but didn't dare sustain it. His eyes were flashing, the wings of his large nose were trembling, his lips were drawn. I knew all the signs well, he was going to explode with rage any minute.

'Well you haven't!' His words wounded my ears, his fingers dug into my arms, his eyes pierced into mine. I looked down, hunched and motionless, floppy as a rag doll. I knew he was going to shake me violently and I let him. 'You haven't, Lulu, you've never grown up, you won't ever, damn you, you've never stopped playing, and you're still playing now. You're playing at being an adult, only you're following some strange rules you've invented for yourself, I don't understand why. You've stopped being a brilliant little girl and turned into a very ordinary woman. I still don't understand why, you got scared and went off to join the mediocrities, but you've failed because you haven't understood – you haven't grown up, Lulu, not you. *We* weren't mediocre, we still aren't, even though you've gone and ruined everything . . .' He let go of me. I didn't dare move. He took me by the chin and lifted my head, but I didn't want to look at him. 'I'll never forgive you, never.'

He turned and walked away from me, but came back, suddenly. I'd leaned against the wall. I looked at him. He seemed devastated.

'You haven't thought about me much, have you?'

Then I realized that he was drunk, completely drunk, at half-past twelve in the morning. He was keeping it under control but he couldn't fool me, and I felt bad, I'd thought that with the redhead and the passing of time, he would have stopped by now. In fact I preferred not to think about it. When I left him, Marcelo wouldn't speak to me for a time – my own brother. They all pointed the finger at me, but Pablo didn't, he never did, but he drank a lot. At that time he used to be drunk all day.

'I haven't got much time left, you know. I'm getting old. I feel more and more ridiculous, hanging around with all these little tarts. I've got nothing to say to them and I don't feel like teaching them anything now, any of them . . . Sometimes I think I'm starting to go gaga. I can pick them up easily enough, that's not much of a problem. It's one of the few things being a poet who doesn't sell books is any use for these days; being a poet who doesn't sell books, picking up chicks and getting free drinks – you know the kind of thing – but I'm tired now, I'm so bloody tired . . .'

I waited for the slightest sign, the slightest hint, to throw myself at his feet, but he didn't say anything more. He turned his back on me and headed towards the sitting room. I'm losing the knack, I thought. At that moment Pablito came out of the bedroom and looked at me with his usual apologetic expression. He'd heard the whole thing.

'Do you want a coffee?' He nodded.

Breakfast was brief. Pablo didn't say another word. Cristina tried discreetly but unsuccessfully to flirt with my guest, who fobbed her off with the utmost ease. Ines was being very tiresome. She wanted us all to play hide and seek, insisting that as there were lots of us it would be more fun.

Pablo didn't even say goodbye to me as they left.

'Was that your husband?' Pablito had sprawled in an armchair. He showed no sign of wanting to leave. I said yes. 'Well, he's really gorgeous, with his grey hair, really attractive, older men have got something special . . .'

At first I didn't know whether to laugh or to throw him out, but I didn't want to be on my own.

Maybe I can't go back now, maybe I'll never be able to go back, I thought.

'Don't you believe it.' I tried to brush the thought aside instantly. 'Your boyfriend's got a much bigger one.'

'Well, that's only psychological.'

'Yeah,' I answered, 'and the Magi[1], they're your parents.'

He looked at me, surprised. He didn't know what I was on about.

'You asked the Magi to bring you toys when you were little, didn't you?' He nodded and I smiled at him. 'And you still asked your parents for toys when you found out that stuff about the Magi was a load of crap, didn't you?' He nodded again. 'And when did you enjoy the toys more, before or after you found out?'

'Before, but that's got nothing to do with the size of your husband's cock . . .'

I burst out laughing, I was having fun.

'Not with his in particular, but it has got something to do with the size of blokes' cocks in general, because both things, big cocks and the Magi, they're the same. They're just a myth. Do you see what I mean?' No, he didn't, I could tell from his expression. 'Look, all that business about the camels, putting your shoes on the balcony, the cavalcade – none of that altered the quantity or quality of the toys, but it added something, you found them more exciting, didn't you? Well, it's the same thing. The size of Pablo's cock doesn't alter the quality or the quantity of his fucking, but Jimmy's got a bigger one, do you get it now? We live in a world full of myths, the whole world is based on them, and you give me that stuff about how it's only psychological . . . Why start with the myth about big cocks? Why demolish that one before any of the others? Myths are necessary, they help people live . . .'

'Well, I tell you something.' I guessed that I hadn't convinced him. 'I'd love to go to bed with your husband, even if his cock is smaller than my boyfriend's.'

'I'd love to go to bed with him too,' I was being serious now, I didn't feel like joking any more, 'but things have been getting more and more difficult lately . . .'

[1]In Spain the Magi are equivalent to Father Christmas in English-speaking countries.

The second time, I turned to Sergio, a recent boyfriend of Chelo's who was a waiter in a fashionable bar.

I wanted to keep away from the crowd, to stay in Malasaña. I felt comfortable there, sure of myself. That was where I'd cut my teeth, sitting for hours on those uncomfortable benches with thin foam cushions, drinking vodka and lime – revolting but terribly feminine in those days – when I'd had my first laughs, my first drunken sprees, my first hangovers. I lived there with Pablo the whole time in a huge loft with exposed beams. He was still there, one of the last survivors. I was almost a part of the landscape. I could go about my business round there completely unnoticed, and I still knew a lot of people, nearly all the old crowd. There were still lots of us left, though many had dropped by the wayside, and we all said the same, 'hasn't this area changed? It's not like it used to be,' but maybe it was only us who'd changed, all of us, ten, twelve, fifteen years on, with the signs of age, bald patches, paunches, grey hair, bras under our blouses, wrinkles that grew a bit deeper every night, our flesh getting flabbier every night, but we were almost the same. We still had a lot of fun, and the square hadn't really changed much – the streets and the bars were still more or less the same.

I wanted to keep away from the crowd because it terrified me to think that Pablo might find out I was roaming around there on my own at night, dishing out money to go to bed with a couple of queers, or three, or four. I was terrified at the thought of him finding out. He had lots of contacts on the street, weird friends, criminals, people he'd met inside prison and out, people who adored him and knew me, people who would have gone blabbing to him at the first opportunity.

I wanted to stay in Malasaña. That was where I'd met Jimmy and Pablito. I'd met a few others there – avid, well-fed bisexuals, not all of them beautiful, but prepared to share their boyfriends with me as an amusement. But the supply soon ran out, very soon, and I hadn't had enough, so I broke the golden rule: try everything once but only once. I hadn't had enough though, so then the worst happened. I gave up acting through intermediaries and I took to finding them myself, with disastrous results. Some of them laughed in my face. They just hung around with me for the drinks – they weren't interested in my body, or my money; my curiosity didn't arouse theirs. Others despised me and openly scorned me. I became notorious, that was the worst part. I got a reputation and some of my friends stopped saying hello. Rumours went around: *Marisa's gone a bit screwy*. In the end an old classmate from university who'd had a bar in the area for years told me straight: 'Look, if you're really after blokes like that, pay out money for them. I'm sure there are plenty around – it takes all sorts – but just don't do it here for fuck's sake. All you're doing here is frightening away my customers . . .'

'Not effeminate, that's the first point; tall, five foot eleven minimum; big, with conventionally handsome faces. You know, the kind of guy schoolgirls go for: slim but muscly, not too much though, no bodybuilders, between twenty-five and thirty-five. One of them can be younger but only one of them, and none of them older. Skin preferably tanned, and dark-haired if possible, with long legs, and not very hairy please, the less hairy the better. I'd rather they weren't in love with each other. Ideally they'd know each other and find each other attractive, though I know you can't have everything. I don't care about race as long as it doesn't put up the price, and no orientals – I don't like them. Ah yes, and if possible, I'd like at least one of them to be bisexual, or if not, then at least capable of doing it with a woman, well, with me, I mean, even if he's not too keen on it. I don't mind. I can't really expect him to enjoy it, and then, well, the better . . . equipped they are . . . well, you know what I mean. See what you can do, cash isn't a problem . . .'

I blurted the whole thing out, stumbling over my words, without stopping to listen to what I was saying, as if it were a lesson I'd learnt for an oral exam.

I wanted to get it over with.

I felt so ashamed to have fallen so low.

He nodded at each of my specifications, as if he understood exactly what I was after, but I insisted once more anyway.

'I want sodomites, not pansies. Is that clear?'

'Yes,' he answered.

He was a sinister bloke. Pablo had warned me about him, but he was also one of the kings of the street. He controlled a lot of people – lots of desperate, naive, beautiful, pathetic little lambs.

I tried to keep away from the crowd. I wanted to stay on the fringe. I tried but I didn't succeed.

When I saw I had no other choice, I took certain precautions. I stopped using friends of mine and rejected the idea of using Ely right from the start, because I knew he would never have let me do it. After all, I was everything he aspired to be. I had everything he wanted to have, and it had cost him so much: so much shame, so much surgery, so many tears . . . He believed humanity was divided into two entirely separate groups, and I was on the winning side. He would never have accepted that I could sink to this.

I made sure I was discreet, arranging meetings in places off the beaten track, avoiding all foreseeable risks, but it took me quite a while to meet the right people in the right places. It was months before I could arrange everything by telephone.

I was panic-stricken at the thought of him finding out, and I took precautions, but they turned out to be useless every time. I've always been cursed with clumsiness.

I came face to face with Ely once at the beginning.

I bumped into Gus, a dealer friend of Pablo's, all over the place, as I too was walking the streets but for the opposite reason, buying instead of selling, looking for something to take to bed with me. I began to think that it couldn't be a coincidence that we were running into each other so often, but I rejected the idea in the end. After all, I had every reason to suppose that some of my best contacts might also count amongst his best clients.

Then, one fine day, Pablito told me about this pimp, Remi.

Compared to him Jimmy seemed like the Mother Superior of a convent, wimple and all, but this didn't prevent us forming a long and mutually beneficial business relationship. The first time, he found me a couple of really gorgeous blokes. They were very good-looking and very pricey. I had a really good time with them. Afterwards, one of them, the older of the two, though not much older than me, asked me politely about my eccentric taste. 'What exactly do you get out of all of this?' were his precise words.

I'd often wondered about this myself and would do so again many times, during the dark, feverish nights which followed the first night. What exactly did I get out of it; what did they give me, beyond the satisfaction of the flesh?

Self-assurance.

The right to say how, when, where, how much and with whom.

To be on the other side of the road, on the pavement with the strong.

The illusion of maturity.

There were other ways, I sensed there were other routes

– less extreme, less intense, less exhausting paths leading to the same place but none was so easy because I didn't really know how far I wanted to go. I'd bumped into them and I'd just let myself go, I thought, that was all. I could turn back at any moment, with no problems or regrets. It was just an innocent pastime, and it made me feel good, so grown up, so superior, so complete, when I played with them . . .

I was scared, though. I was getting more and more frightened, and not just because of the money, which did eventually become a serious problem when the money in Ines's account ran out – money which Pablo put in every month. I'd never asked him for anything. I was happy to share the cost of looking after the kid, but he put more in anyway, much more. I tried not to spend it at first, but my good intentions didn't last long and it was so handy . . . In the end, I got through it very quickly. I spent the whole lot right down to the last penny, so then cash became a problem though it was never my most serious worry.

I was scared, scared of not reacting or knowing how to stop in time. Sometimes I felt I couldn't recognize the line between fantasy and reality. I felt threatened by the shadows of a dirty, alien world, which I never thought I could be part of but which was now closing its cruel, obsessive circle around me.

I knew I should have turned back but I couldn't give them up, I simply couldn't – because nothing could compare to them, to the desire they inspired in me, to the flesh they offered me. Nothing could compare to the pleasure they gave me – they were all I had now that I'd gone back to a difficult, monotonous existence, made up of grey days, all the same. They were an innocent pastime; they were my only possession and my only distraction.

The boundary, a line emerging ever more clearly, was close, very close, and it scared me.

I used to think about Pablo a lot then, because with him everything had always been so easy.

* * *

Their eyes were shining and they laughed at the slightest thing. They both looked so handsome and so young that they looked just as they had twenty years before, that morning in spring when the nuns had taken us to El Retiro to see the Lion House, an excursion – four stops by bus and they called it an excursion, but on a school day it seemed like a real holiday. The cages stank and the wild animals weren't very wild. They were just miserable, emaciated beasts with dull, lustreless coats covered in sores, and flies hovering around their tired heads. The elephant was like one of the family. I'd been to see him so many times and given his keeper a few pesetas so he could feed him a few more bits of stale bread, or a few more peanuts. I was very upset when he finally died of old age, poor thing, just as that joke of a zoo collapsed, after years of falling to bits. I liked it anyway, even though it stank and was very small, so small that we finished too early. We saw the whole thing in three-quarters of an hour, so then they let us loose. They were sitting on a bench in the sun near the pond, the two of them. How I envied them. They should have been at lectures that morning, but at university it didn't really count as bunking off. How I longed to be like them, so I separated from the group. I told Chelo what I was doing: 'I'm going off with my brother.' Pablo was holding a book. He stood up on the bench. Marcelo blew me a kiss, and motioned to me to stop, not to come any closer. I sat on the ground and watched them. Pablo cleared his throat and announced in a clear, loud voice – *Les Fleurs du Mal* – and started to declaim, to bellow in French, waving his arms, hunching and then drawing himself up. From time to time he hid his face against his shoulder, in the grip of a strong emotion, and he addressed me with great pathos, me, his only spectator. Finally a small group gathered round, about eight or ten people. Some of them looked disconcerted, others were laughing. I wanted to look cool so I laughed too, even though I didn't understand a single word. Marcelo was facing Pablo and watching him with admiration, hanging on his every word. His face showed grief, joy, panic, sadness, insecurity, fear, desperation, in quick succession . . . At first I thought they'd gone mad, then when they started to squirm, unable to hold back their laughter any longer, I didn't know what to think. Their laughter grew even louder, and in the end Pablo stopped speaking abruptly and bowed to the audience. Marcelo then got up on the bench, pointed to him and shouted, 'Comrades, this is Socialism!' Applause broke out, long applause, possibly sincere, I don't know. I could hear the voice of my form-mistress in the distance, becoming more and more agitated. 'Maria Luisa Ruiz-Poveda y Garcia de la Casa, will you please come here!' I didn't take any notice. I disobeyed – I just shouted at her, 'I'm going home with my big brother,' and they took me by the hand. There was a policeman lurking so we slipped away discreetly. We went out through the gate without any mishap, and they bought me a drink at a café terrace, Coca Cola and grilled prawns, quite a luxury. It was then I decided to cut off the more aristocratic-sounding part of my surname. Since then I've been Ruiz Garcia, just plain Ruiz Garcia. Marcelo had been signing his name like that for years, just to piss the family off, and he definitely succeeded. My father would fly off the handle every time he answered the phone or took a letter out of our letterbox. He was very proud of the pleasing, aristocratic ring of his offspring's surnames, of the casual coincidence which had given a gloss of nobility to two otherwise perfectly plebeian lineages. He placed great emphasis on the 'y' linking them and did everything to encourage the mistaken belief that we had aristocratic origins, including bestowing several carefully selected Christian names upon each of his children at the baptismal font, in case it might fool anybody. I had four and they were some of the most successful, Maria Luisa Aurora Eugenia Ruiz-Poveda y Garcia de la Casa, but I've been just Lulu Ruiz Garcia since that day when I bumped into them in El Retiro. In Paris they were hurling stones at the police, while *they* contented themselves with declaiming Baudelaire in a public park, but they were young and handsome, their eyes were shining and they laughed at the slightest thing.

'What's up?' Marcelo's voice sounded very far away, but when I turned my head I almost bumped into him. 'Aren't you feeling better yet?'

'Yes, yes, of course I'm better. I haven't got a temperature any more . . .' I assured him. I'd been recovering from flu; that was why I hadn't gone out to dinner with them. 'I was just remembering something from ages ago, that morning in El Retiro, *Les Fleurs du Mal*, remember? I don't know why, but today you really remind me of how you were that day. I'm sure you're up to something and that makes you look younger, I don't know why . . .' This really made them laugh. They gave each other meaningful looks but didn't say a word. 'Are you going to tell me what's going on?'

'No.' Pablo's answer was drowned out by the sound of the doorbell, a clapped-out but deafening device which must have been about eighty years old and which we'd miraculously managed to save.

I didn't know that we were expecting guests but a load of people arrived.

Luis, an old and pretty ugly schoolfriend of theirs who now had a bad case of post-traumatic-stress syndrome after the break-up of a romantic relationship, in which he'd been the injured party, arrived with two girls. One was a small, curvy, extremely feminine blonde, the type he always went for and never tired of. The other one, large and bony, had a South American accent and seemed rather odd. She looked suspiciously like a man, even though she had a high-pitched voice. I tried to find out what her true gender was but Pablo didn't seem to want to answer any of my questions, and Marcelo decided to follow his example.

Luis looked at Pablo expectantly every so often.

I believed I'd correctly asssessed his situation. He's obviously come to lend them a hand, I thought, but he's not in on the secret. He doesn't know what he's got to do.

'Right,' he said at last, perhaps in response to a secret signal, 'who shall we start with?'

'Hah, don't tell me you're still thinking about that.' Marcelo looked at me out of the corner of his eye. He didn't fool me, he wanted to arouse my curiosity. 'Count me out.'

'Count you out of what?' I took the bait, of course. I wasn't going to deprive them of the satisfaction, after all the trouble they'd gone to, getting Luis round and everything.

'Nothing, it's really silly,' Marcelo himself answered. 'The latest fad, half Madrid seems to have gone crazy over it . . .'

'But what is it?' I was beginning to feel curious. 'I haven't been out in the evening for almost two weeks with this bloody 'flu.'

'It's a game,' Pablo smiled at me, 'a silly game, like the one about the pirate with the wooden leg . . . with the lemon half and the chicken giblets. Of course, you were very small, I don't know if you ever played it.'

'Yes, yes, of course, I played loads of times.' I still remembered the fright it gave me. 'It was really fun.'

'How's it played?' somebody asked.

'Oh! It was a kind of initiation game, it's pretty complicated,' I explained. 'You needed at least three people to organize it. One person sat waiting on a chair in a darkened room, with one hand full of blobs of plasticine, a squeezed-out lemon half on his face and a raw chicken neck, the biggest you could get, between his legs, and some other things I can't remember. Oh yes! there was also a stick which was supposed to be his wooden leg. Somebody else would choose the sucker to be initiated and explain that he was going to take him to see the pirate with the wooden leg. He'd lead him to the darkened room, take his hand and pass it over the blobs of plasticine and tell him it was the captain's leprous hand, then he'd grab one of his fingers and stick it into the lemon half, telling him it was the empty socket of the eye the pirate had lost in a battle.'

'How revolting!' exclaimed Luis's terribly feminine new girlfriend. 'And finally you had to guide the hand slowly down the supposed pirate's body so the victim knew at all times where it was going, the stomach, the belly . . . A bit lower down and suddenly his hand would be put round the chicken neck, which the other guy had put in the right place, and I swear to you that it was absolutely exactly the same as a guy's cock, a cylinder of moist flesh, all sinewy inside.' I giggled, remembering the shrieks of laughter with which these sessions usually ended. 'At that moment, a third person would turn on the light and all the mysteries were revealed. It was hilarious . . .'

'It sounds brilliant!' the South American guy/girl seemed really keen. 'Come on, let's play now! Don't tell me nobody else wants to . . .'

'Yes, let's play.' A pale, slim, truly spectacular brunette, squeezed into a purple leather skirt and jacket, who'd arrived with a group of people I only knew by sight, echoed the pleas of our ambiguous guest. The others soon spoke up too.

'But it's rubbish!' Marcelo was refusing to give in to what now sounded like popular demand.

'Right,' insisted Luis, 'who shall we start with?'

'Clarita?' Pablo was addressing Luis's girlfriend. I directed a furious glance at him. He caught it and gave me a wicked smile. He wouldn't dare, I thought, he wouldn't dare. 'All right, we'll start with Lulu.' He hadn't dared. 'I need five big scarves.'

'Six,' Marcelo corrected him.

'No.' Pablo took from his pocket a red plastic ball, slightly smaller than a billiard ball, with a black band or elastic round it, and he made it dance up and down in his hand. 'Only five.' My brother nodded his approval.

'I'll go and get you some right now . . .'

'No.' He stopped me. 'You can't be in here. You've got to go to another room. I've told you, it's just like the one about the pirate with the wooden leg.'

He took me by the arm and led me down the corridor. I grabbed five headscarves from the chest of drawers in my bedroom and then we set off again and entered what I called the guest room, a bedroom with a double bed where Ines's babysitter usually slept.

'I'm going to blindfold you.' Pablo held all the scarves up against the light and chose the thickest one, rolled it up and put it round my head, tying it tightly. 'Can you see anything?'

'No.'

'Sure?' he insisted. 'You mustn't be able to see a thing, otherwise the game's no fun.'

'I'm sure,' I answered. 'I can't see anything.'

A few seconds elapsed in total silence. I sensed he must be waving his hand or something to test whether the blindfold really was effective.

'OK, I believe you, you can't see anything. Lie down in the middle of the bed, on your back . . .'

'What for?'

'I'm going to tie you to the bars.'

'Hey,' it was all starting to make me feel uneasy, 'what kind of little game is this?'

'I'll stop if you want and we can do it to Clarita . . .'

'No way,' I lay down on the bed, 'you must be joking, tie me up.'

Still laughing, he took my right arm and tied my wrist with a scarf to one of the bars at the head of the bed. He then did the same with my left arm. He'd tied me up firmly but fairly loosely. It didn't hurt and I had some freedom of movement, though it would have been impossible to work myself free.

'Don't get all angry with me afterwards,' he'd just tied my left ankle, 'because it's pretty silly, this game. Seriously, you're going to be disappointed . . .'

When he'd finished with my right leg, he lay down by my side and kissed me. It felt very strange because I couldn't see him or touch him and I didn't know where he was. He suddenly pulled his mouth away and I was left with my tongue out, trying to catch him, gulping air. He laughed and kissed me again.

'I love you, Lulu.'

It was then I began to suspect I was going to be sacrificed. I still didn't quite know how or for whose benefit, but I was sure I was going to be sacrificed.

I didn't say anything, though. It wouldn't be the first time.

He moved away from me and I heard him head towards the door. Before going out he stopped and gave me one last warning.

'Don't get cross if we take a while to come back . . . We've got quite a few things to set up.'

He left and shut the door behind him, judging by the sound.

This was all that was missing, I thought. Everything else had come true, except for a few small differences of an essentially financial nature. There's definitely a sensual aspect to money and we hadn't had much in the beginning, until my father-in-law died and we started to reap the benefits of his business, a solid family firm, though it had never seemed terribly important. I'd felt sufficiently loved, sufficiently spoilt and pampered all those years.

We'd never had servants to speak of, just a cleaner, a single mother of two from a village near Guadalajara, not much to look at, poor thing, and a bit neurotic. Of course, she had reason to be, what with all her problems. But everything else had come about, sooner or later.

At first I just couldn't get used to it. I'd go around the house leaving traps everywhere, a packet of cigarettes here, a book there. When I got up in the morning they were in the same place. It seemed like magic. I'd open the fridge door and there was always ice and cold beers – nobody had finished them. I'd buy a dress and leave it hanging in the wardrobe for two weeks, then go and put it on and find that I had to take the labels off – a fortnight later and it still had the labels on. It was incredible, and above all, I had a room to myself. I'd announce, 'I'm going to do some work', and shut myself in my room, a whole room just for me, dear God, that was the biggest joy of all. I just couldn't believe it, I took ages to get used to it.

Having my privacy, something totally new to me, was overwhelming in the beginning.

Pablo found my attitude of perpetual, delighted surprise very amusing, and he encouraged it by giving me unequivocally personal presents, wonderful things for me alone, fountain pens, combs, a musical box with a lock, a Greek-Esperanto dictionary, a rubber stamp with my entire name printed on it in a spiral, a pair of glasses with plain glass lenses. I loved those the best. I've never needed glasses but I was dying to have a pair . . . He couldn't really understand the things that made me happy. He only had one sister, and his parents had always been rich, much more wealthy than mine. He'd never had any hand-me-downs from anyone; he'd always had his own room. He too had always believed that children in large families have a lot of fun and enjoy a particularly happy childhood.

I was five years old, only five years old, when I ceased to exist.

At the age of five I stopped being Lulu and was called Marisa, a big girl's name.

Mummy came home with the twins and that was the end of everything.

I got used to wandering around the house on my own, with a basket full of little bits and pieces, and having nobody to play with, nobody to pick me up in their arms, or take me to the park, or the cinema. *Twins are such hard work*, they'd say.

It was then that Marcelo noticed me.

He's always had a soft spot for lost causes, and I'll never ever be able to thank him enough.

His love, his generous, unconditional love, was the only support I could count on during my premature adulthood.

He was all I had between the ages of five and twenty, and during that horrible grey life I led until Pablo returned and in his mercy took me back to a world of lost pleasures, to the childhood which had been so brutally and unfairly snatched from me.

He never disappointed me.

He's never disappointed me, I thought. This is all that was missing, everything else has come about . . .

And that's when they came back into the room.

I don't know how many or who they were because they must have been barefoot, and also because the sound of scissors quickly opening and closing, click, click, click, cancelled out any other noise, denying me my only means of sensing the outside world.

I felt somebody flop down on the bed by my side, and place a cigarette in my mouth.

'Do you want a smoke?' It was Pablo. 'You won't be able to later on . . .'

I caught the filter between my lips and anxiously made the most of the favour being granted to me. When I'd almost finished the cigarette it was removed from my mouth and I immediately felt something unfamiliar pulling at my left ear.

My mouth was wedged open by what felt like a totally smooth ball probably made of plastic, judging by my unsuccessful attempts to detect any taste with my tongue. Somebody's fingers brushed my right ear and placed something round it. The ball was between my lips, and two threads or strings attached to it were pulled tight across my cheeks.

Even blindfolded, I had no problem guessing what my muzzle looked like.

The red plastic sphere which I had earlier glimpsed in Pablo's hand must have had a hole in the middle. A double rubber band was threaded through it, probably a covered band like the ones used to tie back one's hair, because it didn't pinch my skin, and the ends were slipped over my ears to hold it tight against my mouth. It was a very simple but effective device. It prevented me making any sound at all.

Immediately afterwards, I again heard the scissors opening and closing near me. At the other end of the bed, somebody took off my shoes and stroked my toes, tickling me unbearably. Then I felt something unpleasantly cold under the sleeve of my blouse near my armpit. Snip, snip, snip. The scissors slashed both the blouse and my bra strap. Then, Pablo – I assumed it was him, since the pressure against my side had remained constant the whole time – leaned over me and did the same on the other side. Afterwards, the scissors slipped between my breasts and cut cleanly through the middle of my bra.

This convinced me that it must be Pablo because he loved ripping my clothes. Sometimes I'd ended up seriously losing my temper with him because some things didn't last me two hours, blouses and t-shirts in particular. I'd choose them with great care, taking ages in the shop, hesitating and looking at myself in the mirror, and then I didn't even get to wear them out once. Some months I went through a shockingly high number of pairs of knickers. 'This is costing a fortune', I'd complain. 'Do you have any idea how much this little obsession of yours is costing us?' He'd laugh. 'Don't wear any, then,' he'd answer. 'At least not in the house. You don't need them at all.' I'd always end up doing as he said. I wore nothing under my skirt and I almost never wore trousers – he didn't like them – but I never managed to get entirely used to it. When any guest arrived, like they had that evening, I'd run to the bathroom. I had sets of underwear strategically placed around the house, though I nearly always went round half-naked – he'd got his way there too and now, when anyone else would have chosen to keep the waste to a minimum by unfastening my bra at the back, he slashed it with the scissors and stripped the whole thing off in a couple of seconds.

Then he moved slightly forward.

They stopped touching my feet.

Nobody spoke, nobody made any noise that I might be able to identify. I didn't know how many or who they were, but I sensed that my brother was among them and I didn't like the idea. I'd never known exactly how much Marcelo knew about my relationship with Pablo and I would have preferred things to stay as they were but that night I had a feeling that he was there too, watching me.

The huge silver buckle on my belt, a black suede belt so wide it covered a good part of my stomach, was unfastened in the conventional way.

The scissors then slid onto my stomach, under my skirt, and continued on down, click, click, click, until the fabric had been cut in two right through the middle. Somebody situated at my feet then pulled the skirt and I felt it slip quickly from under my lower back.

I thought he'd finish off the job with his hands, as was his habit, but he again used the scissors. Then they fastened my belt back up.

Then I was left alone on the bed again. For a few seconds nothing happened. I was trying to imagine how I must look with my hands and feet tied to the bars at either end of the bed, my legs spread apart, my eyes covered with a black scarf, my mouth blocked by the increasingly painful muzzle, and with the rubber bands biting into my cheeks and making my ears burn. I felt very uncomfortable and terribly ashamed of how gullible I'd been.

I'd fallen into a clumsy, childish trap, at my age. I didn't seem to learn – maybe I never would. I didn't usually worry too much on that score but that night the thought was particularly depressing, maybe because my brother was there.

I should have been expecting something like this for years, because Pablo always did what he said, although he'd never mentioned the subject again since the first time, that night in Moreto.

'Do you think she's attractive?' His voice expressed a

certain kind of satisfaction which was familiar to me. He always seemed extremely proud of me at moments such as these.

The person he'd addressed didn't answer.

The sharp point of one of the scissor blades began to describe convoluted arabesques on my chest. Then it stopped and somebody started to rotate it on a fixed point, as if it were a compass making ever increasing circles.

I tried to keep completely still.

I wasn't worried. I knew they weren't actually going to harm me, but the contact with the sharp metal blades made me very uneasy. The scissors moved over my entire body, caressing my throat, dancing on my nipples, sliding over my belly, even trapping small portions of skin, keeping me tense, expectant, in the grip of its dangerous caresses, waiting for the shocking outcome which would never occur.

Suddenly I could no longer feel their icy presence. I stopped flinching away from the menacing points. Perhaps it had been nothing but a simple trick to distract me, I thought.

Then somebody placed their hand on me. I wondered whose it was. After an initial light slap, it began to press and knead my flesh, to hold me tight round the waist, squash my breasts, sink into my navel, slide over my thighs and then tease the slit of my sex with its fingers, and finally press its whole palm against it. Then I felt another hand, the second, and a third – that meant there must be two of them. I even thought I felt a fourth hand, though I found it very difficult to tell, because the bed had filled up with people. I could feel them all around me and the bed was creaking as they moved. A pair of lips rested on my neck and covered it in kisses. At the same time somebody else's tongue slid over my armpit, a finger entered me, an arm was slipped under my waist, a hand stroked my right hand, a leg rolled over mine, a knee was pressed against my hip.

I tried to think.

One of them was the South American girl, I was sure.

Pablo was there too, because he had never offered me to anyone without taking part in the game himself, and there must have been a third, another man, I thought because I could feel predominantly male contours, angular and rough to the touch – or maybe the South American girl was a guy after all. I was disconcerted, and whoever they were, they were doing everything possible to make me feel even more disorientated. Their hands and mouths were moving very quickly over my body, instantly switching targets. It was impossible to follow their trail, to guess whether the tongue now appearing over my tortured ear was the same one which had slipped between my legs seconds before, to identify the caresses and bites. I couldn't tell who they were. Something too large for a finger rested against my closed eyelids, over the blindfold, and then pressed against each of my eyes in turn, a male member – this was all I could call it since in that state, unable to see and with my hands tied, how could I tell if it was a glorious cock, a magnificent shaft, or on the contrary, a miserable, shrivelled little dick? Its tip prodded one of my breasts, first circling it then rhythmically banging against the nipple, covering me in sticky slime.

And Marcelo was watching it all.

For a time I tried to restrain myself, not to let myself go, to keep still, not to show my pleasure and to keep my whole body pressed against the mattress, my head straight. I was doing it for him. I didn't want him to see me submitting, but I could feel my skin was becoming damp. I knew all the different phases of the process well: first my skin bristled, then there was heat, a wave which flooded into my belly and spread all over, then sudden shivers behind my knees, on the inside of my thighs, around my navel, a frantic tingling which was the prelude to the imminent explosion, then an imaginary spring suddenly propelled me violently forward, and that was the beginning of the end, the surrendering of all my will. Hardly moving, all I could do was to open up, arch my body until my bones ached. I maintained the same pressure by rocking back and forth in unison with the instrument of my pleasure, whatever it might be, seeking the ultimate fission.

My skin was becoming saturated, and I couldn't fight it.

'Whenever you like . . .' Pablo's voice, uneven and husky, marked the beginning of a new phase. The hands, all of them, and all the mouths, instantly withdrew. Some cool, wet fingers, delicious against my burning skin, slid under one of my ears and released it from the minor torture of the rubberband. The nails didn't protrude beyond the fingertips. The South American girl had short nails. I remembered this because I had noticed her hands earlier, beautiful hands, slender and delicate, out of keeping with the rest of her body. The plastic ball fell from my lips. I felt so relieved to be free of it that, having moved my lower jaw a couple of times to alleviate the stiffness, I felt obliged to show my gratitude.

'Thank you . . .'

Somebody, not Pablo, because he would never have reacted in that way, stifled a laugh. It sounded vaguely familiar but I didn't have time to identify the possible source because barely a couple of seconds later my mouth was filled again.

An unknown male member was slipped between my lips.

'I'm still here by your side.' I didn't need him to tell me this, I knew perfectly well it wasn't his. I could feel his breath against my face and one of his hands slip between the back of my head and the pillow, grabbing my hair and pushing me upwards, moving my head rhythmically against the piston of flesh moving in and out of my mouth, an anonymous cock, considerably bigger than his at the base, but sharply decreasing in size towards the tip, which seemed shorter and narrower.

As the movements of my unknown visitor at times became more jerky, I felt Pablo sit up and kneel by my side.

I thought he was going to join us but I was wrong.

His hands began to tug at the scarf fastening my right

wrist and untied me. Almost simultaneously, other hands, which I could not confidently identify as those of my lover of the moment, untied my left hand. He then removed his penis from my mouth.

Somebody released my ankles from their bonds.

Somebody took both my wrists and tied them behind my back.

I now sensed there were only two of them, two men. Maybe it had only been them since the beginning, I must have just imagined that the South American girl had joined in. Maybe there had only been two men right from the start but now, with so much happening, I no longer knew which was Pablo and which was the other one. I was totally confused once more.

Somebody pushed me and turned me over.

Somebody grabbed me by the waist, pulling me up and forcing me to kneel on the bed.

Somebody penetrated me from behind.

Somebody in front of me took my head in his hands and held it while he put his penis in my mouth. It was Pablo's cock.

'I love you . . .'

He would say it to me at key moments. It calmed me and gave me strength. He knew his voice dissolved my doubts and my feeling of guilt.

Marcelo was watching it all. Maybe he had heard what Pablo had just said but I now felt very far from him, very far from everything. I was almost completely gone, at the point of orgasm.

'Let go, Lulu.' That was a good one, telling me precisely that, to let go, when I could barely move my mouth away from his body without help as my hands were trapped, and my body was trapped too by the pleasurable thrusts piercing me. 'Now it's my turn . . .'

He lifted my head very carefully and rested it on the bed, my left cheek against the bedcover. As if seized by a cruel impulse, the stranger came out of me at the precise moment when my sex was beginning to throb and twitch of its own accord, beyond my control.

'Don't do this to me, now,' I whispered almost inaudibly, 'not now . . .'

'How could you be so desperate, darling?' There was laughter beneath Pablo's words. 'You don't even know who it is . . . Or can you guess?' I answered no, I didn't know who it was. I really had no idea who it might be, and I couldn't care less as long as something or someone filled me again straight away. 'Oh Lulu . . . what a disgrace! To have to witness such behaviour, and from one's own wife – it's too much for an honourable man . . .' The two of them were still there somewhere, not touching a hair on my head. The seconds passed slowly, nothing happened. I was getting more and more hysterical. I had to make some decision, and I chose reluctantly to try and manage without them. I stretched out my legs and tried to rub against the bedcover. I failed spectacularly a couple of times because it was very difficult to make coordinated movements with my hands tied behind my back but I managed eventually to establish continuous, if feeble, contact with the fabric. It wasn't much good. The results were utterly disappointing, as my contortions only served to increase the need I felt in my sex instead of diminishing it. Pablo went on talking, his words exciting me more than any caress. 'You're a real slut, my love. Don't let me stop you, go on, carry on rubbing your cunt against the bedcover but at least tell us how it's going. Does it feel good? What a pitiful sight, Lulu! And in front of all our guests, they're all here watching you. What will they think of us now! You carry on, don't worry about me. I mean, I don't intend to put up with this much longer anyway. I'm off, I'm leaving right now. Why should I stay here and watch you ruin a gentleman's honour? Now, I know you remember this one, you do, I swear you remember.' He leaned over to whisper in my ear but his body remained out of reach. 'I'm going to leave you locked up in here for a couple of days. Maybe I'll even tie you to the bed again but with sticky tape this time, maybe that'll calm you down . . .'

'Please,' I turned my head in the direction of his voice and pleaded one last time, on the verge of tears, 'please, Pablo, please . . .'

Then his hands grabbed me violently by the waist and he turned me round. His fingers sank into my body once more and pulled me quickly towards him. When he was piercing me once more, he again told me he loved me. He said it over and over very quietly like a litany, while he led me skilfully towards my own annihilation.

But they still hadn't had enough.

They penetrated me in turn, at regular intervals, one after the other, in a systematic and orderly manner. Afterwards, the one who wasn't Pablo put his arms under mine and forced me to stand up. I asked him to hold onto me, because my legs were trembling, and he helped to take a few steps, then I heard Pablo's voice, telling me to stop.

He was the only one to have spoken, all along. The other man hadn't yet said a word and I still couldn't see him; I couldn't see anything with the scarf tight around my temples. I felt that if my pleasure had not been so intense my head would have exploded with pain.

Pablo came up behind me and untied my hands.

'Get on top of him.'

He held me as I knelt first on what I assumed was the old, narrow chaise-longue covered in black leather, which we'd brought from my mother-in-law's old workshop. The stranger then took me by the waist and placed me on top of him. He held his penis in one hand and helped me to insert it inside myself with the other. Then he ran both hands over my body for a fleeting moment, after which they seized my bottom, lightly kneading the flesh before parting it so as to open up a second path of entry to my body.

Well, there's going to be a grand finale tonight, I thought, as I marvelled at the calm, natural way both of them, Pablo and the other, shared my body equitably as if they were used to sharing everything.

I was penetrated for a second time almost immediately.

The stranger's body tensed beneath me. He slightly changed my position, forcing me to lie on top of him as he lifted my arms for me to lean my hands against the back of the chaise longue. Then he lay still. Only then did Pablo begin to move, very slowly but very intensely, his thrusts driving me against the body of the other man, who pushed me away from him, his hands gripping me firmly by the waist, and then the whole movement began again, and as they penetrated me with an increasingly regular, easy, fluid rhythm, I felt that my anonymous visitor was preparing to emerge from his passivity. He lifted his whole body toward me, imperceptibly at first, then more noticeably, though still gently, synchronizing almost perfectly with the tempo Pablo was setting from the back.

Their penises moved in unison inside me. I could clearly feel them both, their tips meeting, brushing against each other through what felt to me like a flimsy membrane, a thin wall of skin which was in danger at every thrust, and was becoming more and more fragile. They're going to tear me, I thought, they're going to tear me and then they really will meet, one against the other. I repeated it to myself. I liked hearing myself say it. They're going to tear me. What a delicious idea, the delicate membrane destroyed for ever, and what would their astonishment be when they saw the catastrophic results, their ends united, my body a single cavity for ever more? They're going to tear me. I was still repeating this to myself when I told them I was about to come. I didn't usually do so, but this time the warning sprung spontaneously from my lips, 'I'm coming,' and their movements speeded up, pounding me. I didn't notice anything at first but then I realized that beneath me the stranger's body was trembling and writhing, groans came from his lips, his spasms prolonged my own, then, from behind, a hand tore off the scarf covering my eyes but I didn't open them, I still couldn't open them, not until Pablo stopped moving over me, not until his pressure faded entirely.

Afterwards we kept still for a moment, the three of us, in silence.

Perhaps, I thought, it would be better not to open my eyes, to come off him blindly, to turn round without looking and get into bed, curl up in a corner and wait.

That would probably have been best but I couldn't resist the temptation, and I lifted my head with difficulty, until then resting on his shoulder. I waited a few seconds and looked into his face.

My brother, his features still distorted by his recent pleasure, was smiling at me.

Then he leaned towards me and kissed me lightly on the lips, something he only did on important occasions.

I closed my eyes again.

Pablo then took care of me, as he always did.

He put me into bed, covered me, kissed me, then led Marcelo out of the room. He stayed with him until he left, took Ines a glass of water as she'd woken up, then came back to me and rocked me in his arms, reassuring me until I fell asleep.

In Pablo's mind there was a very definite line between light and dark, and he never mixed the two, but only a dose of each, such was the placid serenity of our daily life.

With him, it was very easy to cross the line and then return safe and sound to the other side. Following the guide-rope was easy as long as he was there, holding me.

Afterwards, all I had to do was close my eyes.

He took care of all the rest.

He was the last person I wanted to talk to. I was tempted to hang up without saying anything, but then I remembered that I hadn't had too many presents that year.

'Marisa?'

'Yes.'

'Hi, it's Remi.'

'Yes, I recognized your voice.'

'I called you loads of times last week, but you weren't in . . .'

'Well, it was my birthday on Monday, and I've been out quite a lot recently.'

'Many happy returns. So how old are you then?'

'Twenty-eight . . .' I lied but then I felt ashamed, so I corrected myself, 'plus three, that's thirty-one.'

'You're in your prime, girl.'

'Yeah,' he himself must have been pushing fifty, 'so they say.'

'Listen, the reason I was calling you . . .'

'Look, I'm sorry, I'd better tell you now before you go on – forget it, I'm totally broke. I really can't go in for any luxuries at the moment.'

'No, it's not about that . . .'

'Isn't it?' I was disconcerted. Right from the start our relationship had revolved exclusively around a single, very clearly defined matter.

'No, this time I'm not calling you about the usual stuff, or maybe I am, it's a bit similar really, but don't worry, it won't cost you a thing . . .'

'I don't understand.'

'Look, I've got this . . . special client, right, a guy from Alicante. He's raked it in selling flats to old Germans and Belgians, you know the sort of thing . . .'

'Yes.'

'Well, as it happens, this guy comes to Madrid from time to time in the winter, to have a good time, you know what I mean?'

'Yes.'

'Look, if you're going to get pissed off, we can forget all about it, OK?'

'No, look, it's nothing.' I realized I'd sounded too abrupt. 'Go on.'

'OK. As it happens, this guy, he's into doing a bit of everything, yeah? And, well, he's asked me to organize a little party, and he wants a woman there too, and I thought maybe you'd fancy coming along. You know all the others – Manolo, Jesus and a few others. Anyway, think about it. It's going to be the day after tomorrow . . .'

'At Encarna's?'

'Fine, if you want we can have it there, at Encarna's, from half-past one . . .'

'That late?'

'Yes, he's got to go somewhere before, dinner with his old mates from the Army or something, he didn't really explain, so we agreed to make it later . . .'

'No, look Remi, really, count me out.'

'But you wouldn't have to do it with him! Not you, he just wants to watch. I mean, he's bringing a kid with him, and a tart, and everything . . .'

'I don't believe you.'

'I swear it's true. Why would I lie to you? It's in my interest to be on good terms with you, you know that.'

'Makes no difference. I don't want to, I'm not going.'

'Well, it's up to you, but if you really are short of cash, you could make a packet out of this . . .'

By supper time, I'd almost decided to go, even though I'd hung up on him that afternoon almost as soon as he'd mentioned money.

At first, I felt terrible. I was completely horrified with myself. I wondered, what must I have looked like for Remi to have dared suggest something like this to me? I felt really terrible but he didn't give up. He rang back a few hours later and he hit me in a weak spot. 'What do you care if you're on one side of the deal or the other? It's all the same, isn't it?' I'd told him once that I found it more degrading paying than charging for going to bed with a man and he reminded me of this, and what was worse, his tone, as he reproached me for being inconsistent, was sincere and impartial, like an older brother. He might have described me, had he known how, as childishly prejudiced or wilfully ingenuous, but he put it another way. 'If you're in this, you're in it right to the end, so don't be an idiot. At least get something out of it. What does it matter? You've done the same thing loads of times, what's different about this?'

By dinner time, I'd almost decided to go.

The line was there, tempting me, exerting an almost irresistible attraction, the call of the abyss, plunging into the void and falling, tens, hundreds, thousands of feet, falling until I struck the bottom and didn't have to think again for all eternity.

Later, at home, when I came out of the shower, I looked at myself at length in the mirror and I realized that I was starting to put on weight.

I wrapped myself in a bathrobe, so I couldn't look at myself any more.

I was overcome by doubts later on in the afternoon, as I was wondering how I should dress for my strange appointment, what type of clothes to choose, something black, short, tight-fitting and low-cut, or an ordinary, everyday dress for an ordinary, everyday woman?

I thanked God that Patricia had offered to go and fetch Ines from school and take her to spend the night at my parents' house.

I wouldn't have liked to see her.

I couldn't decide.

Either way, things looked bad.

He hadn't wanted to listen to me. I tried to explain it to him. I faced him and talked and talked for hours, but my words bounced off him like tennis balls against a wall.

He hadn't wanted to listen to me. He wouldn't look beyond my most recent crisis and refused to listen. He refused to understand. 'I'm sorry,' he said, 'I'm really sorry. The idea was mine, mine alone, it'd been buzzing around in my head for years. After all, Marcelo is my best friend. He had nothing to do with it, though I didn't have too much trouble persuading him. We both thought it wasn't such a big deal. I mean, you're no longer of an age to let yourselves get carried away by a fatal passion, but we didn't reckon you'd react like this. I tell you, if I'd imagined it was going to have such a bad effect on you, I'd have stopped in time. I swear I'm sorry.'

I tried to explain it to him, I really tried. He said nothing while I spoke, for hours. Incest had definitely never been part of my plans and I would never have imagined that Marcelo could act so naturally after something like that, because neither of them made the slightest reference to the subject ever again, neither together nor separately. *Nothing's happened*, their faces and their gestures and their unshakeable calm all seemed to say, *nothing's happened*, and yet things *had* happened, lots of things, but it wasn't only that.

By that time, I'd already begun to doubt the truth of his theory lessons, starting with the very first one, and I was tormented by the suspicion that love and sex couldn't in fact exist as two completely separate entities. I convinced myself that love had to be something else.

Half of my life, exactly half my life, had revolved exclusively around Pablo.

I'd never loved anyone else.

This frightened me. My inexperience frightened me.

I felt as if all my movements, from the time when I jumped out of bed every morning to when I plunged back into it at night, had already been mapped out by him.

This overwhelmed me. His confidence overwhelmed me.

Then I convinced myself that I'd never grow up as long as I stayed with him and I'd get to thirty-five, and then forty, and then forty-five, and then fifty, fifty-five, until I was sixty-six, my mother's age, and I would never have managed to grow up, I'd be an eternal little girl, but not the beautiful little girl of twelve who lived with him in the huge, empty, make-believe house where time stood still, but a pathetic monster of sixty-six, cursed with eternal childhood.

Self-pity is a hard drug.

That's why I left.

But I could never forget that before, at least, I'd been happy.

I finally chose a short black dress, not too low-cut but very tight, made of an elasticated fabric that clung to my body like a swimsuit.

Then the mascara-applicator I was holding in my right hand slipped inexplicably from my fingers, leaving three fine black streaks down my cheek.

I clicked my tongue with annoyance and dipped the corner of a tissue in water and tried to repair the damage.

I looked at myself in the mirror.

I saw the face of a woman in middle age, old even, her mouth tightly drawn into a sneer which was familiar yet different: two fine wrinkles showing my age and experience, a complex combination, the exact opposite of the easy, uncontrolled laughter which used to transform into a grimace, the smile of the innocent, outrageous good-time girl I once was.

I kept my eyes fixed on that woman for several seconds.

I didn't like what I saw.

Things looked bad, really bad.

I turned on the cold water and washed my face with soap. I scrubbed it thoroughly with a sponge, making a lot of foam, until my skin started to pull.

I felt much better.

I needed to hold something, an object that would keep me company, and support and encourage me. I felt I couldn't go back with empty hands.

Suddenly I remembered it, a torn, orange plastic bag which had always had a handle missing. Inside, five pieces of porcelain, two arms, two legs, a head and a body stuffed with wool, a little dirty dress, and a tiny white hat, yellowed with age – the dismembered little Dutch doll, my colleague in the games of eternal childhood which I'd inherited in the cradle from my great aunt Maria Luisa, who I never knew.

I'd been promising myself for twenty years that I'd take her the next day to be mended at the dolls' hospital in Sevilla Street, and I'd never done it.

He'd understand.

It was still very early.

I bought a guide at the kiosk on the corner and turned to the listings section, anxiously looking for a good omen.

In an art-house cinema in Villaverde Alto they were showing *Miracle in Milan*, but Villaverde was too far.

There didn't seem to be any other good old films on anywhere else.

So I chose Fuencarral, my favourite street, and I got in to see a new American comedy, an entirely forgettable piece of rubbish with a splendid character actress playing the hero's mother.

* * *

In the end I decided to use my key.

The house seemed to be completely dark.

I went forward timidly at first, clasping the orange bag with both hands as if it were a shield, until my eyes became accustomed to the lack of light.

I put the decrepit little Dutch doll down in a corner of the sitting room and then went about avoiding obstacles with unaccustomed skill.

I was happy.

When I reached the bedroom I came to a halt in the corridor, my ear against the door, trying to guess who was inside.

I took off my shoes, turned the door handle smoothly and went in on tiptoes.

It took me a while to make sure it was Pablo sleeping there alone, turned towards the middle of the bed.

I took a deep breath and smiled.

This wasn't exactly the best scenario I'd imagined – nobody at home, getting into bed and waiting – but neither was it the worst – finding two people there between the sheets.

I undressed as quietly as possible and searched for the shirt he must have taken off only moments before. I found it thrown over a chair. I looked at it, and touched it, and smelt it, and recognized it, and then put it on and lay down on the floor by his side, which was the best plan I'd been able to come up with while I watched those two idiotic Californians on the big screen getting endlessly divorced and reconciled.

The prodigal daughter returns home, flings herself on the floor like a dog, publicly acknowledges her misdeeds and begs the father for forgiveness, since she knows him to be compassionate and magnanimous.

It wasn't a perfect plan but it wasn't all that bad, given the hurry and the other adverse circumstances.

'I love you,' I whispered.

That's it, I thought, *it's all been very easy*.

The hard floor seemed infinitely welcoming.

I closed my eyes. I was very tired. *Everything's going well*, I said to myself. *Now I'll be able to sleep for hours and hours, and when we wake up, he'll find me here and understand. It's all been so easy . . .*

Then I heard the click of a lighter, followed by his cold voice.

'Get up, Lulu. It won't work.'

At first I didn't dare move. I stayed still, curled up on the floor, trembling, convincing myself that I hadn't heard anything because nothing had been said, but he repeated it in a clear voice.

'It's too late now, Lulu. This time it won't work.'

I got up suddenly, gripped the lapels of his shirt and pulled my arms apart with all my might.

The buttons popped off onto the floor one by one.

I pulled my dress on over my head, stuffed my arms into the sleeves as best I could and dragged it down over my hips. I rushed out into the passage, put on my shoes and carried on running.

'Where are you going?'

In the sitting room, I picked up my handbag and also grabbed the orange bag, but then I realized he had run after me down the corridor and must already have seen her. I didn't have time to hide her.

The old Dutch doll wouldn't be able to keep me company where I was heading so I put her back down on a table.

'Where are you going?'

I went out, slamming the door, but failed as usual.

The door banged violently against the frame a couple of times without closing.

I'd known Encarna for years.

I'd gone a few times with Pablo to her old house in Roma Street, where she'd started off respectably as a young woman with a boarding house for bullfighters, lean, sharp picadors, short, stocky banderilleros, who fucked her with great relish, aware that she might be the last woman of their lives. She remembered if fondly, but she used to say that what with the gorings the matador received, and the fact that they were all bastards who left without paying half the time, it started to prove financially disastrous. According to her, it was from pure necessity that she'd been forced to rent out rooms for another type of corrida.

But Roma Street, though a good place for a bullfighters' boarding house, turned out to be less than ideal for a house of assignations, especially when the area, which was Salamanca after all, started to fill up with Yuppies, the new smart set, even less cultured than the lot before. They didn't appreciate the quaint, traditional charm of an establishment like Encarna's, so in the end she sold it at a bargain price to a film director who managed to bamboozle her, calling her a historic monument and shamelessly fondling her bottom, and with what she got for it she bought a huge flat on Espoz y Mina Street, in an aristocratic old block – she'd say it with great emphasis, 'aristocratic' – and then she brought back from the country a niece of hers, a hairdresser by trade who'd done a correspondence course in interior decorating, and recruited some girls, not over-young or over-pretty but profitable. 'If you're going to do something, do it properly,' she'd say.

When I couldn't go to my place, I'd go round to Encarna's. I got on very well with her.

I took a taxi there because I didn't feel like driving.

I went round the block, walking slowly, trying not to think, to forget that I'd been rejected, but the streets were too lively that night, Friday the third.

A skinny old tart, with a couple of dark marks on her face, grey roots showing through her dyed hair, in a skimpy top too cruelly low-cut for her sad, flaccid breasts, and a light plastic bomber jacket covered in Formula 1 logos, shivering with cold, asked me for a cigarette.

I gave her one, looking straight at her, and quickly turned back the way I'd come.

At the entrance I met Encarna's niece who'd just been out for a drink with her boyfriend, a nice boy who worked in an optician's and didn't suspect a thing.

The mistress of the house was playing solitaire in front of the television. When she saw me, she nodded in the direction of a little room at the end of the corridor, which we both jokingly referred to as the 'bridal suite', the best room in the house.

Encarna was acting a bit odd. She seemed nervous, elusive. I asked her how her arthritis was but she didn't want to talk. She answered my superficial, polite questions in strained monosyllables, claiming she was engrossed in a film on TV, which reminded me that I was late.

I wasn't too keen on the sound of this little party. I'd never been keen on it, I remembered, it had smelt fishy right from the start. I had a feeling I wasn't going to like it but there was no going back now.

I had nowhere to go back to.

* * *

In the room at the end, three old acquaintances of mine greeted me enthusiastically. I didn't respond quite so warmly.

'Where's Manolo?'

'How should I know . . .' Jesus, a short guy with an athletic build whom I'd never found particularly attractive but who was apparently very popular with other guys, looked very surprised. 'As far as I know, he's not coming tonight . . .'

'Remi told me that Manolo was going to be here.' I felt that his absence confirmed my worst fears. 'If he's not here, I'm leaving . . .'

'Come on, Marisa.' The one who broke in on the conversation was one of my absolute favourites – he looked a lot like Lester – a delightful student from a well-to-do English family, who'd been ruined by a dissolute life. I didn't know his real name, I'd always called him Lester. 'What's Manolo got that we haven't?'

'I trust him, but not the rest of you . . .'

Manolo liked women. Manolo found me attractive. 'I'm only in this for the money,' he'd say to me, 'only for the money.' He was young, good-looking and bright, but all within reason, and there was something a bit special about him, not to mention a cock like a hammer. We'd got it together a few times, the two of us, on our own at home, on a purely non-professional basis, and I'd become rather fond of him. He liked me and took care of me. He told me who I should and who I shouldn't go with, what I should and shouldn't do. He wouldn't let me down, not him, I was sure of that, but I couldn't trust the others. I just didn't trust them. I was on the point of turning round and getting out of there, but I couldn't bear the thought of spending the night alone.

Meanwhile, they'd already set to work.

They knew me well, and they knew their job.

The one who looked like Lester stood behind me, put his arms round me and began to caress my body, to fondle me with the flat of his hands, talking to me loudly, pulling up my dress at the back, uncovering my naked flesh with feigned surprise, pressing against me, sticking the flies of his leather trousers against my bottom, moving rhythmically and pushing me forward. Manolo had sworn to me a couple of times that Lester was a pure homosexual and only liked men – he'd never actually fucked me – but sometimes I had trouble believing it.

As if to make up for it, his boyfriend, who was called Juan Ramon and looked like a complete moron, was happily watching the scene. He'd stick it up anything that was put in front of him.

He came up to us and put his arms round me. His hands met Lester's. Their mouths touched over my shoulder. His penis, inside his jeans, which looked as if they were about to burst, bumped against my sex, his caresses included us both.

I couldn't help my eyes closing, my body tensing, my arms, instead, becoming limp, powerless, my sex beginning to swell. I couldn't help it and I didn't even try. I didn't care about anything any more, and they were so delightful, that was the only thing that hadn't changed – they were still delightful when they played with me. They threw my body to each other as if it were a big ball, back and forth, swinging me from one to the other. They squeezed me, they gave me warmth, an easy, basic pleasure. I liked them, I liked what they did to each other and what they did to me. They kissed each other and kissed me; they touched each other and touched me; they sucked each other and sucked me; and I enjoyed watching them look and smile and say things to each other more than I enjoyed them looking and smiling and saying things to me, but I didn't tell them that – they wouldn't understand. They were both a bit stupid, little animals. Their hands wandered under my dress from time to time, and their touch was very different from that of other men. There was no violence, no desire for acknowledgement – they kept that for each other – and their gentle fingers didn't linger over me. All they gave me were careless little taps, if anything, poor, stingy caresses, but just the brush of their nails made me shiver, and I stroked their heads, ran my fingers through their hair. *Poor things, my little boys, you've had a narrow escape. What an incomprehensible aberration of Nature, to have deprived me of the chance of measuring myself against you on equal terms, making me a mere spectator to your innocent games.* They would have lost their innocence with me but it was too late to do anything about it now. Poor things. What a piece of luck, my darlings.

They both tugged at my dress, which they'd wrinkled up above my breasts, forcing me to lift my arms, and they pulled it off over my head. Then they announced amid laughter that they were going to dress me up.

Jesus, who'd never laid a finger on me, was in the corner watching us and wearing a very strange get-up. He reminded me of a comic-book hero, a gleaming galactic avenger, dark and dangerous, but he looked stupid too with those enormous shoulder pads and black leggings open at the front and at the back, like those tights that have holes – tights made for fucking, the harsh truth is that no myth lasts for ever – which they now sell in even the most ordinary shops with the excuse that you don't have to take them off to go to the toilet and they're less likely to get laddered. His penis, all hair completely removed, hung idly against the lurex which clung to his thighs like a second skin. *He* looks ridiculous, I thought, though in fact I liked looking at him. He looked ridiculous but soon I would look very similar myself.

They dressed me in a pair of black boots which came half-way up my thighs, narrow to the knee and then widening out, with outrageously thick platform soles and the finest, highest heels I'd ever seen in my life.

'I'll never be able walk in these,' I warned. They laughed. 'Seriously, you don't know what I'm like. I'll break my neck in these boots, I'm telling you . . .'

The remaining accessories were more comfortable, but

equally outlandish: a belt, decorated with silver studs, from which hung several leather straps, also studded, that had to be done up one by one and crossed over my hips, then a sort of bra consisting of three leather straps which formed a black triangle round my nipples without covering them, and a dog collar in my size, decorated with metal rings.

Lester led me to a mirror. I looked at myself and liked what I saw – all those straps suited me. I thought I looked good and I told them so. They agreed with me, 'You look very good'. They would have said the same if I'd been wearing a potato sack but it was still nice to hear. Then they took me by the arm and led me through to the other room where three figures, sitting on a kind of divan decorated with fake gilded wood, jubilantly greeted my arrival.

The one in the middle, a puny, short, balding man with a very long nail on the little finger of his right hand and the others just black with dirt, with one of those ridiculous, very fine little moustaches barely covering his top lip – the face of a typical pervert – I took to be the property speculator from Alicante.

To his right, a boy of peasant-like beauty, with round, pink cheeks, fifteen, sixteen at the most, sat constantly stroking his clothes. The plastic tag from a label still hung from one of the elbows of his jacket, Italian designer cashmere with enormous shoulder pads.

To his left, a gaunt young girl with her left arm punctured by a string of small bloody dots, hadn't been so lucky.

There was also a very tall man, huge, who looked like a bodybuilder, whom I'd never seen before.

And a tall woman of about thirty-five, with a well-rounded but firm body, attractive in spite of her witch's make-up, false eyelashes, thick, black eyeliner, scarlet lips, her nipples pierced with two silver rings.

It was she who seemed most pleased to see me.

First she pointed at me. Then she arched her eyebrows, pursed her lips and gave me a terrifying smile.

* * *

Somebody had told me the joke many years before and I hadn't found it funny at all – *it's only the first thirty blows that hurt* – but it's true, absolutely true. You only feel the first twenty or thirty blows. After that it's all the same.

I had a good time at first, though, very good, to be honest. I didn't think it would be more than a session of pure fetishism – leather, irons, rings – and that would be all. Judging by the few things he'd said, the guy from Alicante was a simple sort, too simple for any of it to go much further. So I didn't worry when the enormous stranger fixed the end of a chain onto a ring at the back of my collar and hooked one of the links over a thick nail he'd earlier hammered into the wall.

Poor Encarna, I thought. They're really buggering up your place.

I still wasn't worried, and I felt very excited by the dense atmosphere pervading the room, thick, tangible desire, distorting the faces of some of the participants, reducing them to a pair of huge, greedy eyes.

The bodybuilder acted as master of ceremonies.

He grabbed Jesus by the arm, led him into the middle of the room and flung him to the floor.

Juan Ramon slowly came up and put a foot on the nape of his neck to prevent him from getting up, purely a concession to the iconography of the genre, I thought, since the victim showed no signs of objecting to the situation.

Meanwhile, with the affected languor of a stripper writhing in the final stages of her act, the brute stuck his right arm up to the elbow into a long, stiff leather glove covered in small pointed rivets.

Then, smiling to himself, he clenched his fist and looked at it for a time, as if he had to concentrate to appreciate fully the power of the ball of bristling metallic spikes, which reminded me of some terrifying medieval weapon, before heading towards Jesus, who, face down on the floor, had missed the giant's action.

I caught myself smiling, my teeth digging into my bottom

lip, and it frightened me. I immediately altered my expression. I tried to look distant, indifferent, as if it had nothing to do with me, but I didn't keep it up for long.

He did it.

I would never have thought it possible, that a mace that size would fit inside such a small body, but he did it. His forearm disappeared entirely inside the slender athlete, who screamed and writhed, unable to get up due to the foot pressing down on his head. He did it, and not content with that, he began to move his arm inside its sheath, smiling at the screams of pain which he provoked with each turn.

He did it, but he wasn't the only one who seemed to be enjoying the spectacle.

Lester went up to Juan Ramon, leaned languidly against him and began to caress him from behind with his right hand, while with his left he skilfully freed his friend's penis. He gripped it and began to pump it up and down, rubbing the moist tip with his thumb. Soon the same was done to him. Without reducing the pressure of his foot with which he was pinning Jesus to the floor, Juan Ramon managed to undo the row of hooks fastening my favourite's leather trousers, and after lightly caressing his deliciously hard flesh, he sank his index finger in his bottom. 'There,' he said. Lester sighed with a dopey expression on his face. *Isn't he sweet*, I thought, as I felt my sex becoming liquid, my entire being slipping irretrievably between my thighs. I've never been able to resist that sight, never.

The young boy in the brand-new clothes also seemed very excited. He was leaning forward, his mouth half open, panting loudly. He wasn't missing a thing. His owner was turned on too – he was kissing him, touching him up, forcing him to do the same back, and he was talking to him in a choked voice. 'I'm going to do all this to you, every single thing, when we get back to Alcoy. You drive me crazy, but I'll lock you up in the cellar and you won't see the street again, or your mother, or your brothers, just me, when I come down to give you a whipping. I'll piss on your wounds. I'll never bugger you again, ever, I'll find others who're more handsome and younger than you and I'll bring them home, I'll have them right under your nose. You'll never fuck me again, you'll never fuck anyone again. I'll do it with an iron bar. I'll smash you up with it, I'll leave it inside you all night, and I'll make you suck my dog's cock, that'll be the first thing you do when you get up in the morning. You'll see, it won't be any use crying or pleading. You'll get down on your knees to beg me for food, and I'll leave you there to die of hunger. I'll kill you, I'll destroy you with a glove worse than that one there, because you drive me crazy. I'm going to do all this to you when we get back to Alcoy . . .'

The woman with the pierced nipples was sprawled on an armchair, her legs lying across the arms of the chair and her feet in the air and she was masturbating with a black, metal dildo with a golden tip. She looked at me and smiled, then she looked at the junkie. She gestured with her hand, saying, 'come here'. The girl didn't seem to understand, so she said it again, 'come here', and this time she was obeyed. The girl with the injured arm stood up and went over to her. The woman's voice held everyone's attention for a moment, then she removed her toy from between her thighs and pointed it at the mouth of the frightened and inexperienced prostitute who kept her lips firmly shut even when the hard, wet tip was placed against them. *She can't have been on the game long*, I thought, and I felt sorry for her because she wasn't calculating enough. The witch then grabbed her by the hair and yanked her up with a fist. The girl screamed, a chilling shriek, and at last opened her mouth. The dildo was pushed between her teeth, then, keeping a firm hold of her, the woman with the pierced nipples violently pulled her head towards her and the girl's face disappeared from view. All I could hear were the muffled sounds of her tongue licking the bare sex of the other woman, who opened herself with one hand and, with the other, guided the instrument of her visibly intensifying pleasure. She was writhing in her seat, emitting faint cries which, for a moment, made her seem almost human.

The giant tired of penetrating Jesus with his gloved hand and finally pulled it out of his body, soaked in blood. Then he sat on the floor, his legs crossed, just in front of the head of his victim, who hadn't moved, although now free of all constraint. He couldn't move. He squirmed painfully on the floor, letting out anguished moans, but the hand which had earlier penetrated him, now no longer in its glove, rested on his head and ruffled his hair, and, as if in response to a previously agreed signal, the pitiful creature half sat up and threw his arms round his torturer's neck, looking at him tearfully, tenderly. He kissed him at length on the lips, then silently moved his mouth close to his tormentor's thick penis and began to lick it diligently with the tip of his tongue before putting it in his mouth, without uttering a single reproach, and he seemed happy. I understood that he was happy in spite of the red stream steadily trickling down his thighs.

Everything then became complicated. Things moved very fast. The guy from Alicante called to Juan Ramon and said something in his ear. Juan Ramon nodded and the other man kissed him on the mouth, embracing him with sudden intensity, and two new couples formed.

The boy protested at first. He looked tearfully at his master and held out his hand to him pathetically, but it was no good. Juan Ramon took him off into a corner, lay him face down on top of a table and spanked him a couple of times. 'If you don't behave, I'll be really nasty to you, darling.' This calmed the poor little lamb and he kept still. I had trouble making out what happened next – they were too far away. Lester's boyfriend put a kind of spiked, rubber sheath over his cock which considerably increased its already respectable size, and then without warning, he parted the boy's buttocks and pushed it inside him in one go, right up to its base.

The client, now naked, had perched on all fours on top

of the divan, to get a better view of his little favourite being tortured, when mine, Lester, went up to him from behind, his penis, only half erect, in one hand, and with a look of resignation, he pushed it slowly and easily into the enormous hole which opened up in the flabby, ageing body, and at the same time grabbed the feeble prick of his repulsive client in his other hand, and masturbated him mechanically, without enthusiasm.

The guy from Alicante, who couldn't see that Lester was grimacing with disgust for my benefit while he fucked him at the most slack pace possible, didn't seem to notice his lack of ardour, as he was fully absorbed by the scene taking place before his eyes. His little one was screaming and writhing at the bestial assaults of a terrible weapon. Having seen the puny member the poor child was used to, it was easy to imagine the pain it must be causing. Suddenly, though, the victim stopped screaming and began to make very different sounds, as if the pain were suddenly turning into sensations of another sort altogether – it became obvious that it was starting to feel good. He was really enjoying it now. He leaned both hands on the table, arched slightly and began to move. We could all see his stiff cock against the glass.

Then his owner got scared. 'That's enough.'

I smiled inwardly. *It's no use telling him to stop, I thought. You were trying to be clever but now he won't enjoy it with you any more.* He's found out there are better things than you, you stupid fool.

Subsequent events proved me right.

Lester's attitude changed radically when his boyfriend, his penis still hidden, went up to him, smiling and gently swaying his hips, found a place to rest his knees, and penetrated him, stroking his chest with one hand. The guy from Alicante must have noticed the change in the situation, because judging by the joyful expression which appeared on his face, my favourite's cock must have become as hard as a rock and at last have adequately filled the gaping hole. But then suddenly he seemed more concerned by the disobedience of the plaything he'd brought from Alcoy, who, instead of coming and standing in front of him, crossed the whole room on his knees, his mouth open, and humbly satisfied the lover of his lover's lover who had generously opened his eyes once and for all. He started to lick his testicles avidly before parting his buttocks with his hands and sinking his tongue in the central orifice. Juan Ramon, without turning round, grunted with pleasure.

I was really enjoying myself but then, suddenly, I realized there were nine of us, and that eight – all except me – had already joined in the game.

Then I got scared. I became aware for the first time that I was chained up, and I sensed that I was destined to be the evening's main attraction.

She came towards me and grabbed my wrists. She placed my hands round her pierced breasts and did the same to me. She caressed me gently at first, her nails felt very pleasant, but her fingers moved quickly down to my sex, pulled at my lips and pinched them repeatedly with her sharp fingertips. She was really hurting me, so although I knew that the consequences of my action might prove worse than its cause, I flung out my knee and managed to send her sprawling across the floor, and I screamed at the top of my voice, yelling for Encarna. I still hoped I might get out of there unharmed – never again, I swore to myself, never again – but nobody came. The other participants in the party just shot me a brief, curious glance, and showed no intention of intervening on my behalf, except for the junkie who was looking at me with tears in her eyes. She tried but they stopped her in time. It's going to cost us both dear this evening, I thought. The woman finally got up slowly. She smiled, then knelt in front of me and broke off the heels of my boots. I had to hold onto the chain with both hands so I didn't break my neck due to my abrupt decrease in height. I managed to stay upright by balancing precariously on the tips of my thick platform soles, though this meant I had to keep perfectly still. She burst out laughing before punching me in the stomach. I couldn't move. She dug her nails into my breasts and then scraped them abruptly down my body, leaving long, jagged wounds. Later on she chose more subtle methods, like the two pairs of silver pincers, joined by a little chain, in which she trapped my nipples. She pulled on the chain violently and my whole body had to follow my breasts, which felt more and more distant, as if they were going to be torn off at any moment. She played with me like this for quite a while, pulling me backwards and forwards with simple flicks of her wrist, making me sway on my precarious supports. My hands were now rubbed raw by the chain, my arms were getting weaker and my muscles gradually going numb, but she got bored with that too, and granted me a few minutes respite before returning with something I didn't recognize at first but then turned out simply to be a metal shoehorn fixed to a length of bamboo. She smacked it against the palm of her hand. After that I saw nothing more. She turned me round to face the wall and this marked the beginning of a new phase. It was then I remembered that very old, very bad joke, *you only feel the first thirty blows*. She struck my calves first, then moved gradually up to my thighs, concentrating on the area immediately above my boots, then, contrary to what I'd thought, she lingered only a short time over my buttocks and instead unleashed a furious avalanche of blows slightly further up, at kidney level, and the pain reached such an unbearable pitch that I then hardly felt the shoehorn hitting my back – but it still wasn't enough. She turned me to face her again and repeated the process but this time going from top to bottom, savagely thrashing my breasts first – I could see she really enjoyed that. At that moment the giant came up to us and put his arm round my ribs, to lift them and stop them shaking after each blow, increasing the available surface area. She unfastened the pincer from my left nipple and sank her teeth into it. I thought the swollen flesh would be numb, but it wasn't. Her bite proved to me that I was still nowhere near the state of unconsciousness I longed for. The blows intensified, and in the end, he put his arms under mine and held me firmly, so I didn't have to hold onto the chain for a moment and she was able to strike at the inside of my thighs, moving slowly closer to my sex. I'd been expecting this and hoping I'd finally faint then, but I felt the shoehorn on my tense, trembling flesh, and I couldn't escape the pain. I had to endure it for minutes which seemed like centuries, while I comforted myself with the thought that this couldn't last much longer, because if the wounds from the metal shoehorn didn't kill me, I wouldn't have the strength to hold onto the chain for even half an hour more when he stopped holding me up and abandoned me once more to my fate, and I'd end up breaking my neck on the dog collar.

What a shame, I thought, wasting so much drama, so much pathos, on the death of an unfeeling woman who doesn't know how to appreciate tragic endings.

‘Look out!’

She was coming towards me with a red-hot hook she’d heated on a small stove but stopped dead in the middle of the floor.

I came to and told myself it must be a hallucination, it was too good to be true, but then I heard Encarna’s voice again in the corridor, and at the same time, somebody nervously knocking on the door.

‘Look out!’

The sound of a siren filled the street.

She put the hook down on the stove, now extinguished, grabbed a raincoat from a chair, hurriedly put it on and slipped out through a small door concealed in a cupboard, which I knew about too.

Encarna shouted for the third and last time.

‘Look out!’

The guy from Alicante can’t have understood what was going on. He was still sitting on the divan, the boy back in his arms at last, while all the others filed out quickly behind the harpie.

I was crying. I still couldn’t believe it – a raid, saved by a blessed police raid. I’d always looked down and crept past any guy in uniform, even if he was only a traffic warden, and now those angels had had the blessed idea of mounting a raid on that very street, on that very night, at that very time, and they'd saved my skin. God bless them. I kept repeating. God bless the Madrid police, for ever and ever, Amen.

We were the only ones left – me and the three original occupants of the divan.

They were looking at me expectantly. The girl was crying, hunched in a corner. Somebody had ripped her clothes. She must have understood what was going on but she didn't seem to be able to move.

'It's a raid,' I murmured.

The guy from Alicante stood up, grabbed his friend by the hand and they ran out of the door leading onto the corridor. She made as if to follow them, but I stopped her.

'No, don't go out that way.' I was exhausted, I could barely speak. She came up to me and unhooked the chain from the wall. At first, I scarcely felt any relief, I was completely numb. I had great trouble prising my hands away from the metal chain, they were burning. Then I slowly slid down the wall until I was sitting on the floor. 'Look, the third wooden panel of that cupboard is a door. Push it hard and you'll see a narrow staircase. Go right up to the top until you reach the roof. Hide and wait until the police have cleared out and then go down the fire escape. You'll end up in an alleyway that leads onto the street. Run . . .'

'Come with me!' She'd taken my hand and was looking at me with enormous gratitude.

'No, I'm staying. I'm clean, they can't touch me,' I was so tired, 'but you've got to go right now – run.'

She disappeared off to my left, and I was alone.

Somebody was getting a good beating, judging by the pleading and screaming which I could hear intermittently, coming from somewhere.

Then a figure came through the half-open door.

Gus, his fists still clenched and his knuckles covered in blood, came into the room first.

Pablo was behind him, his hands spotless, as usual.

* * *

He'd never hit me.

He'd never ever hit me, and I'd never ever seen him cry.

But he slipped two fingers under the collar, lifted me up, leaned me against the wall and slapped my face, first with the palm, then with the back of his right hand, as two large tears slid down his cheeks.

'Get out.'

Gus, a contemporary eunuch – smack had left him completely impotent – was puffing and panting by my side.

He didn't move.

Pablo looked him straight in the face.

'I said get out.'

Gus returned the look then shrugged contemptuously, turned round and left with bad grace.

We were now alone.

Then he hit me again, still with his right hand, as before, making my head sway violently from side to side. I let him. I was grateful for the blows shattering me to pieces and breaking the spell, destroying the face of the unknown old woman who'd stared back at me in the mirror only a few hours before. With every blow I could feel my skin regenerating, becoming soft and smooth. I was asking for it, I thought, I was really asking for it.

With tears still in his eyes, he pushed me away from him for a second and looked me up and down, then he put his arms round me. He held me tightly. His fingers ran along the weals on my back and he licked the blood pouring from my lips, blood he'd spilt with his own hands.

'Can you walk?'

I shook my head.

He picked me up in his arms and carried me over to a table where he sat me down, removed my boots and took my right foot in his hands, rubbing the sole and massaging it with his fingers.

'You've got horrible feet, much too big . . .'

I nodded in agreement.

He took my hands and turned them palm up, exposing

the glistening red flesh, the blood showing through shreds of dead, blackened skin.

'I've always liked your hands, though.' His eyes were full of anger, and pity. 'It's a shame . . .'

'Forgive me.' He kept his gaze fixed on my raw palms. 'Forgive me . . .'

Finally he looked up at me, took off his coat, put it round me very carefully and held me by the waist as I got down off the table.

'Come on.'

He walked ahead of me down the corridor towards the front door. I tried to follow, but I was too weak to walk at his pace.

Encarna looked in for a moment and shook her head, in both surprise and disapproval, and then disappeared back into the room with the television.

'Hold me.' He'd almost reached the front door and was looking at me. 'Hold me, please, I can't go any further . . .'

He came back, took one of my arms and put it round his neck, then held me by the waist. We got to the door and started down the stairs, very slowly. He was supporting me at every step. Little by little, I was regaining control of my legs, and gradually becoming fully aware of my failure, and his suffering, since he saw it as his own failure, and I felt I'd been so utterly stupid. I was a wreck still haunted by the fear of rejection, and the threat of this was a thousand times more painful than the woman's blows. I felt scared, and disgusted with myself, and exhausted, but mainly scared. We went down the stairs in silence. I didn't dare look at him. Suddenly his words thundered in my ears – there wouldn't be a truce, not yet.

'Ely called me one night. He sounded worried; he wanted to talk to me about you so I asked him over for dinner.' He kept his eyes fixed on the cracked walls along the staircase, as if the filthy, flaking plaster held a vitally important, secret code which only he could decipher. "We both know that Lulu isn't exactly a lady," he said, "but she's mixing in bad company. I'm frightened for her." So then I decided to interfere in your life again, in spite of everything, even though it's none of my business, and I had a word with Gus. He'd seen you around with some pretty unsavoury types too and he needed cash, as usual, so I paid him to keep an eye on you and eventually I found out everything . . . Stop, let's have a bit of a rest.'

I shook my head. I didn't want to stop, I wanted to go on right to the end, to get it over with, so I moved my bare, swollen foot towards the next step. 'All right, if that's what you want . . . Well, anyway, I found out everything and I got scared too, that's why I'm here. Encarna was on the payroll too and she tipped me off. She wouldn't tell me the date or the time, but tonight, when you left the house like that, so suddenly, I realized you'd probably be coming here, so I got in touch with Gus. We had it all more or less planned. At first I'd thought of not telling you all this but now I think I need to. He put up the car and the guns. The guys in the car were already in on it and he didn't have too much trouble finding a couple more to give us a hand and do a bit of shouting in the street. All I had to do was buy the siren – I got one pretty cheap. That gypsy who sells shoes in Vara del Rey, you know the one I mean, he got hold of one for me. The police were in on it too, at no extra cost, though I'm not sure they won't end up arresting those four louts, and then I'll have to pay bail and get them a decent lawyer. I can't just leave the poor sods in the lurch, can I?'

At that moment, I sensed he was staring at me with a fixed, implacable gaze, but I couldn't look up. I was torn between rage and gratitude, desperation and relief, pride – miraculously recovered for an instant – and the desire to submit, finally and definitively. I loved him, but I already knew it, I'd known it right from the start, I'd always loved him.

'Look at me, Lulu. Don't worry, I'll find a way to make you pay for this.'

* * *

All the rest I remember as a confused blur of unrelated images set at a nightmarish pace. I was wandering barefoot in the street. The cigarette seller on the corner looked at us with a bored expression. A powerful wave of nausea swept over me and I lurched forward. Pablo supported me, his hand on my forehead, while I threw up against a tree. The coat fell open, revealing my mortified flesh, and the eyes of an old tramp, making himself up a bed of newspapers on a bench, glittered for a second. I still felt sick. Pablo wasn't saying anything. I was lying on the back seat, trying to work out where he was taking me, which way we were going, once again after all these years, and I fought desperately against a devastating suspicion, which was growing terrifyingly quickly in my stunned mind and coming to resemble the odious certainties, unpleasant truths and indisputable facts one doesn't want to face. I fought it and tried to find a different, more reassuring explanation for that night's dizzying chain of events. I tried to make sense of the real origins of the marks on my skin, of Remi's insistence, Manolo's absence, Encarna's impassivity, the timeliness of the faked police raid, the bloodstains on Gus's fists, and of Pablo's tears, the tears I'd seen in his eyes, the sobs choking his voice, which had sounded very different from the one he used to throw me out earlier that same night. I fought the increasing certainty beneath my suspicion and I could see no alternative – there wasn't one. He'd been there all along, pulling the strings at a distance, but it all seemed too hard, too overwhelming for a fragile little girl. I'm a little girl, I concluded. I'll think about it tomorrow, tomorrow, not tonight. Tomorrow it'll all look much clearer . . .

Mercedes was waiting for us, sitting on the sofa, nervously fiddling with the handles of the old briefcase my mother had given her when she finished her medical studies.

Poor thing, I thought, we always turn to her on these unpleasant occasions.

When she saw us come in she worriedly examined my face, then looked at Pablo, and back at me.

'I was expecting worse,' she said.

Then he took off my coat.

My sister-in-law's hands began to tremble and her eyes filled with tears. I'd never understood how such a fragile, delicate, easily frightened woman could have chosen such a bloody profession.

'My God!' She looked at us both in turn. 'What's this?'

'Nothing.' Pablo went up to her and put his hand on her shoulder, as if to calm her. 'Just the marks left by the measles.'

I woke up with all the symptoms of a massive hangover. Then I remembered that Mercedes had given me an injection to make me sleep.

I was at home, at Pablo's home, and it was daytime. Sunlight was streaming right into the middle of the room through the half-open shutters.

He wasn't there with me.

My wounds were hurting.

The air stank of disinfectant.

I sat up with great difficulty.

Only then did I notice a terribly significant sign, a familiar tightness round the waist. I instinctively touched my chest and smiled.

He wasn't there but under my hand I could feel two butterflies holding a garland of seven little flowers, embroidered with tiny white beads.

I ran my fingers over them, several times. I stroked them and counted them to make sure there were none missing. All of the beads were there, intact, shiny fake pearls, made of plastic but incalculably precious, on my white blouse, a little newborn baby's blouse made to fit a big girl. The batiste was so fine it seemed like gauze.

I lay down again and shut my eyes.

Pablo wouldn't be back for some time. He didn't like being around at decisive moments.

There wouldn't be a decisive moment.

I rolled over the sheets until I was on his side of the bed, and I tried to trace his smell. It wasn't easy – my sense of smell wasn't up to much that morning – but finally I found a revealing hint of him on the pillow. I caught a little piece of the fabric between my fingers and held it against my nose, and I stayed there, curled up, smiling, absorbed by his smell, just letting time pass.

His arrival was preceded by the unmistakeable aroma of freshly made *porras*.

Then he lay down by my side, touched the tip of my nose and waited.

I tried to pretend I was fast asleep but my lips gradually curled into a smile of newly recovered innocence.

He put his head close to mine and whispered.

'Open your eyes, Lulu, I know you're not asleep . . .'